Acclaim for *New York Times* Bestselling Author Francine Prose

"Francine Prose has a knack fo nature."

"One of our finest writers."   y

"Francine Prose has been steadily producing novels, short stories, and criticism shot through with corrosive wit and searing intelligence."   —Scott Spencer

"A world-class storyteller."   —Russell Banks

"Francine Prose is one of a handful of truly indispensable American writers."   —Gary Shteyngart

Praise for *Reading Like a Writer*

"Like the great works of fiction, it's a wise and voluble companion."   —*New York Times Book Review*

"A jewel of a companion. . . . Engrossing—both light and erudite, daringly insightful and, in some places, bust-out-laughing funny."   —*Los Angeles Times Book Review*

"[*Reading Like a Writer*] should be read by everyone who wants to write and, yes, by everyone who loves to read."   —*San Francisco Chronicle*

Marion Ettlinger

About the Author

FRANCINE PROSE is the author of the nonfiction *New York Times* bestseller *Reading Like a Writer* and many highly acclaimed works of fiction, including *A Changed Man*, winner of the Dayton Literary Peace Prize, and *Blue Angel*, a finalist for the National Book Award. Her most recent work of fiction is the novel *Goldengrove*. Her work has appeared in *The New Yorker, The Atlantic Monthly, GQ, The Paris Review, Harper's, The New York Times Magazine,* and the *Wall Street Journal.* The recipient of numerous grants and awards, including a Guggenheim and a Fulbright, Francine Prose was a director's fellow at the Center for Scholars and Writers at the New York Public Library and is the president of PEN American Center. She lives in New York City.

GUIDED TOURS
OF HELL

ALSO BY FRANCINE PROSE

FICTION

Goldengrove
A Changed Man
Blue Angel
Hunters and Gatherers
The Peaceable Kingdom
Primitive People
Women and Children First
Bigfoot Dreams
Hungry Hearts
Household Saints
Animal Magnetism
Marie Laveau
The Glorious Ones
Judah the Pious

NONFICTION

Reading Like a Writer
Caravaggio: Painter of Miracles
Gluttony
Sicilian Odyssey
The Lives of the Muses: Nine Women and the
Artists They Inspired

GUIDED TOURS OF HELL

OF HELL

Novellas

FRANCINE PROSE

Perennial

An Imprint of HarperCollins*Publishers*

HARPER ● PERENNIAL

A hardcover edition of this book was published in 1997 by Henry Holt and Company, Inc. It is here reprinted by arrangement with Henry Holt and Company, Inc.

GUIDED TOURS OF HELL. Copyright © 1997 by Francine Prose. All rights reserved. Printed in the United States of America. No part of this book may be used or reproduced in any manner whatsoever without written permission except in the case of brief quotations embodied in critical articles and reviews. For information address Henry Holt and Company, Inc., 115 West 18th Street, New York, NY 10011.

HarperCollins books may be purchased for educational, business, or sales promotional use. For information please write: Special Markets Department, HarperCollins Publishers, 10 East 53rd Street, New York, NY 10022.

FIRST HARPER PERENNIAL EDITION PUBLISHED 2002.

Designed by Betty Lew

Library of Congress Cataloging-in-Publication Data

Prose, Francine.
    [Guided tours of hell]
    Guided tours of hell : novellas / Francine Prose.—1st Perennial ed.
        p. cm.
    Contents: Guided tours of hell—Three pigs in five days.
    ISBN 978-0-06-008085-3
        1. Psychological fiction, American. 2. Americans—Europe—Fiction.
3. Europe—Fiction. I. Prose, Francine, 1947– . II. Three pigs in five days. III.
Title: Three pigs in five days. IV. Title.

PS3566.R68 G85 2002
813'.54—dc21

                                                              2002024955

08 09 10 11 12 QK/RRD 10 9 8 7 6 5 4 3

TO DEBORAH EISENBERG
AND IN MEMORY OF STANLEY ELKIN

CONTENTS

GUIDED

TOURS

OF

HELL

On the bus to the death camp, Landau searches for an image, some brilliant incisive metaphor for the fields of stunted brown sunflowers, their fat dwarfish heads drooping stupidly on their crackling stalks. These are not Van Gogh sunflowers, these are . . . Anselm Kiefer, their dead round faces fatally kissed by a parching breeze from Chernobyl. These flowers that survived the gassing of the Jews are finally succumbing to the asphyxiation of the planet. Or: These flowers committed suicide to protest the death camp's reincarnation—landscaped, refurbished, a tourist attraction. *Honey, look! The delousing chamber!*

But the truth is: What the nodding sunflower heads really remind Landau of are human heads, specifically, the heads of last night's audience, dropping off to sleep, one by one, all through Landau's reading.

This has been Landau's problem ever since he got to Prague.

Tiny nips of transcendence nibble at his line, but given even the gentlest tug, they slip back into the water, the oily shoals of boredom, ego and resentment, and, let's be honest, fury at Jiri Krakauer, that terrible poet and memoirist whose only claim to fame is that he survived two years in the camp, where he somehow conducted a love affair with Kafka's sister, Ottla.

In the four days—the endless four days—that the First International Kafka Congress has been in session here in Prague, Landau has heard Jiri tell a dozen versions of how he fell for Ottla Kafka, a spitfire and a saint, Jiri sculpts the air with his paws, *Oof*, the curves of a saint, how he was overcome by passion as he watched her breeze through the camp with blankets, water, cups of tea, words of comfort and reassurance. When Jiri tells the elderly rabbi from Tel Aviv or the critic from Toronto, Ottla was kissing the shiny bald heads of the tiny ailing grandpas. But when he tells the feminist novelist from Croatia, the professor of Slavic languages from Vassar—the women hear how Jiri never saw Ottla without a baby in her arms and how he last saw her defiantly heading the children's transport to Auschwitz.

And what did Ottla see in Jiri? No one has to ask. That gangsterish mane of snowy hair, Mr. Larger-than-Life. Eventually everyone wants to know: What did Ottla say about Kafka? And Jiri has no problem repeating himself: Ottla always said how kind and gentle her brother was, how he cared about the workers whose disability claims he processed at the insurance firm, and how the Kafka family worried about his digestion and how boring it was to sit and watch him Fletcherize his food. Jiri imitates Kafka chewing every bite thirty times, and the professors show their slick pink gums and laugh their knowing laughs at this detail so irreverent they know it has to be true.

Well, better chew it a million times, the shit these people eat, no wonder Kafka was constipated, the man never saw a green vegetable. The fat stringy pork, the dimpled yellow pods clinging to the duck skin, the deep-fried cutlets oozing grease, every morsel daring Landau to push aside the most lethal delicious parts as Jiri Krakauer's handsome face wrinkles lightly with scorn. Kafka was permitted his stomach complaints. But Landau, apparently, isn't, so he is trying not to think about the low-grade nausea and diarrhea from which he has suffered since he arrived in Prague, probably thanks to the very same toxins that have turned the sunflowers such a crispy shade of dark brown.

Jiri is several rows back on the bus, but Landau can hear every word he bellows at his seatmate, Eva Kaprova, the Kafka Congress Director. Why shouldn't Jiri tell the whole bus: "This fucking country looked better when I was on my way to the camp!"

And all of Landau's metaphors are pulverized into rubble under the weight of experience that gives Jiri the right to say this. All of Landau's *false* metaphors: In fact the sunflower's problem isn't Chernobyl, their problem isn't the camps, but rather the summer-long heat wave that last week warped the train tracks so that the Kafka Congress had to change plans and hire a bus for the trip to the camp.

Outside, the greasy black landscape streams by, lumpy hills striped with stubble, powdery slag heaps, and compounds hidden behind high walls.

"Pigs!" Jiri announces. It takes Landau a moment to realize they're passing a pig farm.

"Ha, ha," says Landau pathetically, but Jiri isn't listening.

Landau wants Jiri to notice him, wants to ask him a million

questions, Jiri is living history, an eyewitness to what Landau can't even bear to imagine. Unlike the Kafka scholars, those pussies and old maids, Landau would have the balls to ask: What was the camp like, exactly? What single true thing has Jiri left out of all his memoirs and stories and poems?

But it's neither Chernobyl nor the War that's poisoned the air between them. It's ego, Landau's ego, pettiness, resentment. Jiri is a star here, a celebrity based on nothing but bad luck, then good luck, endurance, nerve, resilience, no Survivor Guilt for this guy. Mr. Appetite-for-Life has a story to tell and they eat it up, these pathetic Kafka groupies, these idiots who dozed through Landau's reading of his play *To Kafka from Felice*.

Landau knew that the reading was strange. His drama in letters, his made-up lost half of that brilliant correspondence, was, after all, a one-woman play, to be read by a serious actress, as it was in the off-off-Broadway production that got such terrific reviews. Those female outcries of wounded pride and love were scored for a contralto with a sonorous vibrato for moments of hope and pain (Landau suspects that Felice's voice was a good deal shriller) and not for Landau's tenor, his dash of a Brooklyn accent. But that was no reason for Landau to look out over his audience and see vacant faces, half-shut eyes, the nodding tops of heads.

Only after Landau sat down did the etherized crowd regain consciousness, make a miraculous recovery, and instantly go hog-wild for Jiri's booming oration of his goopy narrative poem about the children's art class at the camp, about a little boy who keeps drawing people burning in a furnace, though that didn't happen at this camp but at Auschwitz, miles to the East, so there was no way the boy could have known, etc., etc. In tears, the audience listened as Jiri ended his poem with the art teacher bravely leading

her students toward the transport to the East, hand in hand with
the tiny artist who had already foreseen this. They rose to their
feet to cheer Jiri's last line, "I was that little boy!"

Afterwards they'd mobbed Jiri, begging him to sign copies of
his books in a dozen languages. No one came near Landau—that
is, no one but Natalie Zigbaum, the Slavic languages professor
from Vassar, who tried to engage Landau in an earnest discussion
of Kafka and Felice, a conversation so screamingly dull that
Landau found himself near tears, especially when he looked over
Natalie's head at Jiri, accepting hugs and handshakes like a star
athlete after a game.

Landau and Jiri have lots in common, even if no one but
Landau knows it. Both are writers, obviously. Both do a little
teaching: Landau as an occasional adjunct at Pace and Adelphi,
and Jiri at Princeton, where he holds an endowed chair in modern
European history. History! What does Jiri know? The history of
Jiri Krakauer! Also, both Landau and Jiri know a thing or two
about women who want to be good: Ottla Kafka, the saint of the
camp, must have shared some personality traits with Landau's
wife, Mimi, a therapist with the lowest fees on the Upper West
Side, a woman who not only works long hours for practically no
pay but volunteers at a shelter where she gives out her telephone
number for battered mothers to call at all hours of the day and
night. She spends so much time at the shelter that Landau often
asks her to bring home the free-meal leftovers in a doggy bag for
his dinner.

Oh, what is Landau thinking! He and Jiri have nothing in
common. Mimi Landau, commiserating with her friends about
their menopausal woes, Mimi who, to her credit, never directly
accuses Landau of having sponged for—how long?—fifteen years

off her hard work and low pay, though she does have one very particular mournful, maddening smile that tells the whole sad story of the years she's supported Landau's self-indulgent arty plays by listening, hour after hour, to New York's most self-indulgent—and cheap—neurotics. Mimi is nothing like Ottla Kafka: always young, always lovely, always heroic and tragic. . . .

Among the letters in Landau's play is one that Landau wrote for Felice in reply to Kafka's nagging insistence that it would be good for her to work with refugee children at the Jewish People's Home. Felice (in Landau's letter) writes that she wants to be good but doesn't have the gift for it, she has no talent for goodness. What she wants is children of her own, she would be good to them, but she knows that Kafka doesn't want children, and she respects his wish, so maybe it will be good for her to work with someone else's children.

Landau knew how this should sound. Mimi had wanted children. He'd read the letter aloud to her, as he had most of the play. She'd gotten up and left the house and didn't return for five hours. Landau was surprised. He'd expected her to be moved by how well he'd listened and translated her pain into art. He'd felt wronged, undermined by Mimi. He went to make a cup of tea and couldn't at first find the tea bags and, until he came to his senses, thought she'd hidden them on purpose.

Three sharp blasts jolt the passengers: static from the bus driver's radio, then a blare of jazz, Eastern European Dixieland, Basin Street with a wailing Levantine gypsy edge. Landau turns to look at Jiri, whose memoirs describe the Ghetto Sultans, the jazz band in the camp, free concerts every Monday, until the drummer and the alto sax were sent to Birkenau by mistake.

But Jiri isn't looking to exchange a flash of recognition with Landau, a shared association on the subject of Dixieland jazz. Jiri is whispering into the ear of the Congress Director, Eva Kaprova, who inclines her head toward him like a gloomy attractive plant.

When Eva shakes the conferees' hands she stares deeply into their eyes, which Landau finds so magnetic that he feels himself tilting toward her. Landau knows she's married, but that is clearly not a concern for Mr. Devour-Life-with-Both-Hands, who was the first to figure out that Eva, fortyish and sexy in that sour Eastern European way, is the Congress's only viable female. Jiri jumped in and grabbed her, which she has evidently allowed, so Jiri's wife back home in Princeton must not be a problem, either.

Eva's speech at the plenary session affirmed the Congress's purpose: to foster peace and friendship between nations and ethnic communities. This, she said, was the true subject of the work of Franz Kafka, who in her opinion was a life-loving guy with a sense of humor and not the quivering neurotic wreck the world chooses to imagine: in other words, like Jiri, not at all like Landau. Eva said all this in the cigarette voice, the smoky tragic tones in which Landau's *To Kafka from Felice* should have been delivered.

Right in front of Landau and the other conferees, Eva and Jiri have begun to plan another conference for some time this winter, a private session just for Jiri, at which he will meet the donors and funders of the Kafka Foundation and work his rough magic on them and persuade them to fork over millions. None of the other conferees will be invited to this event, which Jiri and Eva contrive with the breathless urgency of lovers arranging a stolen weekend, a dream escape that may never occur, but still their faces shine as they find every reason to mention it in front of the women who look at Eva, the men who stare at Jiri to discern what secret quality can make a member of the opposite sex behave so shamelessly, abandoning everything, families, duties, decorum, on the sweet unlikely promise of February in Prague.

Now traffic stalls in a stagnant pool of exhaust that makes Landau's eyes burn. Outside the window, a roadside stand sells huge stuffed animals, plush neon-pink panthers with black button noses sucking up pollution. Landau nudges his seatmate, a depressed Albanian novelist. The Albanian glances over and nods and emits a tragic snort.

Even in the August heat, the Albanian wears a scratchy brown cardigan; a muffler of the same fabric bandages his throat. At the welcome cocktail party, the whole Congress overheard Jiri complimenting the Albanian's outfit, recalling how in the camps he'd worn every scrap of scrounged clothing. If you "slipped into something more comfortable," everything else you owned was stolen. The Albanian had made the same melancholy snort with which he's just responded to Landau. And what is Jiri wearing? An expensive pale blue silk shirt with the top buttons undone, revealing a freckled chest, thatched with white hair, and, even, Christ, a gold chain!

Landau hadn't wanted to go to the camp; he changed his mind ten times, erasing and rewriting his name until he dug a hole in the sign-up sheet. He hates to think of the Holocaust, or rather he feels it too deeply, unlike all those slobs who take dates to *Schindler's List* so they can provide a manly shoulder for their girls to burrow their faces in during the scene in which the naked female prisoners don't know if the shower will spray water or poison gas.

Isn't there something by definition obscene about guided tours of hell—except, of course, if you're Dante? Yet plenty of people visit the camp, for as many different reasons. At the last minute Landau decided to go, to shut up and take his medicine, maybe it would do him good, just as working with children was supposed to be good for Felice. And it isn't as if he's making a special effort, going out of his way to satisfy a ghoulish curiosity. The whole Kafka Congress is making the trip, so it must be perfectly normal. Landau will probably feel left out if he doesn't go. Also he'd hate to look like a coward who can't even visit the camp where Jiri spent three hellish years, which is another reason not to go: The camp is Jiri's kingdom.

They turn a corner, and there it is: a solid brick fortress, not unlike the state colleges built after the Vietnam War, after students like Landau ran around smashing windows. And there is the sign over the gate, *Arbeit Macht Frei*, Work Makes You Free. Oh, the fabulous ironies of the German sense of humor, and how amazing, how incredible that you can see it from a tour bus, which for the first time since they left Prague hits a reasonable speed and zips past the camp, then past parking lots crammed with dusty cars, campers, and fully loaded German-made RVs.

The passengers murmur anxiously. Could they have missed their stop? Wait, this bus was hired to take them where they are going! Eva Kaprova holds up a calming hand. The bus is just going to park—miles away from the camp. How will the frail Israeli rabbi manage the long hike back?

But first they must drive past another tourist attraction. Eva Kaprova points out the National Memorial Cemetery, the tidy straight rows of pale identical markers, over which the state has recently erected a monumental gleaming silver cross. The passengers fall silent and gaze dully at the cross.

Then something startling happens. Jiri lopes to the front of the bus. He turns to mug at his colleagues and, with broad clownish gestures, spreads his arms out wide, as if he is hanging on the cross. But he doesn't look like Jesus. Jiri's in much better shape, a condor about to flap its wings and fly up through the bus ceiling. The conferees gaze at him worshipfully. Why did Landau come here? He'd told himself it would be worth it for the free ticket to Prague, and—let's be honest—he was flattered that he'd been invited, that the news of his little play had somehow crossed the ocean.

The bus squeezes into a parking space; its passengers don't notice. They go on staring at Jiri until he collapses his arms and laughs. The moment's over, they too can laugh and be released to stand and gather their things and follow Jiri off the bus and up the road to the camp.

The Kafka Congress flocks around Eva Kaprova, who collects them on the drawbridge and invites them to look down at the moat that the Nazi engineers designed so they could flood it in an emergency with water from the nearby river.

Landau stares down into the weedy moat, which is dry, of course, and littered with paper, broken glass: Eastern European landscaping. The parching sun sears the back of his neck. He lifts his head too quickly, and tiny black spots swim before his eyes. Oh God, what if he faints here?

"Kafka's castle," says Eva, with a bitter actressy chuckle. But no one's paying attention. Once more they're watching Jiri, who has gone ahead of them and is heading into the camp.

What is it like for Jiri to walk up that cobblestone road and under that soot-blackened stone arch? Could this be the first time since. . . ? Landau can't help wondering. But Jiri's beyond cheap psychology or sentimental melodrama. He enters the camp like its owner, a hero or messenger storming the fortress with urgent news for the king.

The Kafka Congress ditches poor Eva and rushes ducklinglike up the path, scurrying after Mr. Pied-Piper. Even the elderly rabbi lifts his cuffs and hurries. Landau lingers, watching Eva's generous sullen mouth droop even lower as she shades her eyes with her hand and watches the others run away. Landau, her solace, her gallant knight, is drifting in her direction when he nearly falls over Natalie Zigbaum, the Slavic languages professor from Vassar.

It's like tripping over an armchair, an armchair in a brown dress blotched with cruelly girlish pink tea roses, an armchair with long canines, thick spectacles, a helmet of gray hair and a grimly determined smile for Landau, who all through the conference has noticed Natalie finding reasons to be near him, noticed Natalie eyeing him even as he eyes Eva Kaprova, who has been eyeing Jiri Krakauer. In other words, the usual daisy chain, even here in the death camp.

"Look at Mr. Full-of-Shit," Natalie says, jerking her head toward Jiri. She was the one who started it—making up names for Jiri—and now Landau can't help doing it; it's become a new habit, a tic.

"Mr. Resurrected-Saint," hisses Natalie. "Mr. God-the-Survivor. When the whole world knows how he survived, all those confessions—boasts, really—paraded in his memoirs, how he traded soggy matches and leaky shoes for extra rations of bread, how he hardened himself to shaft everyone else, and we're supposed to think: Bravo! Good for him! That's what I would have done! Well, maybe *we* would have given the bread to the dying boy who Jiri knew he had to refuse in that famous chapter from our hero's brilliant memoir—"

"Then *you* wouldn't have survived," Landau says. "Isn't that the point?"

Natalie's face implodes like a puffy doughnut, bitten into, leaving only her increasingly self-conscious and rigid smile.

"Is it?" she says. "Is that the point?"

"Sure it is," says Landau harshly. "The point is: We don't know what we'd do. Nobody knows what accident of fate or DNA or character will determine how we act when the shit hits the fan."

"I guess," agrees Natalie, retreating, and as she turns away, her eyes, magnified by thick lenses, film with gelid tears.

Landau feels awful! Terrible! How badly he has behaved, here where every cobblestone should be teaching him a lesson about cruelty and kindness. Oh, really? Is *that* the lesson? What is Landau *thinking*? The ethical lesson of these stones is that it's smart to withhold your stale crust of bread from a little boy dying of hunger.

What did Jiri do to survive? Landau would rather not know, though he suspects that Jiri's confessions in print are only the tip of the iceberg. There have been some moments since the start of the conference when Jiri has acted in ways that must have distressed even his acolytes and fawning devotees.

Yesterday they were on the tram, headed for yet another reception that would begin with yet another minor official conveying the apologies of a slightly less minor official who was scheduled to greet them but was called away at the last minute. On the tram—because the tour bus scheduled to convey them there had also been called away at the last minute, a scenario so familiar by now that Landau wonders if the Congress budget is lower than Eva will admit, so that she stages these charades in which they wait twenty minutes for a nonexistent bus and then give up and wait another twenty minutes (or more) for the tram. Everything requires waiting, punitively protracted, sometimes an hour for breakfast, though they all get the same plate of slimy flamingo-colored bologna, rubbery gherkins, and pewter-ringed slices of egg, so it's not as if the kitchen has to cook fifty separate orders. The budget must be rock-bottom, judging from the hotel, a grisly state socialist dump untouched by the cushiony strokings of the Velvet Revolution, staffed by a chilly sadistic crew un-schooled in the decadent good manners bourgeois tourists expect, a dank prison to which the conferees are returned each night to bash their aching heads against granite pillows encased in cold damp linen, on beds no wider than coffins.

The grim hotel, the elusive officials, the buses that never come—Hey, welcome to the Kafka Congress (this is the sort of thing that Natalie Zigbaum sidles up to Landau to whisper, along with the news that Jiri isn't staying at their hotel but at a five-star palace not far from Eva's apartment), where, fittingly, they've come to honor the spirit of a man who wrote the book on claus-trophobic living quarters, on thuggish servants of the state refusing to show their faces, and on mysterious obstacles that make it hard to get from place to place.

During the long hot wait for the tram, several conferees sug-gested taking taxis, to which Eva replied that the Russian mob now controls the taxi business; last week a German tourist was stabbed for the gold fillings in his teeth. A rebellious ripple stirred the group, a disturbance that Jiri quieted with the observation that compared to a boxcar, the tram would do just fine. Besides, he said, what camp life taught you was the dangerous folly of simply waiting, of not living in the moment, an idea that Jiri has discussed with the Dalai Lama, who shares Jiri's opinion completely. Jiri name-drops constantly: Miloš Forman. Václav Havel. Still, Landau couldn't believe that Jiri could name-drop the Dalai Lama, whom Landau has always wanted to meet. Oh, unfair! Unfair!

At last the tram arrived, packed full, so it was quickly arranged that half the Kafka conferees would board and the other half would wait another twenty minutes (or more) for another tram. Mr. Every-Man-for-Himself leaped onto the first tram while everyone else was still negotiating, and Eva boarded after Jiri, irresponsibly leaving the remaining conferees to find the right tram and the reception. Landau was swept onto the tram, along with Natalie Zigbaum. As it lurched forward, she fell against him and giggled and stepped away, readjusting her upholstery. Landau had thought—just as he thinks now, walking up the path to the camp—that he and Natalie (squat, bespectacled, American) are a parody couple, a cruel parody of tall, handsome, clear-eyed, European Jiri and Eva.

More people got on the tram at each stop. "Another boxcar!" boomed Jiri. Did none of the Czechs speak English? Everyone stared straight ahead. At the stop in front of the Prague Kmart, three Gypsy women got on, and the other passengers shifted as far as possible from that trio of cackling birds with their bright ruffled plumage. The Czechs emitted clucking noises and muted syllables of threat and warning, and mimed—for the benefit of the Kafka conferees, whom until then they hadn't acknowledged—the wary sensible safeguarding of wallets, pockets, and purses.

Then Jiri went to the front of the tram and spoke to the driver, who was unaware of the crisis. The driver came back and yelled at the Gypsies, who yelled at him, everyone yelled, then the Gypsies got off. The Czechs resumed their blank stares, as if nothing had happened, as did the Kafka conferees, though perhaps for different reasons.

"Did you see that?" Natalie had shouted into Landau's ear. "It took Jiri about five seconds to make the tram Gypsy free."

Landau's only answer was an irritated shrug, as if Natalie were a stinging bug that had gotten under his collar.

Natalie keeps on nipping at him, even now as they walk up the cobblestone road to the camp, and worse, she seems to have read Landau's mind, to know what he's been thinking. How else to explain it—it couldn't be coincidence—when she says, "Did you believe how Mr. Human-Rights treated those Gypsies on the tram!"

Again Landau shrugs, just one shoulder this time. "What were the choices?" he says. "Sit there grinning like liberal schmucks and get our passports stolen?" Why is he defending Jiri for doing something morally vile (although, to be perfectly frank, Landau had felt relieved). Because the people who disapprove of him are people like Landau and Natalie Zigbaum!

"The choices?" Natalie Zigbaum snarls. "Liberal schmucks . . . or Nazis?"

Suddenly fearing that he's bullied Natalie to the point at which her fragile crush (or whatever) on him has been blasted out of existence, Landau feels bereft. Her attention is better than nothing. There is so little sexual buzz going around this conference, Natalie's choosing Landau must mean that he is its second most attractive man.

"Watch your step," warns Landau. "These cobblestones are murder." In fact they are like vicious stone eggs, pressing into Landau's tender arches. Natalie's shoes have thicker soles than his, but she smiles so gratefully, leans so pliantly against him that she could be clicking over the stones in the thinnest highest heels. Landau grasps her elbow and guides her up the path as they approach the dark looming archway in which Jiri stands with out-stretched arms, welcoming them all.

What does the camp remind Landau of? A zoo without animals, maybe. A wide pebbled path lined with overgrown borders and inviting park benches, without the parklike promise of pleasure and relaxation, but rather the zoolike reminder that one is here on a mission, there is sómething to see here, a fixed route to be taken. And how could they go anywhere except where Jiri steers them? Jiri stands off to one side and bows, waving them on. The conferees smile and nod at him, a tiny bit nervous, but jolly. . . .

As Landau and Natalie Zigbaum pass, Jiri whispers, "This way for the gas, ladies and gentlemen."

Landau stops, as does Natalie. The others squeeze timidly past them. Landau says, "What an amazing book! *This Way for the Gas.* Have you read Borowski?" he asks Natalie. "What an astonishing life! Borowski and his girlfriend were sent to Auschwitz for distributing anti-Nazi poetry and miraculously they both survive, are separated, reunited, they get married, and she gets pregnant, has a daughter, he visits them at the hospital and that night goes home and turns on the gas and kills himself."

Some instinct is kicking in here, Landau's showing off for a woman. So what if it's Natalie? She's the only one here to compete for. In one of the letters Landau wrote for Felice, she scolds Kafka for showing off the first time they met at Max Brod's, for bringing along the manuscript of his first book of stories and photos from a trip that he and Max made to Weimar, including pictures of a beautiful girl with whom Kafka had a flirtation. In Landau's letter, Felice scolds Kafka and then confesses that it made her happy; she knew he was showing off for her. But Landau has no plans for a long neurotic engagement to Natalie. Maybe it's Jiri he wants to impress. . . .

"Lying shit," says Jiri. "Borowski was never at Auschwitz."

"He wasn't?" says Landau. But Jiri's gaze skims over their heads, and Natalie and Landau turn to see Eva rushing up the path. Eva *is* wearing high heels, and her stumbling run reminds Landau of postwar Italian films in which beautiful actresses spill out of their ripped flimsy dresses as they flee the smoldering ruins of villages ravaged by battle.

"Jiri," Eva says. "Where did you disappear to?" A thorn of panic snags Eva's throaty voice.

Jiri laughs. "I couldn't wait to get back to this place!" Then Mr. Joie-de-Vivre puts his arm around Eva and sweeps her along, while Landau and Natalie must dazedly pick themselves up and follow. The entire Kafka Congress straggles into the dusty sun-baked courtyard, yet Landau feels that he and Natalie are alone with Jiri and Eva: the homely couple, the beautiful couple, double-dating at the death camp.

"*Achtung!*" Natalie whispers to Landau as Jiri whisks them through a lot surrounded by faded brick walls pocked with dark low entrances without doors, like the holes in a birdhouse.

Tourists rouse themselves from their dreamy sight-seeing just long enough to observe the ragtag parade of Kafka Congress conferees. Then they resume popping in and out of doorways like figures on a cuckoo clock, blinking and bent double.

Jiri points out the high spots.

"Brooks Brothers!" He waves and shouts.

"The clothing depot," translates Eva. "That's where the prisoners picked up their monthly changes of clothing."

"Bastards!" says Jiri. "Bastards!" They pass empty rooms with wooden chairs and desks. Offices? Interrogation rooms? Jiri isn't saying, and they're moving too fast for Landau to consult the map he grabbed as they rushed past the ticket booth. Mr. Live-for-Today had insisted on paying for the whole group, though Eva said, "Jiri, you mustn't do that!" Let the guy pay, thought Landau. Save the money for the Congress. Next time—if there is a next time—they could be put up in a halfway decent hotel and even hire a real bus and skip the charades with the trams.

They turn into a courtyard, a narrow alley lined on one side with cagelike cells and on the other with larger stalls crammed with wooden bunks. Landau thinks again of a zoo, of a decrepit roadside animal park with a pair of big cats pacing their boxes and a few starved monkeys shivering in the corners.

"Here you have your single rooms," Jiri declares. "And here you have your accommodations for five hundred skeletons rubbing together in fifty narrow beds."

"The guy drives me nuts!" says Natalie, clinging to Landau like one of those birds that peck the bugs off the backs of bison. "I will just throw up if I hear him tell one more time about Ottla Kafka leading the children's transport to Auschwitz."

Jiri raises both arms, Mr. Human-Candelabra, flicking one wrist, then the other at the tiny cages on one side, the large holding pens opposite. His face is crimson, streaked with sweat, and the glaring August sun turns his white hair incandescent.

Natalie whispers to Landau, "Eva's got her hands full with him. The guy's had two serious coronaries and a triple bypass. The woman's a wreck. Did you see her face when she came running up to us? She's afraid he'll die on her. Right here in Prague, at the camp! Fabulous for her career at the Kafka Foundation!"

Apparently, sexless Natalie Zigbaum has no idea that Eva's preoccupation and strain is all about Eros, not Thanatos, about her affair with Jiri and not his imminent death! Natalie wouldn't know Eros if it crept up behind her and pinched her ass!

"Don't kid yourself," says Landau. "He's in better shape than we are!"

This time Natalie backs off, and it's just as well. Landau doesn't need her pecking at him as he peeks into the rooms, which he tries in vain to populate with jammed-together skeletal Jews, then peers into the cells on the other side, in which he tries to picture political prisoners in solitary confinement. What efficient cruelty to border one yard with two opposite tortures!

But the ghosts are hiding from Landau. All he sees are walls, scratched paint, bare bunks. No one's staring at him with raccoon eyes, and frankly, Landau's just as glad. The whole trip is filthy, filthy. What people will do for sensation!

Jiri nearly mows Landau down, hurrying out of the courtyard. The group rushes after Jiri, who is standing outside a weathered wooden shack.

"The KB," says Jiri. "The Krankenbauer. Everything in order! First they have to cure us so afterwards they can kill us. My home away from home!" Jiri has written about the ruses he came up with to get himself sent to the hospital, where he could rest and eat slightly thicker gruel before being sent back to work, duties which, as his readers and every literary prize committee know, included pulling wedding rings from the fingers of the dead.

The feminist from Zagreb, who has a gift for investing the most banal utterances with urgent meaning, pushes forward and grabs Jiri's arm. "Did the doctors . . . *experiment*. . . ?

Oh, *please*, thinks Landau, then notices Eva Kaprova watching. Is there a triangle forming? Jiri, Eva, the Croatian . . .

Jiri glares at the twiglike novelist. How can she ask him this? Hasn't she read his work? He roars at her, he blows her away. "The whole camp was an experiment!"

And now, holding her proud head higher, Eva runs after Jiri, again leaving the rest of the group (how fitting that the Kafka Congress should spend so much time chasing blindly after each other) to inspect the hospital and catch up with her and Jiri.

The sick bay is the most decorated, the most elaborately furnished. A certain wax museum aesthetic prevails, Dr. Adolf's Chamber of Horrors, with charming period details, examining tables with real stirrups, leather straps, no sterile chrome imitations, a dental chair, and cabinets with many tiny drawers the perfect size for torture implements: toenail extractors neatly divided from testicle squeezers.

Landau can hardly endure it, but something compels him to look. He finds himself remembering the ophthalmologist he was taken to as a boy, the gloomy office, the shelves of reference books, graphic instructions for tortures involving the eye, the pool-table-green carpet, the leather couches permeated with a sugary alcohol smell, the clunking apparatus that held the prescriptive lenses, looming over you, pressing into your face.

Landau's eye doctor had an accent. Was he German-Jewish? German-German? Landau's parents wouldn't have gone to a German, not in 1950. But there is no one for Landau to ask, his parents are both dead, one heart attack, one cancer, neither much older than Landau is now and unavailable for Landau to ask if there was, as he remembers, a large reproduction Hieronymus Bosch in the doctor's waiting room, so that on the day when Landau finally got his glasses he realized that the framed red blur was crawling with freakish monsters and demons having an orgy.

On Landau's first night in Prague, he'd dreamed that his parents, his grandparents, all his dead loved ones were seated in folding chairs, and Landau went around kissing them, tears of grief soaking his face, and at last he kissed his mother who said, "None of us are alive, but we aren't dead, either."

Even in the dream Landau knew he should be having one of those moments of profound revelation, of overpowering comfort and peace, but in fact he felt lousy, and then violently worse as he moved from the waiting room of the dead to the next phase of the dream, his childhood house, with the whole ground floor redone as a grassy graveyard with rows of tombstones that flipped back and forth, clacking like cheap false teeth.

The doorway where Jiri awaits them is an important doorway. Anyone could tell that, even without Jiri standing outside. An intense inaudible buzz jazzes up the pace as tourists swarm toward the door like pilgrims nearing a shrine.

Landau unfolds his map of the camp, then refolds it without looking. He will know what he is seeing, or, rest assured, Jiri will tell him. He'll tell the world what fresh horror they are about to behold, what new nightmare was the daily routine of Jiri's adolescence. And Eva Kaprova will translate Jiri's blowsy figures of speech into simple damning statements of fact such as Kafka might have written.

The Kafka Congress enters a long tiled hall lined with rows of sinks. Above each sink is a mirror, veined with hairline cracks, missing most of its silver.

"Our beauty parlor!" shouts Jiri.

"The shaving room," explains Eva. "This is where they brought the Red Cross observers on their biannual inspections to show them that the prisoners were maintaining high standards of personal hygiene. Otherwise the sinks were never used—"

"This was where I learned to shave," Jiri interrupts. "And for me it was perfect. My first year in the camp, I only had to shave once every six months!"

Landau watches several women gaze tenderly at Jiri until grizzled old Mr. Character-Face disappears and turns, in those damp female eyes, back into Pretty-Boy-Prisoner Jiri, a strapping Adonis with creamy skin and soft down on his upper lip.

"Seven years bad luck," someone says. "Multiplied how many times?" Of course it's Natalie Zigbaum, who has come up behind Landau with this stunning piece of humor. "*What* bad luck? The Germans have finally conquered the world. Why mess around with a sloppy war when you have corporate buyouts and take over all our supermarkets and half our publishing houses?"

Landau's frosty stare slides over Natalie and past her toward the shaving room, then back at her, communicating with his eyes what he thinks of a person who could stoop, in a place like this, to xenophobic bitching. A place like this? What place like this? There is no place like it.

"If you don't mind," says Landau, "I'd like to be alone here."

"Asshole!" mutters Natalie, and in their shock they stare at the space between them, as if the word has bubbled out of her mouth and is floating there, ready to burst.

Landau escapes from the lock of her gaze, but Natalie is still watching. This makes everything harder as he moves off into the room. What is he supposed to do now? Walk from one end to the other? Stop for a reverent mooning gaze at each nasty sink? Look at one sink, then move along? The possibilities are endless, and none of them seem right. What *is* the tourist etiquette for the shaving room at the death camp?

Then Landau has—well, forces—a vision: skeletons in mirrors, hollow-eyed male bags of bones reflected in rows of dark glass. Another phony metaphor: In fact they weren't skeletons, not the prisoners here, who were kept above starving weight, again for the Red Cross inspectors.

Landau is overdramatizing, getting things wrong again. But isn't that his problem: his falseness, his lack of depth, the reason why, he secretly fears, his play is basically garbage, idiotic, hysterical, just like poor Felice, who wasn't pretty or sexy or smart, she was no match for Kafka, so what did Kafka possibly get out of that drawn-out tortured engagement . . . And how would Landau know, Landau, who doesn't have a clue about why he married Mimi, what youthful vanity she tickled, a year or two of good sex, or why he fell in love with Lynn, the actress who starred in the off-off-Broadway production of his *To Kafka from Felice*. That had seemed like a sensible love. She was an artist, around his age, though not a sensible person, because, halfway through rehearsals, it turned out that Lynn was sleeping with the twenty-five-year-old lighting director.

Landau reaches back to Kafka for consoling proof that the soul food of the artist is sexual torment and deprivation, a theory to which Jiri clearly refuses to subscribe. But who is right? Who is the better writer: Kafka or Jiri Krakauer?

Landau finds himself staring into a mirror at a half-bald, severely myopic gnome with a wiry corolla of clown hair, big teeth, Natalie Zigbaum in drag—it takes forever for Landau to recognize his own face. Where is the chunky determined boy whom girls once found so charismatic, the campus radical known for his speeches at antiwar rallies? Where is the budding playwright surrounded at loft parties by pretty girls asking how Landau understood so much about women! Landau wants to howl in protest. Yet he knows that the cause of his grief is just vanity, egomania. How revolting all that is, here in a mirrored room where the doomed could make themselves presentable for their appointments with Death!

Jiri claps his hands, loud hollow pops that echo off the tiles. Something is coming up here, the next phase of the trip, and Jiri wants to be the one to tell them what to expect.

"*Mesdames et Messieurs,*" says Jiri. "The tunnel to the gallows. Another amazing miracle of Nazi engineering.".

Meanwhile Eva Kaprova is going around to the older conferees, placing her hand on their stooped shoulders, leaning down to whisper in their ears.

Jiri comes up behind Landau. Landau sees him in the mirror, to which Landau has returned for another look, for reassurance that doesn't come, especially not when Jiri appears over Landau's shoulder in all his leonine splendor, thus exploding Landau's last faint hope that the reason he looks so wretched is that the mirror is unflattering.

Gently Jiri turns Landau around to watch the elderly rabbi and critics thanking Eva and leaving the room.

"Another Ottla," Jiri says. "Or . . . another selection. The old and weak get weeded out. And in this case it makes sense; they're better off skipping the tunnel. The damn maze twists and turns underground for two miles, maybe more, and just when you think you're dying, you can't hold out another second, it brings you back up to ground level right smack in front of the gallows. The Nazi version of a cardiac stress test: an oven in summer, an icebox in winter, slanted uphill and so low you had to double over to keep from cracking your head. They'd make you run to your own execution. . . . Everyone heard rumors about all the guys they didn't need to hang because their hearts gave out in the tunnel on the way to the gallows."

"It sounds like a real . . . experience," Landau mumbles stupidly.

Landau is game for the tunnel! He isn't some withered old geezer, hanging on by a thread, some pussy academic afraid of the harder stuff! If Jiri's braving the tunnel, Landau's right behind him, though he's feeling a little . . . well, clammy. Fifty-one-year-olds have heart attacks every day! In Manhattan they're dropping like flies, a colleague of Mimi's, last month. Suppose Landau fell ill in the tunnel underneath the camp? With Northern Bohemian medical care, Landau would be dead meat. He hasn't had a checkup in years, though Mimi often urges him, Mimi, who spends half her life at the gynecologist's office. And Landau hasn't been well here, constant heartburn, constant cramps, his bowels an active volcano. What if he has to take a shit miles underground?

This is not exactly the sort of question he can ask Jiri, who is already loping off toward a low doorway, obviously the entrance to the corridor of death. Someone should save the man from himself! Jiri's the one with the bad heart. But Jiri may be better off than Landau—that is, if Landau discovers in the depths of the tunnel that he too suffers from a cardiac condition that proves to be far deadlier for being undiagnosed.

Landau is already crouching as he jogs stiffly after Jiri. But again he is intercepted by the indefatigable Natalie Zigbaum, who has made it her mission to impede Landau's painful progress, to pour vinegar on the wounds he is sustaining in this Calvary. Peering up through her glasses into Landau's eyes, Natalie says, "Hey, I'm sorry I called you an asshole. Being here is tough on everybody's nerves."

"Not Jiri's," mutters Landau, meaning: Natalie is forgiven.

"He loves it," says Natalie. "It's a real homecoming for Mr. Professional-Survivor." They stand there, silenced by guilt at their venom for this man who has lived through hell.

Landau moves to follow Jiri. Again Natalie restrains him.

"You're not seriously going in there," she says. "Honestly heading, of your own free will, into an underground maze, volunteering for a torture devised by the warped Nazi mind, a forced march, crouched, uphill, bent over. And for what? To have the macho experience of concentration camp survival?"

Has Landau lost his senses? Natalie's perfectly right! It's just posturing—ridiculous!—to follow Jiri into the tunnel. Landau feels a great wash of gratitude for female common sense, for the pure clear heights from which women look down on male games of power and competition, for their bravery in wading in and saving men from themselves.

"Come sit with me." Natalie says, mischievous and faintly subversive, offering Landau an end run around some needless penance. "We can wait for them on those benches over there. The group will have to pass by us on their way back from the tunnel. Eva's been telling the geriatric contingent to meet them on the benches in twenty minutes or so."

Twenty minutes in a tunnel! Absolutely no way! Far better to be included among the geriatric contingent!

Landau follows Natalie to a bench along a cobblestone road lined with dusty plane trees and plots of half-dead zinnias. It's the camp's version of the Champs-Elysées, Fifth Avenue, Unter den Linden. Landau sinks down without thinking. Natalie sits beside him. Their arms almost touch, or maybe they touch, Landau can't tell if some velvety tactile moisture is rising from Natalie's arm and arcing over the space between them. Landau is very aware of her arm, but mostly he is recalling the tingling he used to feel as he sat beside some girl—any girl—in a darkened movie. The warmth and nearness of those arms was as good, maybe better, than sex. Was Mimi ever one of those girls? Landau can't remember.

He and Natalie aren't touching, and yet her body heat raises the temperature. It's unspeakably hot. This is how the Albanian novelist must feel in his scratchy sweater. Landau's stomach growls warningly, then so loudly that Natalie flinches.

Across from them, a line of people file in and out of an entrance. Actually there are two lines, a briskly moving column of men and a slower line of women. This is fantastic! Landau and Natalie have a scenic view of tourists waiting to use the toilet!

A few notice Landau watching, and look away. This is not a situation in which they want to be observed, trudging forward to adjust their clothes and sit, stand, grunt, sigh, piss, shit, wipe their asses, adjust their clothes, wash their hands or not. Better that everyone pretend not to know what is happening here, better glance at Landau and glance away, though Landau can't stop staring at what, he feels, could be a scene staged just for him, at actors hired to reenact the degradations of camp life, the waiting, the exposed public nature of the most intimate bodily functions. This is dehumanizing enough—and it's nothing like the real thing! The world needs writers like Jiri to keep describing what it *was* like. Jiri has a mission, a subject! Unlike *moi*, Landau thinks.

Near the end of the line, a small boy with a pale dirty face yanks his mother's arm like the rope of a bell that won't ring, a curtain that won't open. His mother wears a turquoise miniskirt, a pink paisley blouse, 1970s clothing that goes with her bleached blond hair. Her lips tighten, she rolls her eyes, taps her foot, then smacks her kid on the head, hard enough so that everyone notices and pretends not to. Finally, with a theatrical shrug, she yanks the kid out of line and goes and asks the people up front if her boy can go before them. Her posture grows flirty, obsequious as she talks to her fellow adults, whom Landau and Natalie watch deciding whether to help the child or punish the mother for her garish clothes and what she did to the kid. Deciding against the mother, they don't acknowledge her at all, staring ahead even as she yells one perfect curse and drags her yelping child to the end of the line.

"Did you see that?" cries Natalie. "These people are monsters!"

"See what?" lies Landau. "What did I miss?"

"Nothing," Natalie says. "Forget it. There's a cinema in that building." She indicates the waiting line. "They show a documentary about daily life in the camp. Probably with John Gielgud or a

Theo Bikel voice-over. I don't think I could stand it. Just being here is traumatic enough."

Natalie is hopeless! She thinks the toilet is the cinema! Just as she mistakes Eva's passion for Jiri for concern about his health! The Final Solution almost succeeded partly thanks to morons like Natalie, believing against all evidence that the toilet is the movies, that the death camp was a bucolic resettlement farm somewhere in the East, that the washroom where dead men primped was a bracing Spartan health spa.

But for Landau it's a lucky break. He would love to take a piss, maybe move his bowels. His stomach has been in such lousy shape that he's become very toilet-conscious and registers the location of every stinking latrine like a truck driver noting gas stations at the edge of a desert. Probably he can use this toilet for as long as he likes without returning to the curious glance, the uneasy moment that can occur after someone has gone to the toilet and stayed a really long time. He can take forever, and Natalie will think he was watching a movie.

"I'll go check," says Landau. "See what the film's like."

"Have a ball," says Natalie, whose pout reminds Landau of his own crestfallen face when he and the director of *To Kafka from Felice* went out drinking after rehearsals and Lynn—his actress, his distant star—claimed to be too tired. Later Landau learned that she was meeting her studmuffin lighting director.

"You might want to check on the old folks," Natalie says. "I don't know why they're not here on the benches. I heard Eva suggesting they might want to catch a few minutes of the film. As if such a film were something you might watch to pass a little time, like those vile TVs they have now in airports. Is Madame Kaprova Jewish? That hasn't been established."

"I wouldn't know," says Landau, thinking: Wake up! There *is* no movie, Natalie. But in that case . . . where *are* the graybeards, the Tel Aviv rabbi, the rich Antwerp businessman-donor and fervent Kafka fan? Is that how it was, people disappeared, first the old and weak . . . Landau *is* an asshole! It wasn't like that at all! Those old people were being slaughtered, while these must have found some nice leafy café for a snack and iced tea.

Landau joins the men's line and waves limply at Natalie, who still doesn't seem to wonder why the sexes must separate for the movies. Closer, he sees one guy at a time going in and out of the men's room. They seem to be pissing at record speed, and soon it's Landau's turn to empty his bladder—thank God!—and give his colon a tentative squeeze to see how things are doing.

Not well, is the answer, not well at all; his bowels slide all too quickly, his shit is practically water, and only now does he check for the thin sheets of sandpaper with which these poor slobs wipe their asses. Did Kafka use such paper? Surely Jiri will tell them. Surely that was one of the subjects about which he debriefed Ottla.

The bathroom is buzzing with horseflies so slow and fat it's no surprise that they can't stay airborne but keep landing on Landau's hands, his forehead, his lips. Disgusting! One hears that flies subsist on shit, and there's no doubt about these guys, too sated to leave the kitchen. Landau longs to achieve that transcendental state that lifts us above the sights and smells of alien public bathrooms, an escape route blocked when he recalls Jiri's famous chapter about the brutal choreographies of the camp latrines, the degrading lack of privacy that began on the boxcars.

Finally Landau finishes. Does he feel better or worse? His bowels burn slightly more than before, but at least—he hopes—

they are empty. He's sure his fingers must smell of shit. The thin gray paper is useless, but nothing can induce him to touch the common soap in its filthy string bag or the grimy towel resting on its hook after an encounter with some tourist's armpits. Landau rubs his fingers gingerly under the icy trickle and is still shaking off water when he exits into the foyer, evading the glare of an old man waiting for him to emerge.

Only now does a more relaxed, less preoccupied Landau sidle up to the wall to read a plaque explaining in five languages that this is the former residence of the camp Kommandant, his wife and children, all of whom, Landau imagines, may have used the same toilet, beneath which Landau's innocent excrement is mingling with the Devil's, or at least with that of the demon who shit every day like a normal person, and went off, whistling, to his job of torture and mass murder.

Landau hears the grainy drone of a movie sound track coming from a darkened room. He crosses the hall and looks in. People are sitting on folding chairs, their chins lifted toward a screen, watching a film which is, just as Natalie threatened, about life in the camp, of course not about the toilet habits of the Kommandant and his brats, but about the cruel charades with which the Nazis pretended that the cultural life of their inmates was as tenderly monitored as their personal hygiene.

On screen a chorus of skinny terrified children dressed in fringed vests and cowboy hats are singing—Landau can't believe this—"Don't Fence Me In." In English. The joke sends Landau reeling. Whose sense of humor was this? Or what encoded message were the chorus director and the filmmakers trying to slip past the Germans?

Landau feels a grinding in his gut, as if he's swallowed pebbles.

He almost returns to the toilet, but the men's line has doubled—tripled—and with great misgivings he goes back outside.

"How was it?" asks Natalie snidely.

"Depressing," Landau answers.

"What did you expect?" she says.

"*Brigadoon,*" says Landau.

"That's not funny," Natalie says.

"Oh, isn't it?" sneers Landau. Then the energy drains out of him, from his fingertips down. Is he dehydrated? Anemic? Who cares what his diagnosis is! He has no strength for this quarrel with dull ugly Natalie Zigbaum. He feels that he's back in his marriage: those long morbid Sundays with Mimi. To lose your desire for a woman is one thing—but to lose your taste for fighting! At night Mimi falls asleep, like one of Pavlov's dogs, the minute Ted Koppel comes on. Lying beside her in bed, Landau sometimes wonders how often Kafka slept with Felice. Once? Twice? Never? The point wasn't sex. For Kafka the ultimate turn-on was fucking with Felice's head, insisting that she write him the details of everything she did, every thought she had, what she read, what she ate, why she didn't write him more often—and then pulling back and having "doubts" about their love, their engagement, throwing Felice into despair, then feeling guilty, apologizing, and starting the whole gruesome process over and over again.

But where is the challenge with Natalie? You could drive her insane in five seconds. And their quarrel is so grotesque. What are they fighting about? Whether the former Kommandant's house is now a cinema or a toilet?

Natalie pats the seat beside her. Landau gapes at her plump freckled hand. He could be a kid again, repelled by middle-aged flesh. So what if he's middle-aged, too? He doesn't have to like it. He can't sit where Natalie's hand has been. But what else should he do? Wander off for one more peek in the shaving-room mirror? Catch another round of the children's choir doing great cowboy hits from the death camp?

Landau feels so much like a cornered rat that his breath comes in rodentlike wheezes. He's overreacting, but face it: This is the camp. Even Natalie knows that, Natalie, who keeps patting the bench with a hand that separates from her body, a fat white grub with liver spots, five tentacles stroking the seat. If Landau parks his butt there, he will never get up again.

And then—suddenly!—help arrives. Landau is saved by the Kafka Congress, erupting through the archway that must mark the end of the tunnel. Landau can see from a distance: The little flock is very upset. Tottering on her spiked heels, Eva Kaprova runs sheepdoglike circles around the conferees, shepherding them forward while they stumble over each other, encircling Jiri Krakauer. Some of them walk backward to keep an eye on Jiri, who is also stumbling, dragging himself along, leaning his meaty slab of an arm on the stooped shoulders of the Albanian novelist.

"God in heaven!" cries Natalie. "A heart attack! I knew it!"

"Oh, shut up," mutters Landau, but not so that Natalie can hear. Liberated by disaster from the constraints that normally make him shy around Eva Kaprova, he rushes up to her and suddenly sees that his most repressive inhibitions have been wisdom in disguise. Because now for the first time he truly *gets* the myth of the Medusa, how a woman's face can freeze your blood, turn you into stone. Mimi Landau's darkest looks were girlish mugging compared with the raging furious mask that Eva Kaprova is wearing.

"Chest pains!" Eva hisses.

"Did they start in the tunnel?" Landau's question is too stupid for Eva to dignify with a reply.

As Eva brushes past him, Landau pauses a beat, then ducks beneath Jiri's free arm and takes half the weight from the Albanian, who thanks him with a pained smile. Does Jiri even know Landau's there? Yes! He claps him on the back with a hearty smack that reassures Landau about the state of Jiri's health.

A briny smell comes off Jiri, mixed with floral cologne, and Landau feels slightly woozy, especially when Jiri bears down on his shoulder. How grotesquely ironic if Landau were to die while helping Mr. Unkillable survive, once again on the backs of his comrades.

Landau can't afford these thoughts. What matters is not dropping Jiri and not losing sight of Eva's red hair above her black silk blouse, the rare glimpses of those swaying hips stretching her tight summer skirt. Jiri is very heavy, but they can't stop walking, and the physical strain is turning Landau into a different—a calmer—person. The chatter in his brain has stopped. The only thing, the critical thing, is putting one foot in front of the other, which, as Landau recalls, is a state that Jiri has described as essential for survival in the camp.

The tourists in line for the toilet are staring at the Kafka conferees like extras in some epic costume drama about the aftermath of war, like peasants lining the road to watch the wounded army retreat. Landau is one of those soldiers, supporting his fallen comrade. . . .

Eva collars strangers for swift panicky consultations and runs, then walks, then runs again. Is there a doctor in the camp? After a while she goes one way, and Landau, Jiri, and the Albanian take off in the opposite direction. Is some ghostly magnetic race-memory pulling them toward the camp's former hospital? Or is Jiri guiding them like a glass on a Ouija board?

"No, please, here," Eva shouts crossly at Landau, who has done nothing to deserve her impatience and contempt. Let *her* carry this two-hundred-pound ox all the way back to Prague!

Eva enters a doorway, waving for them to follow. Landau hears the clatter of dishes, and his glasses fog with the steamy school-lunch aroma of cabbage, fried meat, and detergent.

So it's not an infirmary, but some sort of restaurant. What does it say about Eastern European medical care that Eva has decided to bring a sick man to a café? In which case shouldn't Landau be more alarmed about the state of his own health? What if—just what if—his stomach complaints should be masking something more serious, and he too has a fatal attack?

Seated at one long table are the elderly Kafka conferees, eating and making merry, the Tel Aviv rabbi waving his fork as he argues some point with the Toronto critic. The Cambridge don spots Jiri and alerts the others, who turn and stare, alarmed.

Jiri leans down to whisper to Landau.

"Couldn't you vomit?" Jiri says. Reflexively, Landau edges away. But Jiri's referring to the restaurant patrons, their mouths and chins gleaming with grease, wispy beer-foam mustaches lightly frothing their lips. Or maybe he means the room itself, or what-ever it used to be when Jiri knew this tourist paradise in an earlier incarnation. The café is twice, three times as hot as the courtyard outside!

Jiri murmurs something else, spraying Landau's ear with spit, but Landau doesn't mind. Finally, he is feeling a hint of that transcendence that has eluded him before, that swooning sense of rising above the grubby and the small to a place where a saintly version of yourself lets a sick man spit in his ear.

Jiri beckons Eva over, and Landau must perform the complex ballet of moving aside so Jiri can whisper to Eva while Landau stays close enough so that Jiri doesn't keel over; the only way is for Eva to wedge her hip against Landau's groin. Landau feels the faint stirrings of an erection. Well, it's been a dry time since he got to Prague. In fact it's been a dry time for a long while before that. He and Mimi hardly ever have sex, and his affair with the actress, Lynn, was entirely in his head, hungry gazes across the theater, daydreams, and jerking off.

"This was the SS Canteen," says Eva, briefly reverting to her duties as tour guide, briefly forgetting her new role as emergency nurse. Then, remembering, she yells in Czech and, ever the conscientious translator, in English for the conferees: "This man is sick! Someone get us some chairs, a table, a cold rag, and hot tea!"

Eva makes such a ruckus that the other diners give up sawing at their schnitzel and lift their noses out of their beer steins.

The Kafka conferees shift seats, sliding over as fast as they can, an undignified rout requiring much groping for chairs and rearranging of skirts. They make room, lots of room for Jiri. Eva nearly tackles him, pushing him into the nearest chair.

In fact there are several empty chairs, and after many clumsy mistakes, a seating plan emerges: Jiri is in the middle with Eva Kaprova on one side and the Albanian on the other, while Landau is directly across from Jiri, flanked by the Croatian feminist and, of course, Natalie Zigbaum.

They rest for a moment, panting, as if they've all run a long way. Then Eva snakes her nicotine-stained fingers into Jiri's shirt pocket and frisks him, shamelessly intimate, until she snaps her head impatiently and grabs her purse and takes out a bottle of pills. So Eva is carrying Jiri's pills—they might as well be married!

Eva shakes out a pill and fills a glass with cloudy water from a pitcher. Stop! Landau longs to cry out. But surely Jiri must be immune to whatever fiendish microbes have been frolicking in Landau's intestines. Will Eva be hurt if Landau implies that her country's water isn't safe to drink?

Jiri wraps his huge fat hand around Eva's thin one, brings her hand to his mouth and eats the pill out of her palm in a gesture that combines lecherous suggestiveness with pathetic dependence. He takes a sip of water and swallows with great effort; his Adam's apple squirms in his neck like a kitten trapped in a sack. Then he coughs; stops, and coughs again, a bout that lasts long enough for Landau to hear in Jiri's cough the rasping of the dead sunflowers shaking in the hot wind. Jiri coughs for so long that Landau runs out of metaphors and just listens, paralyzed like everyone else, to the sick man's wheeze, which rasps on so interminably they fear it will never end.

They watch the cough consuming Jiri, eating him cell by cell, so that he appears to be shrinking before their eyes, and if there's an ounce of strength left in him, Jiri needs it to push away the water glass that Eva Kaprova slides toward him, now tenderly, now aggressively, while Landau looks on, needing all his own strength to ward off certain images, to keep certain terrible memories from worming into his mind, clearly remembered wrenching scenes from the deaths of his parents: phone calls, doctors, hospital beds, bedpans, sponge baths, glimpses of wasted aging flesh Landau wishes he'd never seen.

As soon as Landau gets back to his hotel, he will telephone

Mimi, to whom he hasn't spoken since he got to Prague, unless he counts the answering machine he informed of his safe arrival. Even if it takes hours to get through, Landau will call his wife and tell her every thought he's had, what's he's seen, what he's eaten, what he's heard, his worries about his health. Isn't that what Kafka wanted from Felice? Mimi and Landau will talk with a candor they haven't shared in years. Mimi knew Landau's parents, she knows who he really is . . . he'll censor only tiny bits, like Natalie Zigbaum's crush on him and his attraction to Eva Kaprova. If he doesn't reach Mimi at home, he'll track her down at the shelter and pour out his heart while women shriek and babies cry and dishes crash in the background.

But even as he imagines this, Landau fears it is useless; he is sure that the world he imagines has somehow ceased to exist. There is no Mimi, no shelter, no Upper West Side, no New York. He will never get to his hotel or beyond this moment of watching Jiri Krakauer cough his lungs out in a café at the death camp.

"Jiri," Eva is nearly sobbing with grief, "Jiri Jiri Jiri!" telling the whole conference they're on a first-name basis, no Rabbi this or Professor that, no Miss Zigbaum or Mister Landau.

Jiri's coughing slacks off a bit, then reaches another crescendo that drives Eva to slam down the water glass and rake her fingers through her hair, a signal for the conferees to ascend to new heights of alarm.

Natalie leans toward Landau and whispers, *"La Traviata."*

Jiri gasps and sputters, and just when it seems that the crisis might be abating, he slumps forward onto the table.

Landau's shocked to find a prayer buzzing through his mind, a plea to no one in particular: Please don't let anything happen to him. Please don't let him die.

When was the last time Landau prayed? When his plane made a rocky landing in Prague. He wants to think he's praying for Jiri, but he knows it's for himself. If Jiri recovers, they can all go home and forget this. But if Jiri dies here, if he's come back to die in the death camp, Landau feels that some part of himself will be stuck here forever and ever.

Eva half-rises out of her chair and flings herself on Jiri's back, but Jiri ripples his shoulders and shrugs her off.

Back from the dead, Jiri raises his hand. It will take more than this to kill him.

"Please," croaks Jiri. "Everyone eat!"

On cue, a gang of waiters rush over. A menu is slapped down in front of Landau, while more menus sail past him like Frisbees. Rushing waiters? Flying menus? In this country where waiters scurry away if you happen to catch their eye and hide in the kitchen and move only in the slow-motion crawl of scuba divers?

One day the conferees went to a café in Old Town Square, where the waitress ignored them for so long that they twice got to see the astronomical clock put on its hourly performance. Finally Jiri stood and began to follow their waitress, duckwalking behind her like Groucho Marx. The waitress ignored him for a while and then turned on her heel and gave Jiri a long cold stare and came over and took their orders.

Maybe these waiters are just relieved that Jiri has stopped coughing and isn't dying. Or is he? "Everyone eat!"—what perfect last words for Mr. Zest-for-Life, campaigning with his final breath for a posthumous Nobel Prize, while Landau, that worthless flea, that grub, begrudges the last unselfish thought of this man who plumbed the depths of darkness and bobbed up to the surface and is going down one last time, thinking only of his comrades.

Dying, Kafka begged his doctor not to leave him and then reconsidered and said, "But I am leaving you." Felice's dying words went unrecorded, of course, so Landau had to invent them: "All I wanted was your happiness, Franz." He can still hear Lynn whispering that sultry *Liebestod*, and the audiences' quiet gasps, and the sounds of sniffling. Those sniffles couldn't have been faked! They didn't know Landau was watching!

What if Landau died right now? What would his final words be? He hasn't spoken since he asked Eva Kaprova if Jiri's chest pains began in the tunnel. How lame and moronic he'd sounded! Oh God, he'd better say something quick or be remembered (by whom?) for that.

Jiri opens his menu. Covered with imitation leather, big as the Magna Carta, the menu trembles in his hands and falls onto the table. Eva picks it up and holds it in front of Jiri, who clumsily bats it away.

"You decide. Please," he gasps. "Can't you do anything right?"

Eva looks at him and looks away. The intimacy with which she'd stared into his eyes as they'd planned their forthcoming Kafka Congress à deux has entirely disappeared. Who is this man? What does he need? Eva hardly knows him.

"Give us a minute," she tells the waiter, who grimaces with scorn and then resumes staring impatiently at her.

Someone taps Landau's shoulder hard, and he turns around. His waiter is a stocky old man with tiny porcine eyes, a semicircle of cropped white hair outlining his shiny head. He looks like Nikita Khrushchev, he looks like . . . every former concentration camp guard whose photo Landau has ever seen in the papers. What was this sweaty old sadist doing during the war? Landau pictures him stepping out of his black tie and tails—the poor schmuck wears a tuxedo at a tourist joint in a death camp—and putting on his old uniform and going to work at the camp, maybe as a switchman, waving in the trains.

The old man sneers at Landau and points disdainfully at the menu. Landau forces a brittle smile and turns the heavy pages. Columns of letters hold still for an instant, then swim off in every direction. Landau needs his reading glasses—unless he wants to remove his regular glasses and press the menu against his nose. He pats his pockets—they aren't there! Where the hell could he have lost them?

Not in the toilet, he certainly hopes. When did he have them last? He's horrified to think of his glasses left in the camp without him: like fingernail clippings, a lock of hair left on the voodoo priest's doorstep. He should leave at once and start searching— how will he replace them in Prague?—but he's reluctant to make a scene or even explain his wimpy problems: farsightedness, forget- fulness, misplacing his pitiful specs while Mr. Historical-Tragedy is having a coronary and dying.

The waiter sighs and rolls his eyes as Landau scans the blurry menu. Could he borrow someone's glasses? He and Mimi used to exchange reading glasses when they still pretended that growing old was a little joke between them and not (as it would soon become) a crime each blamed on the other. Poor Mimi, farsight- edness isn't her fault!

Natalie's wearing reading glasses, smudged with fingerprints and flecked with tiny white dots. Landau wouldn't borrow hers, not if he were starving and this menu listed the last food on earth! His starry explosion of sympathy for Mimi, back home in New York, has failed to rain droplets of charity down on Natalie Zigbaum.

Anyway, Natalie's busy, speaking Czech with her handsome young waiter. Pointing at the menu, she's debating her selection. She must think she's in France or Italy, some country in which it makes sense to have informative chats on the subject of food for which you will soon pay tons of money. She must have forgotten that she's here, where the only choice is between the deep-fried pork and the deep-fried chicken. Landau can hear his arteries wheeze, strangling along with his bowels. The minute he gets back to New York, he'll go in for an angioplasty—forget the stress test, the heart monitors, cut directly to the chase.

"Yes?" says Landau's waiter. Landau looks across the table, thus bringing to four the number of men—Jiri, his waiter, Landau and his—boring into Eva with impatient hostile stares.

Eva implores the waiter in Czech, touching her stomach and breast in the universal language for whatever a culture believes the sick and weakened can eat. Eva too must imagine herself in a country in which a cook can conceive of anything edible prepared without gobs of salt and duck fat.

"Meat," Jiri whispers. "I need meat. Not water! Not gruel! This bitch is trying to starve me."

Jiri is speaking English, but the waiters understand and are glad to be able to cut the bitch loose and deal directly with Jiri. Several talk at once in Czech, no doubt listing a selection of animal organs, available charred or deep-fried. Jiri's too ill to care. Again he covers his face with his freckled truck driver's hands, covers everything but his ears, with which he listens until at last he raises his chin and nods, still without looking up.

Now both waiters focus on Landau.

"The same," says Landau, his teeth clenched so tight that he has to repeat it. "The same." *These* will be his last words now: I'll have what that other guy has. "The same" translates into Czech, it seems, and the waiters trudge toward the kitchen.

Eva has to call them back to say that she too will have the same thing as Jiri and Mr. Landau.

Then urgently she tells Jiri, "What you've ordered is terribly heavy. Very hard to digest. Do you really think you should—?"

Jiri slowly peels back his fingers and rotates his face toward Eva. "Is this about money?" he says. "The conference saving a couple of kopecks? That's all right! Thanks! We'll skip the meat course! Grandpa will just have the soup."

"Jiri!" cries Eva. "Calm yourself! Please!"

"I'm calm!" says Jiri. "Calm enough to see through your fucking plans. Persuading Jiri Krakauer to pimp for the Kafka Foundation, if there *is* a Foundation, if it isn't the private account of Madame Eva Kaprova, maybe toward a hot new car or a week at some nudist beach in Dalmatia—"

Eva covers Jiri's mouth with her hand, which he promptly pulls away, and the lovers struggle while the conferees stare. Landau feels a sort of vibratory hum rising from Natalie Zigbaum, an energy that builds and builds until it rockets her out of her chair. Grabbing the table edge, she leans across toward Jiri. From Landau's perspective—looking up—she's the figurehead on a ship's prow, an avenging mermaid with shelflike breasts plowing through the water.

"You know . . . ," Natalie tells Jiri, "you can be a real shit. You know that?"

Jiri's look of dazed annoyance reminds Landau of a cat, distracted by another cat and fooled into losing his mouse.

Jiri and Natalie regard each other. Something primal is transpiring. Natalie and Jiri facing off are the cobra and the mongoose, the shoot-out at high noon, lightning bolts zinging back and forth between the sorcerer and the witch. Natalie's crashing her broomstick right into Jiri's face, and Landau watches with new respect as the staring contest continues until—amazingly—Jiri surrenders by smacking the table and laughing.

"Very good," says Jiri. "I like this babe. Who is she?"

"I'm Natalie Zigbaum," she replies. "We've met. Several times, Mr. Krakauer."

"Of course!" says Jiri. "I remember. Can't a guy make a joke?"

"Hilarious," Natalie says.

"What's her problem?" Jiri asks the group.

Landau's plastic placemat is red and white, checked bistro-tablecloth style, dabbed with smears of dried gravy. A fly crawls out of a dish of salt and lumbers unsteadily from square to square of the Albanian's placemat. Landau thinks: I know that fly, he's followed me from the toilet.

Meanwhile Jiri's eyes widen with mock or genuine wonder as he seeks an explanation for Natalie Zigbaum's problem, silently asking the conferees and finally turning to Eva, who is not about to explain that Natalie's problem is how Jiri treats Eva. Natalie Zigbaum—Eva's defender. How humiliating that must be!

Distress exerts its downward pull on Eva's attractive features, a gravity lost on no one, not even Jiri. He smiles forgivingly, though he's the one who should be asking forgiveness, and, taking Eva's chin in his hand, he gently prods and squeezes her cheeks like a peach he's testing for ripeness.

"God," he says. "This place. This place. None of you know what it's like for me. This was the SS Canteen."

"I told them," Eva interjects nervously.

"Told them what?" says Jiri. "That being sent on an errand

here was a risky mission? Listen: The only way to survive in this camp was by forgetting your former life, blotting out what you used to have, what you used to love. It was much too dangerous, a death sentence if you remembered. Memory lowered your resistance, made you vulnerable and weak, remembering and hoping were the worst things you could do. That was the reason for what happened to me. Is *that* what you told them, Eva?"

"No," murmurs Eva, looking down.

"What happened to you?" breathes the Croatian feminist.

Scornfully, Jiri puckers his lips and plants a loud smacky kiss on the air. "It was safer to forget you'd ever been anywhere but hell. And the trouble was that the SS Canteen was a vision of heaven. Walking in the kitchen door brought back sensations deeper than words, memories of another world with warm stoves, hot soup, a world of tiny potatoes baked in their jackets, duck and chestnuts, Linzer torte, pear tarts with frangipane.

"That was what they ate here—and not only on holidays! Where did they get such ingredients? I wondered then, and I still wonder today. The Camp Kommandant was Viennese! He insisted on his pastry!"

Ah, the Kommandant, thinks Landau. He and I have shared a toilet.

"I too ate Viennese pastry," Jiri says. "With my mother, before the War. In this lovely little café, just the two of us, Mama and me. But if I'd let myself remember that, I never would have made it. . . ."

Landau's disturbed by a vague sense of something not quite right. . . . Then suddenly he realizes: All this business about forgetting the past in order to survive—It's from *Survival in Auschwitz!* Jiri's ripping off Primo Levi!

And now Landau can't control himself, the words burble out of his mouth. "Come on. Viennese pastry? Are you asking us to believe that there was a gourmet restaurant in a concentration camp in wartime Northern Bohemia?"

Instantly, he's sorry. Has he lost his mind? Jiri turns on him with the same stagey outrage, the precise same slow burn he did on Natalie Zigbaum. It strikes Landau that Jiri has a narrow repertoire of gestures and facial expressions. But who can blame him for trying to simplify? The pressures he must be subjected to, the demands, the expectations! Why bother learning new tricks if the old ones work, getting the laugh or the tear or the victory over the pitiful heckler?

But is it just Jiri stealing from Primo Levi or is it a . . . full-blown déjà vu, a little tug at the edge of that silky tablecloth, Time, rattling Landau like a saucer. Did something like this happen before? It didn't happen to Landau. It's Jiri who was here in the camp. Is this what Mimi means when she talks about clients losing their ego boundaries?

Jiri stares at Landau with his watery basset hound eyes, which visibly dry and brighten as they register Landau's discomfort. Anger resurrects him, reminding him of his stature, the historical experience that authorizes him to tell Landau to go fuck himself with such smug uninflected politeness.

"I wouldn't say gourmet," Jiri says. "Let's just say they ate well. Another one of their little jokes." As Jiri resumes his story, Landau can't help thinking he sounds . . . rehearsed. Isn't there something monstrous about Jiri telling this over and over, the Holocaust as a party piece to amuse one's dinner companions! But isn't that the point, in a way: to tell it again and again and never stop repeating. . . . It's Landau who's the monster, judging Jiri for sounding practiced.

Jiri says, "You took your chances when some SS bastard asked you to get him coffee and a slice of *Apfelkuchen*. It was always the biggest shitheads who sent you to the canteen. What they liked more than the coffee was to drink it in front of the prisoners. So you had to watch yourself when you'd just been in the canteen, dipping into that bright world that tricked you into remembering a life in which you ate when you were hungry. You had to make sure this old self didn't sneak into your face and give it the wrong expression while you watched the SS eat."

"What could the right expression have been?" Eva Kaprova mutters, as if to herself.

"My point exactly!" cries Jiri. "Okay. I met a pretty girl who worked in the canteen kitchen. She was Jewish, a pastry chef, also Viennese. Her other qualification was that she was the Kommandant's girlfriend. And very pretty. Did I say that?"

"You did," says Natalie Zigbaum. "Several times."

"Just once," says the Croatian feminist.

"So," says Jiri, "I began to *like* going to the canteen. I'd enter through the kitchen, where my girl always had something for me, some days a pastry horn stuffed with cream, some days almond custard. Not exactly what you want on an empty stomach. Did I say empty stomach? I was starving to death! But as my cute little pastry chef stuffed eclairs into my mouth, I persuaded myself that this was dessert, that I'd already eaten the whole fabulous meal that came before it.

"This girl and I would smooch all over the kitchen. We'd fuck leaning back against the shelves of the pantry. Once a box of powdered sugar fell down, and we licked it off each other. . . ."

Landau has never heard such sexual boasting in his life! He can't look at Natalie Zigbaum. If he catches her eye, he'll laugh. And then he sees: Natalie's leaning forward, drawn in by the story. Even as Landau was making plans to exchange a covert smirk at Mr. Camp-Casanova's expense, Natalie has been falling under Jiri's spell.

Okay, so the guy has charisma! It's unfair, but some people do, and not always good guys, not always Gandhi or the Dalai Lama; obviously there was Hitler. . . . Once, at a party, Landau met a reporter who covered the Oliver North trial for a New Jersey paper. He described going into the courtroom prepared to hate the little fucker, and after listening to him for ten minutes, thinking maybe he wasn't so bad.

But Jiri isn't Hitler. He isn't Ollie North. He's a guy who lived through hell and has every reason to be bitter and filled with hate, and instead embraces life, food and sex and women. And Landau's sitting here hating *him*, so who is the hateful person? It's not exactly surprising that no one, not even Natalie, is staring into Landau's eyes and hanging on *his* every word.

The color is back in Jiri's cheeks. In fact, he looks flushed, warmed by his own spicy story. Once more something's ringing a bell; it's clanging inside Landau's head. What does this scene remind him of? Has Jiri already written this? Jiri sounds so practiced he might as well be reading aloud:

"The whole kitchen knew what was going on, but they looked the other way, even though, believe me, we were giving them something to look at. My girlfriend was a good pastry chef, a hard worker, uncomplaining. And who wanted to tell the Kommandant what she was doing with me? It was easy to kill the messenger. They were killing everyone else. If the Kommandant learned the truth, all our lives would change, and the first rule of camp life was that change was never for the better.

"But this girl made me forget everything I'd learned in the camp. Not to hope and not to plan and not to trust in anything or anyone but yourself."

And now Jiri has the whole table—and half the restaurant— gazing at him like disciples at the feet of a master.

"I forgot myself," he says. "I hoped. I planned. I believed that no one would have the balls to tell the Kommandant. We got more and more outrageous. Our big thrill was having sex in the kitchen while the Kommandant was out in the canteen, nibbling chocolate cream puffs. We were young—what did we have to lose? We were going to die anyway."

The waiters bring small glass bowls of wilted salad, iceberg lettuce and soft tomatoes glued together with white cheese. Jiri makes a face at his salad and pushes it away.

Eva catches a waiter's eye—Landau's waiter, as it happens. Landau wonders if the waiter too feels he's heard this story before. Possibly he's worked in this joint since he used to bring the Kommandant's Sacher torte. Though probably his wartime duties were worse—unspeakably worse—than serving coffee and cake.

"Did we order this salad?" asks Eva. She and the waiter bark at each other in Czech, and then the waiter shrugs and begins to clear the salad bowls from the table. Landau stares after the salad that, a minute ago, seemed disgusting. Now he feels like Tantalus watching the grapes fly out of his reach and all the water in hell drain away as he bends to drink. When did Landau eat last? He truly can't remember. The ghost of the vanished salad lingers on the table, filmy shreds of green and red under a gooey white caul, lost now because of Eva Kaprova saving a couple of pennies at the expense of their happiness, their health. This is what Landau's worried about, here in this crummy café where, if one believes Jiri, the devil dined on lemon cream pie in the center of an inferno packed with the starving and the dead.

"Rabbit food!" shouts Jiri. "Who eats that shit, I ask you?"

"It's good for you," says Natalie Zigbaum, with a coyness bordering on flirtation that plunges like an ice pick straight into Landau's heart. You'd think Landau was in love with her, that's how grief-stricken he is now that she has shifted her burdensome affection from Landau onto Jiri's capable shoulders. When Landau found out that Lynn was sleeping with the lighting director (everyone but Landau knew and assumed he did, too) he used to look at the guy's twenty-five-year-old muscles squirming under his T-shirt and ask himself how a bright mature woman like Lynn could choose a . . . *back* . . . over Landau, with his talent, his experience. He was the fucking playwright! He'd met Mimi at a loft where a group of left-wing actors performed his play about Stephen Biko, a better version of the story that, years later, another playwright trashed and got onto Broadway.

"Good for old ladies!" Jiri booms back at Natalie, jolting Landau out of his reverie. Will Natalie take this personally?

"Good for everyone," she answers sweetly. Eva Kaprova nods, twice. So what if she's just sent the salad away? They're united in this, two women allied in a noble attempt to make Mr. Juicy-Carnivorous-Blood-Lust eat fiber and live forever.

"Where was I?" Jiri asks, and from down the table the Toronto critic calls, "Your little pastry chef in the kitchen!"

"Thank you, my good man," says Jiri. "Right. My little pastry chef. One day I showed up, she wasn't there. She'd been taken away. Two SS guys had finished their coffee and crullers up front and then come back to the kitchen and got her. I took the place apart. I went nuts! I raged like a bull. I threw pots, pans, flour. The cook looked like a snowman.

"Someone stepped in front of me. It was the Kommandant. He had flour on his overcoat sleeve, on his evil Hitler mustache, on the big red wart at the tip of his nose. I used to think about that wart, burrowing into my girlfriend. And now there he was, the son of a bitch. He looked at me, cool as a cucumber.

" 'Are you hungry?' he said.

"I also was a son of a bitch. You had to be to survive. I stared right into his squinty eyes. I said to him, 'Fuck you.' "

Jiri translates into Czech what can only mean *fuck you*. Loud, in case the whole room missed his heroic act.

Wait! thinks Landau. None of this is true! There was no Viennese bakery, no Kommandant patiently playing games with some Jewish kid. . . . It all leads back to the question of what Jiri Krakauer did to survive, not just survive but triumph and come out the other side seeing himself as the kind of guy who could sleep with the Kommandant's girlfriend, trash the SS kitchen, and live to tell (or invent) the tale.

"What happened then?" Eva asks.

"When?" Jiri smiles an odd half-smile.

"You know," Eva says girlishly.

"Say it," Jiri insists. "Say what I said."

Eva takes a deep breath. "When you told the Kommandant: Fuck you."

She might as well have said: Fuck me. That's how turned on Landau is by this intimate scenario of power and compliance.

"What happened next?" says Natalie. "Please! Don't leave us hanging!"

Jiri says, "Nothing happened next." Is his story over? He covers his eyes and shakes his head. Is he thinking about the dead girl? This is how he ends his stories: with the pretty pastry chef vanishing, the tiny art student marching off to Auschwitz, with great gushes of sentimentality, like coming all over his audience. And Jiri can get away with it because his subject is beyond literary criticism, beyond plausibility, kitsch, way beyond good or bad taste.

"Where's the food?" shouts Jiri. "We're dying here!" And once more Landau is shaken by what must be the world's most protracted déjà vu. Did he read this scene? Did he live through it? It's all so bizarrely familiar.

A pair of waiters—not Jiri's or Landau's—appear with several orders, ready ahead of the rest. No doubt they'd been sitting there cooling off until Jiri asked. Landau peeks over the top of the plates. Well, better the rabbi's noodle soup be a little cool. Don't want the old guy scalded as he sloshes soup all over himself, offering Jiri his bowl.

"No thank you!" Jiri scowls at the rabbi's soup. A few more plates of food arrive, though not for Jiri or Landau. It must be taking longer to cook the vast hunks of meat they've ordered.

It turns out not to matter who has been served and who hasn't. Jiri won't let anyone eat, won't let them escape into their slippery duck or the rubbery potato croquettes spurting geysers of grease.

"Excuse me!" he says. "It's not over. Listen, please, while I finish!" Forks drift down as gently as snow.

"Years later I saw the Kommandant. This was in the Catskills. Many years after the War." He turns to Eva Kaprova. "Do they know about the Catskills?"

Eva knows the answer, but she's lost the energy for translation.

"The Catskills," Natalie Zigbaum speaks up, addressing the crowd, the entire Tower of Babel they've erected in Kafka's name. "Like Karlsbad. Karlovy Vary. Marienbad. Yalta. For the health."

Landau whispers to Natalie, "You're right. The same healthy chopped liver diet, though without the healing waters, unless you count the Olympic pools. . . ." It's the kind of thing that Natalie would have whispered to Landau in that lost golden age before she just ignored him and kept listening, enraptured, to Jiri.

"I was with a girl in the Catskills," Jiri says. "On vacation. From my wife."

Ah ha ha, the Toronto critic gets this, and the Croatian feminist, even the Albanian novelist emits his depressive snort. Only Landau, the chump, considers Jiri's wife, left home so that Jiri can have his Borscht Belt fling. Why is Landau taking the wife's side? He might as well be Mimi, always siding with the wife, especially when Mimi *was* the wife. . . . Did Mimi know about the nights Landau waited till she was asleep and, under the cover of Ted Koppel's drone, crept into the living room and lay on the couch and thought about Lynn and jerked off. It was all so embarrassing, how easily he—at his age—could become obsessed with a woman. And was it any more or less depressing that he could forget so fast? He hardly feels anything anymore. . . . Did he think it would last forever? Nothing that embarrassing will ever happen to him again, which, he thinks, may be the most depressing part of all.

Mimi paid close attention whenever he mentioned Lynn and whenever he didn't mention Lynn. And he captured the tremor of pain and rage he heard in Mimi's voice and used it in the letter he wrote for Felice in the final week of rehearsal, the letter in which Felice describes the nights she lies awake, afraid that Kafka has stopped loving her and fallen for her go-between, her best friend, Grete Bloch.

Landau understands women. The critics—and many women Landau knows—have always agreed on this. No one has ever said as much about the great work of Jiri Krakauer. Landau understands women so well he never gets laid, except once a decade by Mimi. And Jiri so misunderstands them that they plaster themselves all over him, even Natalie Zigbaum.

And what's the point of understanding women? Or anyone, for that matter? Kafka was the first to admit he didn't understand himself. Yet he understood exactly what it was like to wake from a night of troubling dreams and discover that you had become a giant cockroach. Landau feels another twinge, another tug of déjà vu, announcing itself with an aura, like those displays of northern lights that precede Landau's migraines.

"We were in love," Jiri explains, in case his listeners have the wrong idea and imagine him betraying his wife just for hot sex at The Concord. "There was nowhere for us to go. *Why* was a very long story. I couldn't believe it, I was out of the camp, and still I couldn't find a place to take the woman I loved."

In other words, Jiri earned it. He had the right to take as many girls as he liked to love nests in the Catskills.

Jiri says, "Our intellectual refugee crowd would never go to a vulgar resort hotel, so I thought my girl and I could relax there and feel safe. This was before my first book came out, before strangers recognized me. . . . I saved up my money. We took the bus. We got there Friday night. On Saturday morning we stayed in bed late—and then went down for breakfast.

"And there, in a monkey suit, pouring coffee for our table, there he was, the Kommandant, big red wart and all!"

A voice screams and screams inside Landau's head: *The son of a bitch is lying!* This lousy café in a death camp was never a gourmet bistro! Its Kommandant never turned up as a waiter in the Catskills! Real life never dabbles in such corny absurdities, such perfect ironies, cheap coincidences . . . though Landau has to wonder: Who is the cornier writer—Jiri Krakauer, or real life? Probably Jiri got the idea when, like Landau, he saw the older waiters and speculated about what they did during the War. But unlike Landau, Jiri's pretending that his fantasy happened.

Landau's on his own here, out here all alone. No one else thinks Jiri's lying, not the Croatian feminist nor the Toronto critic. The Tel Aviv rabbi must question the Talmud more than Jiri's story.

"What happened next?" cries Natalie.

"Nothing happened," says Jiri. "What should have happened? What was I supposed to do? Shoot the guy? Beat the shit out of him? Go directly to jail? Devote my life to bringing him in, testify at his trial? Hey, I'm not Simon Wiesenthal. Please. I'm only a poor struggling writer. What happened? My girlfriend and I ate our bagels and lox. He poured us plenty of coffee.

"Now listen. Here comes the juicy part: the dessert, so to speak. It was our waiter's, the former Kommandant's, job to bring round the pastry cart!"

Jiri is sitting up very tall, recovered, alive and then some. He shakes his head and grabs the air, intoxicated by the gorgeousness of this detail. His mitts inscribing the very same curves he made earlier in the conference, encircling the yummy memory of Ottla Kafka's hips. Hot sun streams in the window, backlighting his thick white hair.

I know who he looks like! Landau thinks. *He looks like Kafka's father, except with longer hair!*

"The pastry cart!" says Jiri. "Can you believe it! Maybe the guy asked for that job. He was still a big lover of pastry. . . .

"So I had a little fun. I ordered the lemon cream pie. The Kommandant brought the lemon pie. I took a bite. I waited a minute. Two minutes. Then I asked for the chocolate chiffon. And I took one bite of that. And so on. The banana. The blueberry. The apple. Our table was covered with pies and cakes. My girlfriend couldn't imagine what the hell was going on."

"Excuse me," the Albanian interrupts in a gentle voice, slightly rusty from disuse. "Did this waiter, this Kommandant—did he recognize you?"

Jiri pretends to think about it, as if he's never wondered, as if he's never been asked, as if he hasn't told this story a thousand times before.

"I guess so," he answers at last. "I think you'd remember the little bastard who fucked your girlfriend! No?"

For the first time, the Albanian laughs from the gut. Ho ho ho, the men love this, the critics, the rabbis, the professors, the scholars, and third-rate poets, they turn to Landau to gather him in this all-male embrace that includes all the men in the room, in the world, even those little bastards who poach on the next guy's erotic preserve, even the little-bastard lighting director who turned out to be porking Lynn. If that little bastard walked in the door right now, Landau would like to imagine that he wouldn't give a damn—though he might feel as if he'd instantly grown ten years older and ten pounds fatter.

"We're dying of hunger!" Jiri cries, alerting the whole café. In another minute he'll storm the kitchen and fetch the remaining orders himself.

"Please, trust me," Eva says desperately. "You know this place. It is coming."

"Damn right I know this place!" Jiri says. "That's what worries me."

Just then, a waiter brings Natalie's food. Landau, Eva, and Jiri stare with curiosity and then longing at her plate of sliced roast pork with a trickle of brown gravy, nicely lumpy mashed potatoes, and some kind of berry relish. Food has come to Natalie, but she doesn't look happy to see it. While Jiri was telling his story, he belonged to the whole group, but now that his story is over, he's reverted to being just Eva's.

Landau clears his throat, then says, "That pastry chef—was she before or after Ottla?"

People stop chewing and hold their breath, creating a silence that's audible above the din of the café.

"Excuse me?" says Jiri. "Excuse me? Before or after *whom*?"

"Ottla Kafka," says Landau. He can't believe how crass he sounds, how crude and leering and slimy. He feels he's been suckered into it by how the men were talking about little bastards fucking your girlfriend. Several times, as a schoolboy, Landau was taken in by classmates who said they would all play some trick on the teacher and then bailed out and left Landau to play it all by himself. That's how he feels now, alone in his dirty trick. He's guilty, and he deserves it when Jiri wheels on Landau.

"What's it to you?" Jiri says. "What's it to you who I fucked, and in what order, while I was fighting to stay alive in the midst of a giant killing machine? Not just staying alive but stealing a moment for tenderness, for love. What difference does it make to you if I fucked one and then the other, or both at once, if I started fucking one girl two seconds after the other was sent to Auschwitz. What's it to you, you little—"

"Nothing," says Landau. "It's nothing at all. I'm sorry. I had no business . . . I don't know what I was saying."

He can't believe he's done this; he's finally got the attention he's craved from Jiri and the others, but with a question that's reduced this hallowed ground to dirt, reduced a saint, Ottla Kafka, the sister of a saint, to the kind of slut men joke about in the locker room.

"You neurotic American guys," Jiri says. "You shitty writers and academics and bloodsucking so-called intelligentsia. The dirty truth is, you envy us, you wish it had happened to you. You wish you'd gotten the chance to survive Auschwitz or the Gulag. History has picked up our lives and given them hard little kisses, while your generation has been left virgins, unkissed, on the shelf. And what have you done? Played cops and robbers during the Vietnam War? Then gone on, making money, not making money, writing your silly poems, your . . . plays, your bullshit. You know your lives have no meaning, so you distract yourself with sex. Did I say sex? I don't mean *having* sex, I mean having sexual *problems* that you whine about in your books and . . . plays,

no wonder nobody goes to see them! And you want to think that
Kafka was a lonely guy with problems just like yours.

"But guess what Ottla told me? *Kafka fucked like a bunny!*"

Everyone's looking at Landau now, or rather at Jiri and Landau,
asking themselves which of the two is more important, more
attractive, the better writer, more of a . . . man. Handsome old
Mr. Spirit-of-Life with his flowing white hair, his gorilla's shoulders and hands, his dramatic story? Or the middle-aged myopic
golem with the migraines and diarrhea, the guy who gave the
most boring reading of the entire conference, the pathetic yelp-
ings of some babe Kafka didn't want to marry?

Which is what Jiri is saying: "The guy just didn't want to get
married. Meanwhile he was fucking every girl in Prague, society
women, whores, going to health spas and fucking patients and
nurses. Because that's what you do in the face of death, and his
sister was the same way. She had all her brother's genius, which
she used, when I knew her, for finding ways we could be
together. . . . Not like you pussies, you . . . creeps . . . having sex
in your head, complaining because you had the bad luck to miss
out on the great tragedies and get stuck in your boring lives—"

So now it's clear: Landau *is* Felice. No wonder he could write in
her voice. *Madame Bovary, c'est moi.* He's the dumpy woman with
braces on her teeth, whom Kafka didn't want to marry but got a
kick out of torturing by mail, tormenting himself in the bargain.
Landau's the reject, the spinster, unworthy of being alive. So what
if Mimi chose him? That was years ago. So what if a lousy critic
or two said his plays weren't too awful?

But why should Landau feel this way? What has he done to
deserve this flood of wrath and resentment and spite, of more

venom than Jiri (if his story is true) spewed on the former Camp Kommandant? Landau tries, but can't quite convince himself that Jiri doesn't mean him, Jiri doesn't know him, he shouldn't take this personally, Jiri is enacting some primal battle, some generational father-son thing: Abraham and Isaac, Oedipus Rex, Kafka and his father.

And now Landau figures out what's been eluding him all along. He's not having a déjà vu. They're *living* a Kafka story, specifically, "The Judgment," the passage in which the weakened babylike father suddenly recovers and swells into a giant and starts to shout and humiliate Georg, the son who has been carrying him in his arms.

Feeling someone come up behind him, Landau swivels around and rams his elbow into the waiter bringing his lunch. His food has arrived on an individual wooden chopping block streaming with juices and grease. A modest dish of fried potatoes accompanies the largest piece of meat Landau has ever seen.

The waiter slams it down before Landau so that the potato dish rattles. The meat bounces up in the air and lands with a daunting thud.

Just what part of the pig was *this*? A whole shoulder or a haunch, a heart-shaped hunk of serious meat under a crispy foreskin of fat, shot through with an arrow of bone, thick as a human thighbone, but stubbier and more clublike. *Treyf, Treyf,* bad for you, unclean, in other words delicious, the caramel crust of meat and fat, the juicy meat smell in the air.

Only now does Landau notice that Jiri and Eva haven't gotten their food. It's as if there is a God, watching over Landau, or as if the ex-Nazi waiters are angels who know that Landau has been abused and are tending to his needs first.

But are they doing him a favor? Or is this a new and ingenious form of torture? Perhaps this prodigious piece of meat was meant for Jiri, the celebrity, and Landau got it by mistake, and now what should he do? He should pass his chopping block across the table, conveniently saving himself from having to eat in front of the others, from having to chew and swallow this slab of pork fat big as a grown man's head, from subjecting his system to this, after all his poor stomach's been through, diarrhea in the Kommandant's toilet and now a cholesterol fest! Landau shouldn't eat the meat, maybe just the potatoes. He should pass his food on to Jiri . . . or possibly Eva? Should he offer his meal to the sick man, or be gallant, ladies first . . . ?

Landau is still puzzling this out when Jiri rises out of his chair and plunges his fork into Landau's meat and sails it, dripping, high over the table and plunks it down on his placemat.

"Wait a minute . . . ," Landau says weakly.

"Wait nothing," Jiri says. "This—this!—is how I survived in the camp! Meat! You Americans don't know what it's like to not be able to have it. You get no pleasure from meat or food or sex or love or anything except making fine distinctions. I'll have this and not that, thank you, this isn't good for me, thank you, I don't think I'd better, thank you. . . ." Jiri's voice is high and tremulous, his mouth twisted in a savage imitation of . . . Landau? Landau doesn't sound like that, doesn't look—

"And here's the most pathetic thing," says Jiri. "How small you are, how microscopic. . . . Here you are, Mr. Landau, here you are in the death camp, tromping on the unmarked graves of innocent women and children, and you're fighting some little fight in your head, squabbling with me, or maybe with Papa, some ridiculous ego drama about writing or women or who gets to sleep with

Mama or something equally childish, and your smallness is so gigantic it blocks the whole horizon, blocks your view of history, of the world, and you won't let go, you won't let go, till you suck me into it, too—"

Jiri's fork is still stuck in the meat.

Landau stands and glares at Jiri. He's dimly conscious of Natalie's steadying hand applying itself to his arm.

"Liar," Landau hears himself say.

"Pardon me?" says Jiri.

"You're a liar," Landau repeats. He can't believe he's doing this—he's doing it for Kafka! This is what Kafka should have done, stood up to his father, that bully—and not just in a letter. Landau's heart is pounding, a belt cinched round his chest. Is he having a heart attack? No, he feels terrific! He feels like a hero, gearing up to tell Jiri that his lies must stop, that having survived those years in the camp doesn't put him above the truth, doesn't let him appropriate and distort an event so profound and important, doesn't let him turn the Holocaust into kitsch, into bad— terrible!—art. . . .

Jiri looks at Landau, long enough for Landau to shrink under Jiri's chilly gaze.

"And what have I lied about?" Jiri says evenly. "About the six million dead? Don't tell me you're one of those loonies who say the Jews are making it up, the whole thing never happened. Herr Professor Landau, the first Jewish Holocaust revisionist."

Of course, Landau doesn't think that. But of course he can't say so. He can't say: I believe in the Holocaust. He'd feel like an absolute jerk. What did he think he was doing? Defending the six million against this dying mediocre writer? The dead no longer need Landau, nor do they need Jiri. They are way beyond caring about who's telling the truth and who's lying.

As Jiri stares at Landau, blood rushes into his face: The bright red of a flashlight switched on beneath his skin. A blurry distraction fogs his eyes, as if he's just remembered something; he opens his mouth, attempts to speak . . . and crashes forward onto his plate. Silverware clatters, tumblers spill. Landau jumps up to escape the rivulets of water and beer trickling toward him across the table. Eva also leaps to her feet and grabs Jiri's wrist and starts screaming in Czech.

Is she saying that she can't find his pulse? Is Jiri dead? Landau backs away and nearly collides with a waiter, who curses at him and then joins the group of waiters converging on Jiri. The canteen's patrons stand to watch this alarming drama in progress. . . . Landau backs farther away. No one turns to look. Eva doesn't run after him the way she runs after Jiri. Not even Natalie notices or cares where Landau is going.

Is his leaving an act of cowardice? Could Landau help save Jiri by staying? What is Landau thinking? He's the one who may have killed him!

Just outside the door, he stops. All right. Okay. What now? The sun has ignited the whole camp in a flare of nuclear white. Landau can't go back in. He can't go on. He can't just stand here, frozen. His instinct is to get out of the camp. Okay. Fine. Follow that.

But the camp isn't making it easy. The heat and the cobblestone path conspire to make each step an effort. Imagine if there were guards here with orders to block his escape. But the guards are busy taking tickets, selling postcards and souvenirs.

Landau was right not to want to come. This place truly is hell. Well, not hell, exactly. A former hell, remodeled. The smoldering pit where hell used to be has closed up like a wound, and crowds of people pay money to inspect the jagged scar. Jiri should have known better, too. He overestimated his powers if he allowed himself to think he was stronger than the camp. How foolish of him to imagine that he could outlive or outrun or outsmart it, when the camp was waiting all those years, biding time until it could claim him. . . .

Amazingly, Landau's picking up speed, half-jogging toward the exit. The up-and-down motion is good for his brain. Slowly it eases the searing burn of what Jiri Krakauer said, and of what Landau said—and couldn't say. What could he have answered? There was nothing to say.

Only now does it start to sink in: what has—what may have—happened. The deadweight of sorrow and loss and dread presses on Landau's stomach. The grief that overcomes him is so intense, so shocking—Landau hasn't felt like this since his parents died! He longs to go back and pull Jiri out of his chair and gather him in an embrace. The urge is so strong Landau groans aloud. But what would he tell Jiri? He wants to say: I prayed for you. I prayed you wouldn't die.

What did Jiri do to Landau to deserve the coup de grâce that Hitler and all his armies weren't able to deliver? What was Landau so angry at? Jiri's lies, his exaggerations? Who appointed Landau to be the righteous avenger, safeguarding the fragile honor of the dead? Did he imagine for one second that all six million were saints?

Unlike Landau, the world knows better than to believe that all six million were heroes, the world isn't fooled, the world doesn't care if Jiri was less than perfect. They'll mourn him, mourn this hero's death, and they'll be especially moved by the bitter irony of his returning to die in the death camp. Every magazine, every newspaper will carry Jiri's story, and not one of them—Landau is sure—will note that his final attack was precipitated by an obscure, pathetic playwright, a worm so small that he's still competing with Jiri, even after he's killed him!

But maybe Landau's being too hasty, too quick to bury Jiri, maybe Mr. Survivor will live through this, too. . . .

Landau lowers his head and keeps going. He runs out onto the drawbridge, thinking: Now it's *just* like "The Judgment." After his father's tirade, the son, Georg Bendemann, runs from the house and over a bridge streaming with heavy traffic. He shouts, "Dear Parents, I always loved you!" and vaults over the rails and into the water.

This is perfect! It couldn't be better! The stage is set for Landau to leave the death camp via the wooden bridge and fling himself into the deep trench that the Nazis dug to be flooded in case they needed a moat. Landau would land with a sickening crunch amid the Coke cans and brown paper bags, his head at that rag-doll angle in a tangle of thorny weeds.

Landau's not going to jump, no way! He knows what he's going to do:

He'll wait near the bus for the rest of the group. He won't even leave Prague early. He'll stay the last two days, grinning, eating shit, mourning Jiri—if he's dead—or else pretending nothing happened, as if anyone cares what Landau pretends, not even Natalie now. Then he'll board the plane and travel ten hours in a flying anchovy can with foul air, lousy food, someone's screaming baby. He'll take the bus from JFK to Grand Central and splurge on a ride home in some maniac's taxi, and let himself into the apartment, where maybe Mimi will be asleep, or maybe she'll be at the shelter. On his desk he'll find stacks of bills, requests for letters of recommendation from students he can't remember, notes from theater directors explaining why they can't consider *To Kafka from Felice* for the upcoming season.

Landau stops and stares into the chasm, at a grape-colored plastic bag turning ashen in the sun. The parking lot is before him, and just beyond, the cemetery with its silver cross gleaming over the orderly rows of the dead.

Landau will join them soon enough, and none of this will matter, just as it no longer matters to those already there. But for now, it's all that counts, and for now, Jiri is right: Landau would feel better, he would have been better off if something or someone had picked him up and thrown him into the abyss.

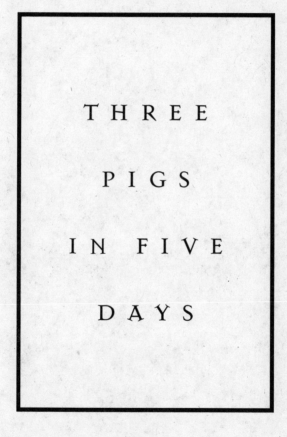

THREE

PIGS

IN FIVE

DAYS

Every time she turned on the TV, someone was killing a pig. Tonight it was an elderly Provençal couple, like Russian nesting dolls, the farmer who would have fit so neatly inside his bowling pin of a wife. Their pig was a very docile pig, unlike the pig last night, which the elderly Alsatian couple had slaughtered, also on TV.

When the Provençal farmer bopped his pig on the head with a mallet, the pig nodded, as if remembering, then sank to its knees and died. The Alsatian pig had struggled and squealed and bled all over the snow, and the Alsatian couple had also yelled as they ran around lunging and grabbing.

But even that was quiet compared with the woman next door to Nina whose all-night screaming orgasm had kept the hotel awake all last night. Nina slept between crescendos and woke in fits of grief or rage, though it had never bothered her, all her other times in Paris. Screaming was something Frenchwomen did, or else there was a sex tape that French hotel owners put on to impress American tourists.

Nina had said that to Leo, the last time they were in Paris. They'd heard a woman that time, too. They'd both known she was faking. Because they knew what the real thing was. Intense, the opposite of noise, it made the whole world get quiet.

That time in Paris they'd hardly gone outside except to change hotels, the five—or was it six?—hotels the famous dead had slept in, Oscar Wilde, Fitzgerald, Hemingway, Edith Piaf, supposedly in the same rooms Nina was writing about for *Allo!*

Allo! was Leo's newsletter for American Francophile tourists. Leo said he'd started it as a scam to keep going to France and, after he hired Nina, a scam to keep taking her with him. France was a passion for Leo—as was Nina, she'd hoped. He made his money from other newsletters, on investments and health.

They'd met at a crowded party, actually, a wedding. The bride was Nina's former boss, the publisher of *Squeeze*, a downtown arts magazine that she had just folded in order to travel the globe with her elderly rich new husband. What a coincidence that Leo needed a writer-editor and Nina needed a job! They exchanged cards (Leo's) and scribbled phone numbers (Nina's) with much checking to make sure that they'd really completed this apparently simple transaction. The wedding was held on a tour boat that lazily circled Manhattan while Nina and Leo paced tighter, watchful circles around each other.

Nina started work that Monday. On Friday Leo took her to dinner at his favorite bistro, Chez Josephine—dark and narrow as a railway car, with low tin ceilings and ribbons of peeling paint like party decorations, in fact the only decorations except for some faded group photos of French soldiers—or were they Boy Scouts?—lined up behind panes of smudged glass. For one fleeting instant Leo struck Nina as a little sad: this fast-talking, aging New York guy pretending to be in Paris. Then halfway through the curried mussels he reached over and took her hand and tasted the briny curried cream sauce from the tip of each finger. The desire that flooded through Nina bypassed any notion that this was corny—and also perhaps a bit sudden for the first hour of their first date. And any thoughts she might have had about Leo being sad were alchemized into passion for the sad beauty that was Leo.

That first night, at Leo's loft, he picked two CDs from a rack and played one selection from each. The first—surprise!—was Edith Piaf. But if Nina had expected that, her smugness was soon blown away by the sheer raw ache of Piaf's eerie warble. The second was Billie Holiday singing "Don't Explain." Her lullaby voice crooned Hush now, Don't explain, Just say you'll remain, Fire don't explain, forces of nature don't explain and neither does her man, forget the lipstick, the cheating, he's her man, she's so glad he's back, and she loves him. . . .

After one verse, Leo said, "I can't stand this. It makes me too unhappy," and rushed out of the room.

Nina assumed that what he couldn't stand was the depth of his own emotion, his sympathy for the singer's, the woman's broken heart, for the abject pure nobility of her languorous self-debasement. She assumed that his reason for playing those songs was to convey a message he couldn't say: that what was about to happen between them was not only about sex, but about romance, love beyond reason, love beyond death, love beyond the reaches of time, the love that still haunted the voices of these women, dead for so many years. He was telling Nina that she was capable of such passion. And that same night, in Leo's bed, this turned out to be true. That anything could feel like that had focused Nina's attention and convinced her that her whole life, prior to that moment, was a ripped magazine she was leafing through until her appointment with Leo.

But later, she listened harder—of course she went out and bought the CDs and played them over and over—and began to think that Leo's playing the Billie Holiday song was less about his ideal of love than about his idea of how a woman in love should behave. After a blissful few weeks when they were constantly together, she'd come to believe that the lyrics were meant to be prescriptive: an etiquette lesson on what Nina should—and shouldn't—do and say. Hush now, don't explain if Leo disappears for a whole weekend. Hush now, don't explain if he doesn't answer his phone. Nor will Nina be asked to explain. Well, she *won't have* anything to explain! She'll spend the weekend by the phone, waiting for Leo to call.

With subtle expression changes, brief sharp withdrawals of interest, Leo had taught Nina that some things were not to be discussed. And Nina was such a good student they never *had* to discuss them, so there was never any unpleasantness, which Leo wouldn't have liked. At her most uncertain moments, Nina had to wonder: *Was* she a passionate person . . . or an evasive proud one, only too ready to play by the rules that Leo had set down?

But what should she have done that first night? Turned and run for her life while Leo was off in another room, hiding from Billie Holiday's pain or discreetly hanging back while Billie gave his new girlfriend instruction by example?

She could never give Leo up. Their love was worth it, all worth it. How many people felt a sexual buzz just going to work in the morning? *Nina* did, she was joyous—because she knew that Leo would be there. That was almost the only time she *did* know, except when they traveled on the research trips that were merely excuses to devour each other in a series of French hotels. She'd never been happier than she was on these trips! But she couldn't even say *that*.

They'd been to Paris three times in the last seven months. But now he'd sent her here by herself, to check out the Hotel Danton and write a piece on the small new hotels and secret bistros of Montparnasse.

Two weeks ago, just before Halloween, he'd called her into his office. All that morning, at her desk, Nina had entertained herself by recalling moments from the night before with Leo. What made it all the more erotic was that they'd arrived at the office and gone directly to their separate rooms. There was a game they played: who could hold out longest, until Nina went in to see Leo, or the light flashed on her phone.

Nina had run down the hall, then stopped to catch her breath outside Leo's door. When she walked in, she was embarrassed, as if he knew what she'd been thinking all morning. That he alone in the world *could* have known made it all the more thrilling.

Leo sat, smiling, behind his desk. How oddly handsome he was! For a man who worked in an office and hated sports and had never, as far as Nina knew, been in a physical fight, Leo looked like a veteran of bar brawls in every seedy port on the planet, or like one of those French move stars—Eddie Constantine, Yves Montand, all those craggy, ravaged guys with tire tracks on their faces. His nose seemed to have been broken and left to mend on its own; his face was deeply lined; small fleshy pads sat like callouses on his occipital ridge.

A greasy cold October mist had nuzzled Leo's many windows, but his office was warm and brightly lit.

"Five days in Paris?" Leo had said.

"I'd love to," Nina said simply, and then sank back into a chair, overwhelmed by gratitude in advance for the pleasures before her, starting with certain pleasures that no one else might enjoy: the happiness of being packed in with him for eight hours on the plane—precious hours during which she would know exactly where Leo was.

The first indication that something was wrong came when he gave her the tickets. Normally, Leo kept them in his inside jacket pocket, along with both their passports and all their traveler's checks. But this time he handed Nina the envelope—in which there was only one ticket. And he seemed to be telling her that she was going to Paris without him.

"You could write about . . . Montparnasse," Leo murmured dubiously, as if to himself. "A neighborhood with an arty past, a little frayed at the edges, maybe, but comparatively cheap and convenient. . . ." Nina listened in misery as it grew progressively clearer that this wasn't an invitation but rather, an assignment. "I'll be eager to hear what you think of these. . . ." He scribbled a list of bistros on a memo pad and then with an absentmindedness that was startling, even for Leo, crumpled up the paper and threw it in the trash.

A hot little fist of disappointment knotted itself inside Nina's chest, yet she managed to keep smiling. Nothing was to be shown. She kept the same pleased expression as when she'd

thought they were going together. Now the trip seemed like torture, a desolate hell of boredom. But this was their understanding,
the etiquette between them: It was impolite to act as if what the
other did mattered.

Well, it didn't matter! Anyone would be glad to have a job with
so many free trips to Paris. She would go without him and have a
wonderful time! It was just so surprising and painful that he would
choose to be without her. That he was capable of it made tears
pop into her eyes. She turned and looked out at the blurry lights
of a million office windows.

"Nina," said Leo. "I'm over here."

As she'd hurried from his office, he'd called after her, "See you
soon." So even though they'd been lovers for months, he apparently wasn't someone she knew well enough to ask what he was
doing. Was he getting rid of her, or what? Why wasn't Leo going?

Nina spent the next two weeks rehearsing imaginary interroga-
tions of an imaginary Leo, but whenever she came face-to-face
with the actual Leo—in bed with him, for example—something
stopped her and she couldn't ask, couldn't get out the words. It
was a matter of pride for them both that their romance was based
on passion and not on tedious analyses of every gesture and word.
If he'd wanted that, said Leo, he could have gotten married. There
were always so many mysteries about what exactly Leo intended.
For example, why had he raved on so about the Hotel Danton?

On TV the Provençal farmer was slicing open the pig's belly.
His wife reached in and pulled out the entrails and tossed them in
a bucket. The Alastian pig had been noisier but afterwards less
gory. The Provençal couple were up to their elbows in blood. At
least Nina *thought* it was blood. The TV was black-and-white.

The jittery black-and-white TV had been the final blow. It had taken Nina strangely long to realize it wasn't in color, and then she watched as if color might yet appear, like in *The Wizard of Oz*. She was seized with desire to grab the TV and hurl it through the window. Fortunately, her windows were covered by immovable wooden shutters. Who wouldn't want to keep the sun from shining into this chamber of horrors?

Three of the walls were wainscotted halfway up to a dusty ledge that bordered the scuffed peeling wallpaper in a lotus-bamboo pattern. Shelf paper covered the fourth wall in silver tweed, though not the tweed of the carpet. The thin shag bedspread was the hairy off-white of a blanket scrap some toddler had been chewing on for months. The bathroom smelled of mildew with an edge of urine that instantly ruined the illusion of the virgin hotel room, anonymous and newly minted.

The television had been the last straw, or so Nina had thought until she leaned back and then sat up and her hair stuck to the headboard. And it was then that the woman next door had begun to gasp and moan. . . .

Was Leo a sadist whose idea of a joke was to pack her off for a couple of days to an actual whorehouse in Paris? That would contradict everything she thought she knew about Leo. He could be cool, even distant, but he was not the sort of person who would bother dreaming up inventive ways to be mean: A free trip to a Paris brothel—a neat way of saying, We're through!

But Nina had discovered that men could suddenly reveal unsuspected alarming traits you surely would have noticed, so maybe they weren't old traits at all but new and drastic mutations. For a time she'd dated a filmmaker from Havana who one night knelt by the bed and asked Fidel and the Virgin to have mercy on them both. What did you know about anyone? Obviously, you knew strangers more intimately than loved ones, and the person you knew least well was the one you were in love with.

Why had Leo informed her: She was going to like this hotel! He said he'd heard about it from a friend in London. Even after it was clear that they weren't going together, he went on cruelly, endlessly, about how charming it was. Hey! Nina was fully capable of deciding that for herself! At *Squeeze*, she'd made all the decisions about whose art was interesting, whose work was getting better. Cindy, her boss, hadn't cared about that; she was mainly concerned with finding the latest club where a downtown girl like herself could find an uptown husband like the one now escorting her around the world.

Leo always tried to tell Nina what to think. She could admit that now. Every dinner they ate, the French movies they saw—he said: You're going to love this. And he was right, she *did* love them. There was no point even trying to solve the Zen-like riddle: Would she have loved that meal or that film if she hadn't been with Leo?

The Provençal couple lit a fire. Soon cauldrons of water were boiling and hunks of flesh and bone hung from a laundry line. Now their pig was only a memory trotting around the barnyard.

Nina pretended for as long as she could not to hear the woman next door, starting in for a second night with a sort of hysterical gulping. Nina lacked the nerve and the language skills to call downstairs to complain. She would be up another night, sleep through another day. And sooner or later—sooner—she would have to stop pretending that the reason she was still in bed was just an aggravated case of jet lag.

Now, finally, Nina could hear the man who was giving her neighbor such pleasure. He was growling down in his throat, a rhythmic whirring and stopping, like someone trying to start a car on an icy morning. Leo had been very silent but so had everything else, as they fell on each other in those beautiful rooms, the room in which Piaf slept with Marcel Carné, the room in which Colette awaited Mistinguett, possibly the very room in which Ernest cheated on Hadley.

The same rooms! Leo had checked in advance. Every hotel had promised. But for all Leo's fuss about booking those particular rooms, he never mentioned their previous occupants when he and Nina were there.

Nor had Nina tried to commune with those ghosts, to see what traces of them remained. Nina hardly gave a thought to the souls who had stayed in those places. She was too busy thinking about sex with Leo, or having sex with Leo, that is, not thinking at all, hardly even noticing as the voices quit, one by one, first the voice of the woman next door, then the voice of the clock, then the nattering voices inside Nina's own mind. You couldn't make that happen with just anyone, someone you'd picked off the street. And wouldn't you *have* to feel something for someone with whom you could?

The Provençal couple was eating now, steaming platters of *boudin noir*, meat with sauce—delicious, even in black-and-white. Nina could hardly remember the pig. Anyone would have killed it.

The camera zoomed in on the Provençal farm wife, laughing,

enjoying her food. You could see she was missing some teeth. Then she spotted the camera. Her face set, and she stopped laughing. In the quick half-second before she scowled and shut her shining lips, her eyes had that look of remembering, ingested, along with the pig.

Children were buried, standing up in a row, their heads budding out of the ground, and the Provençal farmer raced back and forth, playing them like a marimba. As he hit their skulls with a mallet, the children began to sing, percussive chimes that turned into the sound of someone banging on Nina's door.

Nina flew out of bed and opened the door before she'd had time to wonder why anyone would be knocking. In another hotel she might have assumed it was the maid, come to clean.

Reassuringly, the man at her door was carrying a tray.

"*Bonjour, Madame,*" he said. The man wore a houndstooth jacket, a slicked-back shelf of dyed red hair, and the smile of a friendly iguana. Had he been downstairs when she checked in? Nina would have remembered—if she could remember checking in.

But now she did remember, though mostly what she recalled was how different it had been this time, checking in without Leo.

Together they used to generate a faint sexual commotion, showing off and leaning close together over the swift exchanges of credit cards and keys. Alone, Nine thought it best to keep the lowest possible profile, to occupy no space at all and at last become invisible as the nun's cell of an elevator came to spirit her off to her room. Nina was fairly relaxed in hotels, but you'd have to have no animal instinct whatsoever not to be alert: sleeping in a new place, alone, completely surrounded by strangers. And now one such stranger—a peculiar one—was at the door of her room.

"*Bonjour, Monsieur,*" Nina said.

The redheaded man brushed past Nina and set his tray on the dresser. On the tray was a bottle, a coffeepot, a glass. The rest was draped in plastic wrap. You rarely saw that in France. She watched the man take in the musty room, the slightly grimy white bra she'd slipped off from under her sweater when she'd crawled into bed in her clothes. That was a whole day and night ago. It was morning again. That is, Nina hoped it was light outside beyond the heavy shutters.

One problem was that Leo had very clear ideas about what to do, and in what order, on arriving in a new city. Nina used to have her own ideas before she and Leo were together. She'd gone to London and Berlin, to interview artists for *Squeeze*. But as soon as she'd started traveling with Leo, she'd surrendered her passport to him and become dependent on *his* jet lag cure, which involved going straight to bed in the pretty hotel rooms, making love for an hour or two until the change in time was just another detail peripheral to Nina and Leo. Then they would nap for a while, go out and walk around, have coffee, then dinner, then bed again, and by that time feel totally normal.

"Madame is over her jet lag?" asked the redheaded man, in English.

Nina's mind was racing. Was there a bill to sign? A tip to give? Leo always took care of that.

"*Oui! J'espère!*" Nina was almost shouting.

She hadn't slept at all on the flight. A disturbing thing had happened.

There were many Hasidic passengers who were going on to Antwerp and who kept rushing to pray in back of the plane as if on an urgent mission. One of the men bumped into Nina. But she wasn't annoyed at all. She was grateful to him and his friends for the prayers that were keeping the plane in the air.

Evidently, this feeling was not shared by the three couples across the aisle from Nina; Belgian, Italian, Austrian—they had just met and were playing cards. Each time the Hasidim rushed by, a nasty pause fell over the game and the cardplayers shuddered and sneered, and then everyone burst out laughing.

Nina wanted to yell at them or say something brilliant and cutting. But what would she have said? Also there was a good chance that whatever Nina started might get ugly or scary, and continue or escalate for the rest of the flight. She was guiltily relieved that Leo wasn't with her.

Leo blamed what flaws he found in himself—sinusitis, anxieties, a lack of athletic ability—on his being Jewish. But he also seemed to blame Nina for *not* being Jewish. And so whenever the subject came up, a wedge of distance and rancor would insert itself between them, and many kisses and caresses would be needed to work it loose.

Nina had grown up in New York. Everyone she *knew* was Jewish! She'd never given it any thought until Leo made her so self-conscious that now, whenever she tried to describe to herself the sort of person Leo was (smart, articulate, sensitive, sensual, chronically anxious) she wondered if she were actually seeing him, if she were *capable* of seeing him—or was she just falling back on a series of vile anti-Semitic clichés.

It was Leo who'd made her worry that she might be anti-Semitic. Nina wasn't anti-Semitic! The few times she had dozed on the plane, she'd been jolted awake by a shock of adrenaline and hate for the card-playing couples. That must be why she'd slept so much ever since her arrival to Paris.

Nina considered telling the red-haired man the story about the airplane, and even about Leo. Or she considered it up to the point at which her ability to speak was snuffed out by his fixed patient smile. Did the breakfast he'd brought, if that's what is was, come free with the room? Or was there a bill she was meant to pay? Did someone imagine she'd ordered this? And why was the man just standing there? Was he being solicitious—or sinister? Their attention drifted to the flickering TV. Nina must have turned off the sound and fallen asleep with the picture on. She and the man watched some French parents embracing children with a fervor suggesting that the children had just been released after a perilous hostage crisis. Following this came a montage of attractive, ravaged-looking Bosnians carrying wounded comrades and family members away from street fights and battles.

"Terrible." The man sighed breathily.

"Really bad," said Nina.

The redheaded man held Nina's eyes in his neutral gaze. "Would Madame like the shutters open?"

"That would be nice," she said.

Did he not know what was out there? What was in his mind as

he wrestled open the shutters so that he and Nina could look down on a layered geometry of flat sandy roofs pocked with oily puddles and black pipes belching smoke and gas? On the largest roof three cats scrabbled around in circles, clawing at a sheet of plastic wrap the wind lifted and spun between them.

The plastic wrap guided Nina back to the dresser and the food tray. On the tray an individual box of breakfast cereal sat in a bowl at a jaunty angle, beside a metal thimble of cream and two baggy tangerines. The Perrier bottle was open and—was Nina still dreaming?—half-empty. She looked quizzically at the red-headed man who looked quizzically back. Not everyone might complain about the cereal and fruit, but the open bottle was inarguably over the top.

I'm being tested, thought Nina.

"Uh . . . did I order this?" she said.

The man straightened his jacket collar. "Compliments of the hotel."

So Leo had alerted them. He did that, more often than not, dropped some reference to *Allo!* while making reservations that translated into fruit plates, champagne, and love notes from the management. He'd said it was essential if you had to be sure of sleeping in the actual room where Sarah Bernhardt slept in her coffin. Besides, whom did it hurt? Travel was not a science experiment requiring that one be strictly objective. They had integrity, they would tell the truth even if the hotel was bad.

The redheaded man said, "Madame Cordier would like to invite you for coffee. She will meet you at ten-thirty sharp, an hour from now, in the bar."

This was the downside of the fruit and champagne: the annoying phone calls from hotel managers asking what they

could do, and was there anything special Leo and Nina wanted—
when all they desired was each other, and they could hardly say
that. The obligatory handshake, the stiff chat in the lobby . . .

"Thank you," said Nina. "I mean, please thank Madame. But I
have a million things to do."

What things? Nina hadn't left her hotel room since she'd got
to Paris.

The man said, "Madame is especially eager because you have a
friend in common. . . ."

And now Nina experienced one of those moments of blank-
ness, like the brief lag it took her to process the fact that the TV
wasn't in color, the split second before the Provençal farm wife
noticed the camera watching. This slight lapse threw Nina off, so
that when at last she understood, she recoiled as if the red-haired
man wouldn't stop yelling Leo's name, though in fact he had said
it only once, and without raising his voice in the slightest.

Every part of Madame Cordier seemed to be tapping at once: her fingernails on the table, her foot against the floor, her high heels on the linoleum as she stood and straightened her skirt and tapped over to shake Nina's hand.

She was small, in her early forties, doll-like, crisp and perfect. Her cap of blond hair, her dove-colored suit with its nipped waist and tiny skirt made Nina acutely conscious of having slept in her clothes. Everything about Madame was outlined in sharp pencil, while Nina, all in smudged charcoal, exuded an oily ring onto the page. She shuddered with furious regret. Why hadn't she bathed and changed?

"Are you cold? We can turn up the heat," said Madame in a high fluting voice. The woman who'd been screaming all night cried out once in Nina's mind. Surely that wasn't Madame Cordier, who surely didn't live here. In fact, what was she doing here, this stylish overbred woman, in this unreconstructed crummy hotel on the far edge of Montparnasse?

The breakfast room had low tables and upholstered armchairs, like in a good hotel. Perhaps they'd been bought or stolen from a good hotel and left among the grimy mirrors, the scabrous checked linoleum, the spotty glare and furious buzz of the fluorescent tubing. Behind the small bar were two shelves of liquor bottles glued shut by dust, their labels stained sugary brown.

"No, thanks, I'm fine," said Nina. "I think I'm still a bit jet-lagged."

"In this direction, it's terrible," said Madame. "The other way I quite like it. Waking up all ready"—she widened her eyes—"at three o'clock in the morning."

Ready for what? All at once Nina was certain that Madame had been Leo's lover at some time during the decade or so that Leo had lived in France. What was Leo up to now? What else, what new bizarre trick did he have planned next for Nina?

It was uncomfortable being with Leo's ex-mistress in a foreign country, her country, a cheap hotel, her hotel, which for some reason Nina seemed unable to physically leave. But it got Nina's attention. She gave Leo credit for that. And as Madame sat down with a single gesture that left her back and shoulders straight, her knees perched at a graceful angle and the ideal distance from the awkward low table, Nina had a moment of near happiness: She liked being here in Paris, agreeing ever so smarmily with this chic Parisienne that transatlantic jet lag was an everyday inconvenience.

Madame motioned for Nina to sit, then smacked a bell on the table.

"Deux cafés," Madame told an Arab girl. "With milk?" she asked Nina.

"Un café au lait," Nina said. The waitress looked at her, uncomprehending.

"Un café au lait," said Madame, with more success. "Your flight was smooth, I trust."

"Sort of," Nina said. What would she add if Madame followed up on that *sort of?* Would she say that the Belgian couple had pushed in front of her twice, once at the check-in counter, once again while boarding, so she had focused on them, despised them long before they began their anti-Semitic eye-rolling knee-slapping good time?

Did that call into question that purity of Nina's response to their filthy sneering race hatred? Would Nina find some subtle means of signaling Madame that she wasn't Jewish? Oh, Leo was right to have left her and to have devised this wicked good-bye, packing her off to his former mistress in a sleazy whorehouse.

"Always it's *sort of,*" said Madame. "Unless one takes the Concorde."

"This was coach," said Nina.

"Pity," Madame said. And then, after a pause, "You *are* writing for *Allo!*?"

Nina nodded vehemently. "Low budget. We always fly coach."

That *we* hung in the breakfast room like a hive of hostile bees shifting and thrumming between them. Madame tossed her head and raked her short blond hair with her fingers.

"How is dear Leo?" she said.

How did normal people navigate these conversational shoals when the current seemed to be spinning you toward the churning rapids of confession? What if Nina surrendered and told Madame the whole story: How, from the night she'd met Leo, she'd felt helpless, out of control, how once she'd run twenty blocks to a bar from which he'd called, wanting to see her. At first she'd been playacting, pretending that nothing else existed, nothing mattered beyond the well of white light in which she lay with Leo, until at some unguarded moment the game changed and became real, and she looked away from Leo and the world had ceased to exist, or at least his absence had bleached out all its color and now turned all Paris a muddy gray and left her a prisoner in her hotel room.

Telling Madame *that* would certainly change the terms of their brief acquaintance, ratchet their level of intimacy up a notch or two. Perhaps she would even mention that conversation in Leo's office, how her silly pleased smile had stuck on her face like a fly trapped in amber. She wished she could remember when exactly she'd figured out that their romantic long weekend in Paris was a trip she'd be taking alone. She would describe how he'd made her cry, his *Nina, I'm over here.*

And perhaps she would discover: The same thing had happened to Madame! Then they would be more than intimates. They would be sisters, fellow victims. Why not fling herself at Madame's feet? Leo had made her realize that she was a passionate person.

But wait. Wouldn't it be far worse to see Nina's private tragedy reduced to one of Leo's bad habits? And whom was she going to tell all this to? Leo's former mistress? Nina wasn't one of those people who confessed their darkest secrets to the first person who made eye contact with them for more than half a second. She hadn't needed Leo to enroll her in the Billie Holiday school of manners, to tell her that mystery and passion lasted longer if one refrained from discussing one's *relationship*, from analyzing one's *feelings*. What amazed her most was that—in light of everything that was occurring—it still cheered her immensely to recall that she and Leo had this . . . reserve . . . in common.

"Oh, Leo? He's fine," said Nina.

"I am sure Leo's fine," said Madame. "The streets will be littered with corpses and Leo will still be fine."

"Pardon me?" said Nina.

The waitress had brought their breakfast. Nina poured her coffee with what she hoped was panache but the pot was soon leaking a fecal ring onto the snowy white tablecloth. Her first bite of croissant scattered buttery flakes all over her chest. Madame tore off the end of her croissant and nibbled at the crusty fang, all the while gazing at Nina. The subject was not to be changed.

No other conversation would be permitted until Nina said, "How do you know Leo?"

"I know Leo many years," Madame said. "I met him in Tours. I was married, with three little children. My husband was a professor; we lived in a house with many students. This was the sixties. Sixty-eight. Leo came to visit. There was a big demonstration at school, but one of my children was sick. I stayed home and Leo stayed with me. Everyone in the house was arrested at the demonstration. And by the time they got out of jail, I'd taken my kids and gone to Paris with Leo."

"Wow," said Nina. The envy she felt was so instinctive, so pure and unalloyed, it was like hearing that someone you hate had just been given a prize or a fortune. But what was she jealous of, really? That Madame Cordier had once had a chance to wreck her life for Leo?

"Yes. Wow." Madame Cordier curled her lip, a reflexive tic of nostalgia. "Leo had a tiny apartment. My children slept in the kitchen. My kids were very good kids, but Leo couldn't bear it. One morning he said he was leaving. Leaving me. Leaving Paris. Going to Provence, to Arles, to try and finish his novel."

"Leo was writing a novel?" Nina loved this new view of Leo as some corny bozo who'd left New York and gone to France to try and write a novel. She was, however, depressed by the unseemly fervor with which she'd latched onto this sudden chance to sneer and look down on Leo.

"All the American guys were writing novels," said Madame. "Novels about American guys who come to France to write novels."

Madame Cordier and Nina laughed, mirthlessly. "I stayed on with my children. I was very sad. Very blue. I was drinking lots of red wine. Bad wine. Then I got hit by a taxi."

Nina winced, but Madame held up her hand. "It knocked some sense in my head. When I got out of hospital, I was in a cast, on crutches. So I got my children from my mother's and moved in with a man, the only man I knew with a street-floor apartment. No stairs. He was a friend of Leo's. He was nice to me and the children. Then one day Leo came to the door. My new boyfriend wasn't home. Leo and I went to a hotel, a hotel like this one. . . ." Madame looked around and shrugged. "It took me no time to realize that my new lover was a mistake."

So there it was, what Madame and Nina shared, not just a distant mutual friend. Surprise! What they had in common was that sex with Leo had made everything else seem like a mistake. Not that Nina knew what exactly "sex with Leo" meant—what exactly she and Leo had done that he might have done with this other person. It was so hard to remember sex; you remembered your surroundings, the distractions, the interruptions—strangely, the very things that you forgot about first, at the time. At home, Nina still had notes on the rooms, as if what had happened between them had anything to do with Colette's bed, with Oscar Wilde's bathtub.

"I would never have gone back to Leo," Madame said. "Except that I found out there had been an unfortunate misunderstanding. I thought that Leo had left me—left me! But when he came back into my life, he swore that he had told me: He would be gone only three months, and then he would return. He swore he told me to wait for him, to wait for him in Paris. But don't you think I would remember that? Wouldn't a woman pay attention when her man is telling her when he will be coming back?"

"You'd think so," Nina said weakly. How was she supposed to know what had been said or not said, understood or misunderstood, what had fallen into the gaps between Leo's French and Madame's English? But she was right: You *would* pay attention, you'd want to get those facts straight.

That afternoon in Leo's office, when he told her she was going to Paris, Nina had been attentive. But obviously she'd found it hard to follow what Leo was saying. Maybe Leo was someone who had trouble making himself clear. But the Leo she knew valued clarity: People made investments, medical and travel decisions based on what they read in his newsletters. Maybe it was all a simple, regrettable misunderstanding. She should have asked if it meant anything, his sending her to Paris without him. Any sane person would have asked. But not, apparently, Nina, who was too proud and too well schooled by Leo to ask this seemingly basic question.

"And then?" said Nina.

"And nothing," said Madame. "I am a passionate woman. Those were romantic times. Every girl in Paris wanted to be Jeanne Moreau. Or Jean Seberg. Or Anne Magnani, Maria Callas. Anyway, a martyr."

Madame turned down the sides of her mouth, her Jeanne Moreau imitation. And indeed she did have that preoccupied look of fatigued, combustible brooding. She said, "There was a Billie Holiday song that Leo used to play. . . ."

Oh, great, thought Nina. "Don't Explain." Leo had probably played it for a whole harem, a whole lifetime of passionate women. It had never occurred to Nina that this was what Leo was *really* doing. He wasn't playing a song that moved him so deeply he couldn't listen, a song that expressed the romantic potential of Nina's passionate soul. He wasn't even instructing her in how he wanted her to behave. He was just employing a time-tested seduction technique that he had been using on women—successfully!—for over twenty years.

"Was this when Leo was married?" said Nina.

"Married?" Madame Cordier frowned prettily. "Maybe Leo was married. Yes. A skinny American girl, maybe she had money. When Leo spent his last traveler's check, they always fell madly in love again."

Madame smiled, flashing pointy teeth like the white tips of Halloween candy. There had been a bowl of candy corn on Leo's desk that day, a lovely Japanese bowl in a high-glazed mossy green. Leo loved ironic gestures like that: pop, cross-cultural, stylish. After his *Nina, I'm over here,* she'd turned back from the window and counted the triangular striped candies until she'd regained control of her face and could calmly get up and leave. *See you soon,* he'd told her. . . .

Nina gazed coolly at Madame Cordier. Nina didn't even have a savings account, so that couldn't be why Leo liked her.

"I am glad I am French," Madame said. "We are practical. Hard-headed. I buy and remodel hotels. I never thought till this moment that maybe this is why I go into the business. That maybe it had something to do with that hotel I went to with Leo. But I don't think so. No. Do you? Really, it's too ridiculous!

"Years later a close friend died and left me my first hotel. One thing led to another. . . . Pretty soon I have six hotels. All in different arrondissements. My newest hotel, not counting this, is a very historic hotel, many great people stayed there. Sarah Bernhardt, Colette."

"*We* stayed at that hotel!" Nina said. "Last time, with Leo. We loved it!"

She'd meant it as a compliment, a gesture of recognition. A hotel owner would want to know if you'd admired her latest acquisition. But the mention of Leo made everything double-edged and suspect. Was Nina complimenting Madame's hotel—or boasting about Leo? If that was what Nina was doing, claiming Leo, pulling rank, why not take it all the way, pull out all the stops?

"It was very romantic," Nina said.

She kept her eyes on Madame's as they entered the next round in their game of dueling hotel rooms with Leo. In fact her apparent compliment was a statement of possession. And why not? After Madame's allusions to those life-changing afternoons with Leo, those afternoons that pried her away from a husband and a lover, it was Nina's turn to stake out her postage stamp of sexual territory.

But what could Nina claim to possess? Certainly not Leo. That she had been with him most recently ultimately counted for nothing. In fact it counted against her. That Madame's grief was long in the past, that she'd had years to recover from Leo made the whole conversation so much less painful for her.

"Frankly," Madame said, "I am very surprised that Leo would send you here now when I made it perfectly clear to him that I am just commencing renovations. After next week this hotel will be closed for six months. I cannot imagine what is in Leo's mind."

At least Madame wasn't blaming Nina. She was suggesting they both blame Leo.

Nina said, "It's sometimes hard to know, with Leo."

This was Nina's chance—perhaps her last chance—to describe what Leo had done to her, especially now that Madame Cordier had confided *her* Leo story.

The moment lingered in the air. Madame gave Nina a searching look. Nina waited for some conspiratorial glint. But nothing like that was forthcoming.

"This hotel was a whorehouse," Madame said.

"I thought so!" said Nina. Madame stared at her.

"Quite a few of my hotels were whorehouses. That's just the hotel business, what happens. Obviously, it is premature to write about this for *Allo!* . . . though maybe this could be an article for some other publication, the grand old whorehouses of Paris. They are history, too. No? Many sad things happened here. For example, what room was it . . . some poor girl jumped out the window."

"Probably room twenty-eight," said Nina. "My room."

"Hmmm," said Madame. "Maybe."

"I can come back when the renovation's done," Nina said. "There's no harm seeing it now. Perhaps a before and after piece...."

Madame rang the bell and rose and briskly shook Nina's hand. "I hope you enjoy your stay in Paris."

"I'm very glad to have met you," Nina said, and in fact she was. She was grateful to Madame Cordier, not only for showing her several new and unattractive aspects of Leo, but for getting her out of bed. What was Nina's problem? What had yesterday been about, spending the whole day sleeping and watching bad French TV? She was getting paid to travel, given a budget—okay, a tight budget, but a budget—from *Allo!* She was in Paris, free, on her own. Why had she thought she needed Leo?

"Wear warm clothes," said Madame Cordier. "The weather is very cold. Very bitter."

It had never been cold or bitter when Nina was here with Leo. The rain had fallen in warm oily drops and thoughtful cooling showers. But this time, Leo had warned her a few days before she left: "The weather could be beastly. But even if it's freezing and wet, better Paris than here!"

Nina had nodded. Yes, of course. By then she'd spent two weeks on the edge of tears that welled up and spilled over whenever she thought about asking Leo if they were really breaking up. Even if it was freezing and wet, better Paris than here. Nina could hardly disagree with that incontestable statement. Everyone loved Paris, rain or shine. With Leo or without him.

With Leo or without him. The most idiotic thing would be to let that bogus distinction warp her whole time in Paris. The Luxembourg Gardens with Leo vs. the gardens without, boulevards she'd walked with him vs. the same avenues alone, the Mona Lisa smiling at Leo or, less mysteriously, at Nina. The narrow lanes it was best to avoid for fear of suddenly coming upon a bistro she had eaten in with Leo, or had been too nervous to eat in, too busy looking at him. With Leo or without him. How small that difference was compared with other, more major differences. For example, the weather.

The air here had always felt sweet on her skin, even when it was gritty and polluted. But now the rain fell in cold needles, and the damp breath of the stones was the secret slow revenge of all that historic beauty. No one liked being outside, and people got it over with quickly, slipping into doorways as if on secret missions.

Last May Nina kept catching glimpses of the city as it must have looked once—and still looked in Doisneau and Brassaï photos of Paris in the '40s and '50s. Girls in pretty dresses, lovers embracing on the street, *La Vie de Bohème* with a fashion makeover involving nose rings, fishnet, and dreadlocks. But Paris in November seemed much closer to New York: Everyone wore the same winter clothes, the same harried expressions, as if all of them were late for jobs they were already in danger of losing.

Nina wandered for a while, vaguely toward the river. It was not unpleasant except for the problem of not knowing where she was going or how she would know when she got there and could give up and go back to the hotel. Having no destination made her unsure and self-conscious, as if someone were observing all the confusions and worries that showed plainly on her face.

The first time they'd walked in Paris, Leo talked about Rimbaud and the demonic marathon walks that left holes in his shoes and his feet. Nina had known about Rimbaud's walks, but she smiled and let Leo tell her. For all she knew, Leo was planning a walk just as frenzied and manic for them.

Leo was a fast walker, no maps, no red lights, no split-second hesitations; there was never any doubt that he would decide the route they would take. But then he would put his arm around her, and they'd begin to walk very close, their hips and upper thighs rubbing beneath Leo's jeans and Nina's thin dress. Pedestrians moved over. It must have been very clear that Leo and Nina should get off the streets and go directly back to bed.

Nina would visit the Louvre. That was a destination. She imagined telling Leo she'd been to a show of one of his favorite painters, Tintoretto or Carpaccio, the largest canvases, the biggest collection assembled anywhere ever. But wait! The second most idiotic thing would be to fill her time in Paris like an empty sack with glittery things to catch Leo's interest. What about *her* favorite artists? She'd always liked the French Orientalists: Géricault and Gérôme. But now it seemed depressing to go to the Orsay and stare at pictures of naked Moorish girls being bathed and perfumed for some pasha.

She stopped in front of a window in which exquisite shoes were arranged at angles that made them appear to be taking off or landing. Her eyes tracked to a pair of red suede high heels so elegant and graceful they could afford to flirt with an edge of the cartoonish and the Minnie Mouse.

She and Leo often window-shopped but never really went shopping in Paris. What would be the point? Shopping was about the future: a sweater to wear tomorrow, a bowl in which to put apples at home. But they'd had no reason to want anything beyond the present moment. And of course the future was banned as a subject for thought or discussion.

Did *this* count as shopping: That last trip, they'd gone to a Monoprix for the graph-paper notebooks Leo bought by the dozen. They'd passed racks of dresses and skirts, intriguing French cosmetics, packs of hosiery spouting puffs of beige net and black Lycra. They were walking through the underwear department when Leo stopped and gave Nina a questioning look. And she'd shrugged, embarrassed, but not saying no. Leo wandered off and meditatively browsed the cheap pretty bras and panties.

She watched him from a distance. It was such a tired cliché, guys and their underwear fetish. But Leo's rapt concentration drew her in, and she realized with surprise that his intensity was fixed on her, on her body and what they would do, until gradually her clear view was heated and blurred by desire, and she looked around uneasily to see if strangers were watching.

That was the trouble with sexual drift: Such thoughts could function like radar, sending out loud, deceptive, misreadable signals to the rest of the population. Now, for example, her erotic reverie about Leo seemed to have attracted a man to the shoe store window, a nice-looking guy in a leather jacket who took in the whole window and then—she could see this from the corner of her eye—focused on the red suede shoes she'd been gazing at all this time.

He looked at the shoes, he looked at Nina. At the shoes, at Nina. Was he about to offer to buy her the shoes in return for some sexual service so degrading and baroque that even this handsome Frenchman couldn't get a woman to do it for free?

"Quels beaux souliers rouges," he said.

Nina smiled and nodded as he spoke to her in French. The man who'd brought her breakfast had spoken English, as had Madame Cordier, so this was almost the first French she'd heard, not counting announcements at the airport, the taxi driver who drove her into town, and the TV narrators with their monotonous play-by-plays of happy peasants slaughtering pigs. Nina understood nearly everything people said, but was shy about speaking. Leo's French was fluent, so she always let him talk.

Eventually she realized that the man was saying something about "The Red Shoes," the Hans Christian Andersen story, and then *The Red Shoes*, the Michael Powell film about a ballet based on the Hans Christian Andersen story.

What an amazing coincidence! *The Red Shoes* was Nina's favorite film, that is, the favorite film of her childhood. Nina gasped with surprise, an intake of breath that must have sounded like horror.

She turned and hurried away from him, her heart pounding with shame and regret. Why am I running? Nina thought. Let's be objective here. The guy was better looking than Leo. He liked her favorite childhood movie. (What was it that she had liked so much? The romance? The ballet? Another story, like *Anna Karenina*, about a woman so jacked around by men that the only sensible solution was to fling herself in front of a train?) She and this Frenchman could fall in love. Her whole life could change. He probably had a spacious attractive apartment into which she could move. She could shop in the markets, buy flowers, breads, cheeses . . . and then what? In her luxurious Paris flat, in the gathering dusk, she could pine away for Leo.

Oh, none of this would be happening if she were here with Leo! Passion gave lovers license not to engage with the world as they coasted through it in their little cocoon-made-for-two. But the world lay in wait for them. And as soon as they were alone—on their own—it got them back with a vengeance. It was so risky, being shut off in some little love capsule, losing contact with the truth, losing your faculties, your judgment. It was dangerous, like joining a cult or a fascist army of two.

Crossing the intersection, Nina saw that she had somehow landed directly outside La Coupole. It could have been an accident, or some masochistic homing instinct. She stared into the enclosed porch of the bright café, at morose couples cradling tiny cups and gazing out at the street, and at others who'd chosen to be inside, to be warm and look at each other.

Nina thought of Simone de Beauvoir hanging out in this very café, writing or talking or reading amid a smoky blue haze of ideas, black coffee, and Gauloises. She saw de Beauvoir trying her hardest not to think about Jean-Paul Sartre, off somewhere with a beautiful, much younger, female philosophy student.

This was one of the problems with love! It could narrow your field of vision and limit your intelligence to the point at which you were insulting everyone else's. Imagine, reducing Simone de Beauvoir to a country-and-western torch song, the existentialist Tammy Wynette standing by her Sartre! All right, de Beauvoir's affair with Sartre was a little . . . problematic. But what about her writing? Her books? Her international reputation? Nina thought of Billie Holiday. *Hush now, don't explain.* Those four words, the first line of the existentialist national anthem.

Not long ago, Leo had told Nina that Simone de Beauvoir's grave had become a shrine for young French feminists who left flowers and handwritten notes on her tomb, asking her for advice and favors. Maybe that's what Nina should do. Go search for Simone de Beauvoir's grave. She was in the mood for something like that, some pilgrimage or symbolic act or oracular consultation. But she couldn't imagine what she would write in a note to leave on Simone de Beauvoir's grave. *Please send Leo back to me.* Nina would be ashamed! She'd always thought of herself as a feminist. It was something a woman just naturally was, if she had any brains. But what kind of feminist was Nina, unable to think of anything to ask this saint of women's rights except to intervene and, please, oh please, make her boyfriend love her again? De Beauvoir would have understood. She knew all about patience, about men who disappeared, about waiting for them, believing in them . . . outlasting the competition.

Nina walked into the café and ordered black coffee to keep up the buzz from the coffee she'd drunk with Madame Cordier. Several times this morning she'd had to pause on her walk while a frolicky hiccough interrupted her heartbeat. She hoped it was a caffeine overdose and didn't mean that she was dying.

Nina eased off her coat and looked around, but got no farther than a young couple nearby who were causing quite a scene. A pale girl in black with orange hair and dark roots shouldered a video camera trained on her Arab boyfriend. As she talked into the microphone, Nina understood her so easily that for a moment she thought her French had improved until she realized that the girl was American, speaking English.

"Tuesday morning," she said. "Eleven A.M. Achmed is eating breakfast. Achmed has ordered coffee. He's about to take his first sip. Let's go in for a close-up. Monsieur Achmed, please. Look at the camera."

Achmed raised one weary shoulder and half-hid his regal face, slouching down in his chair till his long legs reached across the aisle and under the next empty table. Nina was openly staring now, but Achmed didn't return her gaze, though he was aware of her watching. His lidded eyes were like half-lowered shades covering the windows while the house's owner waited inside for guests to arrive and adore him.

Of all the people in Paris these two had been ordered up and sent here expressly for Nina. This girl on her junior year abroad videotaping her boyfriend reminded Nina of herself, taking notes on Hemingway's sink and Oscar Wilde's bathtub. After Achmed was long gone, the poor girl could watch the tape, just as Nina— at especially self-tormenting moments—could reread her piece on historic hotels in a back issue of *Allo!*

Simone de Beauvoir, Billie Holiday, and now this girl in the café. Next it would be Jean Seberg, Héloïse, Maria Callas, Piaf, every woman who'd ever gotten famous for suffering over men. But wasn't it always like that? The world showed you what you were looking for, what you were tuned in to see. Once Nina had had a redheaded boyfriend, and for that time and long after, she was shocked to find the streets of New York crowded— teeming—with redheads. This morning a man with copper-colored hair had brought her coffee. But it was no longer a message, just the color of someone's hair.

Nina signaled for the check. Wait. She didn't have French francs. Her legs went weak, even after she recalled that she'd changed fifty dollars at the airport. What did she think they would do to her if she didn't have cash? Surely the café took credit cards. Probably traveler's checks, too.

She paid the bill, left the café, and walked on with no idea where she was going and only intermittent clues about where she actually was. She wandered into crooked lanes lined with yellow restaurant signs and placards picturing platters of couscous or glossy Vietnamese stir-fry, a deserted side street of dusty shops with vintage printing presses, a block of bland concrete apartment houses. At last she rounded a corner and found herself in the place de la Contrescarpe.

Getting her bearings encouraged her, as did the lovely square. Hey, this wasn't so bad—being in Paris by herself without a care in the world! And let's hear it for magical thinking! Once more, it was as if her thoughts affected her surroundings, as if the improvement in her mood had managed to conjure up this curving street of bookstores, this shop window full of glossy volumes on Flemish painting, these bins of wispy botanical drawings in crackling cellophane slips. The rain had stopped. From time to time there were even coy hints that the sun might break through.

Nina walked on and got lost again and at last had a panicky moment when she came out of a dark narrow street and into an open square and looked up and saw the Eiffel Tower looming above her like Godzilla. All right! She knew where she was now! Not where she wanted to be! In the wrong direction completely and much farther than she'd intended.

But what was she so scared of? At any point she could find the nearest metro station and take the subway back to the hotel. What stop *was* nearest the hotel? That was something Leo would know, one of the many travel facts he would have on file in his mind. Probably he would also know where exactly the hotel was. *This* was scary, Nina saw now, how quickly one could surrender charge of the most basic information.

Once she'd got lost with Leo. Even Leo was lost. They'd come out on a grimy boulevard jammed with buses emitting black smoke. Leo sent her to look at the street sign, and when she came back and told him the name, he gritted his teeth and snapped, "Spell it!"

An elderly gentleman stopped and helped them, a pleasant

man who seemed to Nina still to be living in Paris in the '50s, a city of lovers so wrapped up in each other they often wound up lost and had to be set back on course. He beamed and warmly grasped Leo's elbow, and soon Leo and Nina forgot their quarrel and were grinning at each other and at the old man, whom they kept turning around to wave at.

Now, reaching a corner, Nina looked down a street of pale dignified houses. It was the neighborhood—the street—on which she'd stayed with Leo. Halfway down that block was the hotel in which Edith Wharton entertained Morton Fullerton while waiting for the plasterers and parquet-polishers and stained-glass installers to finish work on her home. Now the hotel seemed magnetic, drawing Nina to it. And for what? To gaze in at the lobby with a lump in her throat?

Nina remembered Leo pointing down the street and noting that the Rodin Museum was just a few blocks over. He said they had to go there, but they hadn't gone anywhere. They'd stayed in their room and joked about Nina writing a piece for which she didn't have to get out of bed. They never went outside—not once—except to move to the next hotel. So the neighborhood was harmless enough if Nina steered clear of that one building.

She would go to the Rodin Museum. And she would try, she would really try not to get suckered into thinking about the tragic life and death of Camille Claudel.

Leo loved the story of Camille Claudel having been Rodin's student, his mistress, then his colleague, a gifted sculptor, then going mad because he wouldn't leave his wife. Just before they put her away in the mental ward forever, she destroyed her own work, trashed her entire studio and her most brilliant sculptures.

Nina liked the story considerably less than Leo did, yet now the thought of Camille Claudel made Nina feel reassuringly in control. She was still a long way from going certifiably insane over Leo! Were there Claudels in the Rodin Museum? Nina couldn't remember. But she wanted to find out. It was similar to, but better than, a pilgrimage to Simone de Beauvoir's grave. If this was what Paris was giving her, Nina might as well be gracious and take it. De Beauvoir, Claudel, Madame Cordier, Achmed's girlfriend, Nina—sisters under the skin, in this city of women who love too much, Paris, city of broken hearts!

She walked around the block to avoid the Edith Wharton hotel and was afraid she was lost again when she took a turn—the wrong one, surely—and found herself alongside the smooth cement wall that bordered Rodin's gardens. This experience of being lost and lost and then suddenly found had happened to her in Venice but never before in Paris.

Somehow she'd found the Rodin Museum! But the heavy doors were half shut. The ticket booth was empty. Was the museum closed? Nina might have turned away, but at that moment a chill autumn sun burst through the clouds, which (thinking magically, again) she took as a message of personal encouragement.

Several people were in the garden, too far away for Nina to see if they were museumgoers or workers. On the opposite side of the building was the famous statue of Balzac in his voluminous robe, staggering beneath the prodigious weight of his own genitalia. From a sagging rope connecting two trees hung scallops of tricolor bunting and a banner announcing the hundred and fiftieth *anniversaire* of the *naissance* of Auguste Rodin.

Nina ventured up the walk between the plane trees, up the steps, through the doors, and into the huge foyer. The wintry light streaming onto the parquet floors and the scrolling staircase was refracted at crisp brilliant angles by the antique glass in the tall windows.

A young man was sitting at a desk. After a while he looked up. He was desolated to tell Nina that the museum was *fermé*.

"Pourquoi?" said Nina.

"Une fête," he explained. *"L'anniversaire de l'artiste."*

"Ah, oui! D'accord!" said Nina. She felt she should seem more happy about the great sculptor's birthday than disappointed for her own selfish reasons, being shut out of the museum. But why hadn't they posted a sign outside or closed the gate completely? Why had they lured her in so this young man could reject her in person?

Just then a door opened, and an elderly woman ran out and shook Nina's hand.

"Welcome! Welcome! *Enchantée!"*

Obviously, she was mistaking Nina for someone else. But in the rush of the moment Nina couldn't say so. First there was the challenge of putting it in French. And something about the woman's age made Nina hesitant, lest the woman assume her mistake was a sign of decrepitude and decline. Or was Nina the decrepit one? Her own self-doubt was so intense that for a moment she wondered: Maybe they *did* know each other, and Nina had just forgotten. Lately she often found herself greeting strangers warmly or failing to recognize people who seemed to have known her for years. She often believed and trusted the other person more than she trusted herself, and had had many friendly bewildered chats on the phone before the caller inquired if she might like to sit on his face. All this had set her up for Leo's telling her what to think, all the more so because she thought of herself as having a mind of her own.

"Je suis Madame Arlette Martin," the old woman said.

Nina smiled and inclined her head. There was no need for her to say her name—that is, whatever name was supposed to be hers.

Madame Martin addressed the young man in French, too fast for Nina to catch it. Like Madame Cordier, the old woman was wearing a suit, but hers was a severe dark blue. A tiny medal winked from her right lapel. Another little sparrow, the same species as Madame Cordier, a different breed from the peasant women who slaughtered the nightly pig.

A silk paisley scarf was tucked artfully under the collar of her jacket. Her penciled eyebrows were sketched in with a feathery hint of surprise repeated in the bright blue eyes that widened as she said, *"Parlez-vous français?"*

"Je comprends," said Nina. *"Mais je ne parle pas."*

Madame Martin smiled ruefully. She understood why Nina might not want to speak: shyness combined with an understandable respect for the beauties of the French language.

"Je suis désolée! Je ne parle pas anglais." Well then, it was settled. She could just speak French to Nina and not have to listen to what Nina said.

And Nina might not have to reveal that she wasn't whoever this woman thought. Because by now Madame Martin had taken Nina's coat and they were rapidly passing the point at which Nina could gracefully bail out. And what if she didn't? At parties, everyone pretended to recognize people they couldn't place and watched helplessly as the last moment for a confession sped by. Obviously, whomever Nina had been mistaken for was entitled to be welcomed and given a private tour of the museum that was closed to Nina. And as Leo used to say: Whom was it going to hurt?

Had Nina had a good flight? Madame Martin began in a French that sounded as if she herself were learning it phonetically.

"*Oui*," said Nina. "*Très confortable.*"

Madame touched her heart and said, It is his birthday. Already her speech had been slightly sped up by an influx of emotion.

It occurred to Nina that she could write a piece for *Allo!* on the centenary and a half of Auguste Rodin's birth. *Allo!* readers adored that sort of thing, invitations to make their own pilgrimages to honor the first appearance or demise of romantic cultural figures.

Madame Martin stepped back so Nina could precede her into the museum. And now it was definitely too late to find out who she thought Nina was. Probably some American art historian or curator or writer. Writer? Had Leo alerted her, too? Relax, Nina reminded herself. He couldn't have known she'd come here.

Nina drifted into a gleaming salon, then stopped so abruptly that the old woman almost stepped on her heels and gave a stifled yelp of alarm. A moment later, Nina paused before a marble sculpture of a crouched woman, leaning forward, spilling her long hair onto a rock. Her white marble back was smoother than skin. The hollows at the base of her spine made Nina's hand ache to touch them.

Last summer, Nina rode up in the elevator at *Allo!* with a man who had a beautiful tattoo, an elaborate apple tree dropping an apple that reappeared twice as it rolled down the length of his suntanned arm. Nina could hardly stop herself from reaching out to press the apple with the tip of her finger. The man wore black short shorts, a leather cap, a leather lace-up vest. He probably wouldn't have minded. Leo would have misunderstood; he would have thought her wanting to touch the man's arm was about sex. But it was more about childhood, when the world had a sexual buzz, the air, the sun, the bees, earthworms, dogshit, and you wanted to touch it all, before you learned that you shouldn't.

An old girlfriend of Leo's had joined a cult and now wrote him letters saying that she was experiencing nonstop sex with plants and rocks and trees. Leo told Nina, and they'd had a good laugh about that. They knew what real sex was. It wasn't about vibrations from rocks or about the vegetable kingdom. Nor was it those women shrieking behind every French hotel room door!

He loved women, someone said in French. Madame Martin had come up behind Nina.

Madame spoke faster and faster, and soon Nina was losing crucial connectives. Sometimes she would follow whole sentences and then miss one critical word. What made it even harder was the talking and stopping, talking and stopping, the peculiar rhythms of speech while walking through a museum. Half the time Nina's back was turned as she moved from one work to another, in this case from naked body to naked body or group of naked bodies, lovely smooth athletic torsos, one sex sculpture after another, here a couple embracing, tipped back on their knees, his face buried in her breast, there a young man with his robe open to just above his groin.

The gist of what Madame Martin was saying was what a genius Rodin was, his work was entirely original, entirely new, like the cave paintings at Lascaux, like the Renaissance, Leonardo. Never in art history did the human body have the life that Rodin gave it. How sad it was, how long it took for the world to recognize his gifts. First they accused him of casting from life, and then called his work obscene. Madame threw up her hands and shrugged. Then she said something Nina didn't quite get, something about people, Paris, rumors accusing Rodin of being Nijinsky's lover. . . . Was Rodin Nijinsky's lover? The next few sentences streamed past in a current that Nina could only observe until the word *Rilke* leaped out like a gleaming silver trout.

"Yes, Rilke!" Nina said. *"Son secrétaire."*

You didn't have to be a psychologist to understand that Madame Martin was madly in love with Rodin. Well, who wouldn't adore this genius who so worshiped the female body? There were photographs on the walls that Nina and Madame Martin studied together: Rodin, incredibly handsome at every stage of his life.

In one photo he sat on a park bench. He'd grown stout and looked very much the Artist in his bushy white beard, long morning coat, and straw hat. He was sketching a Thai or Cambodian dancer, a lovely girl of about eleven, in costume, with her toes turned out, her delicate hands curled like temple spires. In the background, two policemen looked on, fascinated. Leo would have loved this photo with its graphic representation of Eros on the periphery of the domain of Law and Order.

It was sad, Madame Martin was saying. Fame ignored Rodin in his youth; old age cut him down in his prime. His mind went, he was not himself, and just before his death he finally married Rose Beuret, who had been his mistress for forty years and bore him a son, and in the beginning wet down his maquettes so that the clay wouldn't harden. Madame Martin doused one of the sculptures with imaginary water: a naked woman crouched like a cat on the chest of a naked man.

"Madame Rodin," Nina said. *"Sa femme. Après quarante ans."*

Was Nina's French so unintelligible? The old woman looked bewildered. At last, she nodded vigorously. Ah, yes, Madame Rodin, the old shoe worn for forty years and married mostly for comfort, the good fit of the broken-in. Madame Rodin posed no threat; she was no one Madame Martin had to contend with.

They reached a group of figures in bronze, and perhaps Nina already knew whose work it was because she leaned over and checked the caption though she hadn't, with the others. Of course, it was Camille Claudel's, this trio of tragic figures, a man trudging forward, suffering, refusing to be consoled or dissuaded, though a nude kneeling woman pulled at his arm, begging him to stay. He forged onward into the protective and smothering embrace of a monstrous old hag with wings, a witch pretending to be an angel.

Maturity, the piece was called.

"Give me a break," said Nina.

"Pardon?" said Madame Martin.

The sculpture was technically excellent. But not nearly so good, not half so good as the worst piece by Rodin. But of course. His work was all about sex, and this one was all about grief. Who would choose this sculpture over a Rodin, except perhaps for a melancholic, suicidal adolescent?

But that was unfair to Camille Claudel! Her life was so much harder than Rodin's, as she progressed through the frustrating stages from student to apprentice to famous artist's mistress. A childish voice whined in Nina's head: At least she had Rodin! Nina remembered Leo saying how they'd found Claudel in her studio standing amid the shards of clay and chunks of broken marble. Maybe she overlooked this sculpture or wanted it to survive: her wrenching transparent comment on losing Rodin to his wife.

"*C'est triste,*" Madame Martin said.

"*Oui, c'est triste,*" said Nina. And now she felt bitterly sorry for poor Camille Claudel, dead and buried in the ground while they patronized her with their pity, Nina and this old woman who loved Rodin herself and was secretly glad that her major rival was out of the way for good. Wasn't this just another version of the jealous unspoken competition that had made for such a lively breakfast this morning with Madame Cordier?

As if Claudel's grief were contagious, Nina felt tired and chilled, and her guide wasn't nearly so frisky as she'd been a short while before. But then Madame Martin had a happy idea.

"*Venez, venez,*" she said. Nina trotted after her, outside, across the garden and into an adjacent building.

"*Son atelier,*" Madame announced, and now it was Nina who touched her heart.

"His studio," she translated for herself.

"*Oui,*" said Madame Martin.

Elegant track lighting spotlit selected parts of a long dark room with a central island partitioned into segments—not unlike a salad bar. But this salad bar held clay body parts, thousands of thumb-sized legs, knees, shoulders, tiny forearms and tinier noses. They reminded Nina of *milagros*, those silver cutouts of feet, heads, and eyes that, in Latin countries, the faithful left on their altars to let the saints know which organs were in need of miraculous cures. In his office Leo had a giant wooden cross encrusted with *milagros*—practically his favorite possession. He said one reason he loved it was because he was Jewish. But unlike *milagros*, those icons of damage and disease, these arms and legs were healthy. In fact they were in motion, wriggling around in their cases, seeking their lost living bodies.

"Toujours, toujours," said Madame Martin. She held out her hand and flexed her fingers as if kneading clay, and she and Nina stood there watching her knead the air. Always Rodin had clay in his hand, always he was making something: a body out of nothing.

Nina walked along the cases and stopped at a tray of breasts, the shape and size of gooseberries, walnuts, grapes, or cherries, each one different from the next, every one of them pretty. The old woman noticed where Nina had stopped.

He loved the body, she said.

And now she was nearing a part of her story that she so much wanted Nina to hear that for the first time she acknowledged that Nina might not be following every word. She slowed down and repeated everything several different ways.

It seemed that Rodin often made love to his models in his studio. And when he did, he put a sign on his door that said: ABSENT, VISITING CATHEDRALS.

She looked at Nina, expectantly.

"Quel homme," said Nina, shaking her head.

"Quel homme," Madame Martin agreed.

Still speaking deliberately, she made sure Nina understood that cathedrals were important to Rodin. He wrote a book on cathedrals, he believed that the body was a cathedral, that the great cathedrals were constructed on the principles of the body.

Absent. Visiting Cathedrals. Whose heart wouldn't be won forever? Still, Nina wondered sourly if he had one Absent, Visiting Cathedrals sign that he recycled for different women, or if he bothered making a new sign for each new model he made love to, or if by that point Rodin and his model were in such a fever of desire that she preferred him to use an old sign rather than take time to scribble a new one.

"*Venez,*" the old woman said, and graced Nina with a puckish grin. She groped along a dark wall.

"*Et voilà!*" she exclaimed. She pushed a button, and a hidden door in the wall swung open. Then she ushered Nina into a long narrow room, surgically clean and bare but for a row of sliding compartments on each side and perpendicular to each wall.

Madame Martin slid out a heavy vertical flat. Nina started to help her, but Madame waved her away. Nina stepped up to look at the sketch on the flat, a drawing in soft pencil of a masturbating woman, shown only from the tops of her breasts to the middle of her thighs, her long torso arched diagonally across the heavy paper.

"Oh, my goodness!" said Nina.

"*C'est beau, non?*" said Madame Martin.

"*C'est beau. Oui,*" Nina said.

Why had the old woman brought her here? Why was she showing this to Nina? Or really, to whomever she thought Nina was? That probably explained it. She had mistaken Nina for some curator who warranted the cellar-to-attic tour: the sculptures, the photos, the atelier, and now the dirty pictures.

Nina had known these drawings were here. In fact she'd been thinking about them—expecting to see them—when Madame Martin opened the door in the wall. Leo had spoken of Rodin's erotic drawings locked away in the museum. Maybe he'd even mentioned it when he'd pointed out the museum from a distance. And now Nina was getting to see them. Wait till she told Leo!

The old woman stood on her toes and strained as she pulled

out the flats, each of which contained one drawing: women on their backs with their legs spread, their hands behind their heads, two naked women, face-to-face, one on the other's lap.

It could hardly have been weirder, being here in total silence except for the creaking of the flats, with this genteel, proper Frenchwoman and these intensely erotic drawings. The only way to deal with it was to have the out-of-body experience that was learned behavior for looking at art in museums. Asexual, clinically detached, like going to the doctor's. As if the naked people on canvas weren't naked people, as if what Rodin put on paper had had nothing to do with sex. Nina and Leo used to talk about this. What was wrong with those poor critics and art historians who had such a stake in denying that certain artists loved the body? Some problem with *their* own bodies, perhaps? No problem with Leo's and Nina's!

The drawings were spectacular, and again there was no mistaking that the man who had drawn them was madly in love with every curve and fold, every inch of the flesh that he so tenderly translated from three dimensions into two. Probably there were critics who saw the story of Camille Claudel as the case history of a misogynist: clinical evidence that Rodin secretly hated women. Let them take a good look at these drawings and see if they still believed that! But no doubt they'd already seen them and remained unpersuaded.

Given the drawings' subject matter, it was not at all surprising when Madame Martin reverted to her dearest subject: how much Rodin loved the body. He wanted to be God, she said, making Adam and Eve out of clay.

Gradually, Nina understood what Madame Martin was doing: She was showing Nina what she had, how much she'd been given to live with. Like a house-proud wife or widow taking guests on tour of her magnificent home: Look at what my man bought for me, look at what he left me. As if Rodin had meant these drawings for Madame Martin to hoard in this museum. Not for Camille Claudel, not for his wife—and certainly not for Nina. He'd done all this for Madame Martin to cherish and use as she pleased.

Finally they rolled back the last flat. They both felt a little drained. Madame Martin walked Nina out through the atelier and back onto the wide path lined with plane trees. She invited her to stroll through the gardens, spend as long as she liked, go through the museum again if she needed more for her essay.

Her essay! Nina nodded. She could agree to that—with genuine conviction and an easy conscience. She would write an essay for *Allo!* But not the essay Madame meant. She could hardly tell *Allo!* readers about the erotic drawings, fill their heads with envious dreams of what they would never see. She thanked Madame Martin, who smiled briskly and gave her head a sparrowlike shake and mimed that she was shivering and hurried back indoors.

Nina had gotten away with it. She'd been taken around the museum without being found out as someone other than the person whom she was supposed to be.

A moment later Madame Martin reappeared. Nina's heart skipped a beat, assisted by the black coffee and the fear that the woman she'd been mistaken for had arrived in their absence, or else a phone call had come in, and Nina's game was up.

But Madame Martin had merely remembered that she still had Nina's coat. She ran, with the coat stretched across her arms, the way war victims on the TV news ran with wounded children. Nina hurried toward her, to spare her a trip across the garden. It was all very awkward, getting her coat back. Nina thanked her even more warmly. They said good-bye several times more.

Nina felt as if she were being watched by someone who might be offended if she turned and left. She walked beneath a bare pergola down the length of the garden. The lawns and flower beds were undergoing major excavation. Huge areas were dug up and roped off with neon-orange plastic net, and the ripe smell of sewers and wet cement hung thickly in the air. Shouldn't they have finished before the sculptor's birthday? They'd be done by spring or summer, when the tourists came back.

After a decent interval, Nina left the grounds and returned to the deserted street. She looked around. Where to? What now? Leo would know where to go.

But what made Leo so special? Who was Leo compared with Rodin? And what was sleeping with Leo beside what she'd just experienced, the orgy she'd taken part in, the lustful entwining of bodies and limbs that Rodin set in motion: ecstatic, blissful, unsatisfied still, all these years after his death?

Using the same navigational system as before—lost, hopelessly lost, then found again, Nina somehow resurfaced on the boulevard Saint-Germain.

Cars and pedestrians chased each other down the crowded avenue, darting between pale shadows and patches of cold silver light. Was it morning or afternoon light? Nina couldn't tell. How much time had she spent at the museum? Where was her watch? Had she left it at the hotel? Well, it wouldn't have helped her now. She knew that she hadn't reset it.

She stood on a busy corner, watching people go by, trying to guess the approximate hour from the looks on their faces. Were they going to lunch? Returning? Leaving work and heading home early after a miserable day?

Nina wished she'd brought the list of restaurants that Leo was scribbling as he told her how much she would love the Hotel Danton. She would have had to rescue the scrap of paper from the trash. She hadn't wanted to get that close, to risk brushing elbows or knees, though in the past they'd clung to each other behind that very desk.

Did his absentmindedness betray what they both knew but couldn't acknowledge, that his packing her off to Paris wasn't merely business as usual? Why had he sent her here, anyhow, when he could have simply done what normal men did: told her that it wasn't working out and he needed to see other women. Looking out at the city lights, Nina had imagined that there were other offices in which lovers were making each other unhappy, but none in which men were buying women off with free trips to Paris. Why had he picked the Hotel Danton? Did he want her to meet Madame Cordier? Was there some lesson he meant her to learn? Or possibly, some secret?

Nina would feel competent, tracking down an enticing bistro, studying the menu, ordering, taking notes on the food and wine. They used to alternate taking notes. Leo was less circumspect. In fact he made a production of requesting souvenir menus, asking pointed questions so that anyone would realize that he had some professional interest. Soon, delectable morsels—compliments of the chef—would appear from the kitchen, plates of buttery *amuse-bouche* with caviar and crème fraîche, balls of exotic fruit sorbet, expensive bottles of wine.

Several times Nina asked Leo if that was ethical. Weren't they supposed to re-create the experience of a typical *Allo!* reader, humble and anonymous and likely to be mistreated? Leo said there was nothing wrong in letting the restaurants do their best, and that the experience they were re-creating was that of a typical *Allo!* reader on an atypically lucky day.

She should head back to Montparnasse and find those secret

bistros and write them up for *Allo!* The smell of wine and tobacco, the clink of silverware and glass, voices rising and ebbing—it might be cheering, a comfort. Nina imagined several appealing dishes: slices of duck breast cooked rare, anything with venison or wild mushrooms, or stepping down, roast chicken and *frites*, any place could do that. But they seemed appealing for someone else to eat. Nina wasn't hungry, which was worrisome and unusual, considering she'd eaten nothing for the last two days except a bite of croissant, half an overripe tangerine, and an ocean of black coffee.

Perhaps that was why she felt so weak. Honestly, she was exhausted. Could one still have jet lag after sleeping for two days?

Nina should go back to the hotel and take a refreshing nap and wake up in better shape to write her article. She had two more days left. She could still pull herself together in time to fly back home and suffer jet lag in the opposite direction.

But she couldn't go back to the hotel. She was too tired to walk there—even if she knew where it was. She could ask at the metro ticket booth: What station was nearest the Hotel Danton? Her French was good enough for that, but the idea made her sleepy, and soon she was too lethargic to consider it at all.

She drifted over to a shop window and looked in at racks of couturier dog sweaters on hangers, puppy jackets with epaulets, turtlenecks, tartan blazers. Pet baskets lined with sprigged Provençal cotton were heaped up on the floor.

Behind the counter a woman was kissing a large toucan whose blue and orange feathers spilled down her arm as she brought the bird close to her lips.

Then, as Nina watched, the bird's neck shot out like a jack-in-the-box, and the bird bit the woman's cheek. Nina saw the woman scream, though she couldn't hear it. The woman put her hand to her face, and her fingers tracked a smear of blood from her cheek to her chin. She looked up. Her eyes locked with Nina's.

Nina started running, although she tried to appear as if she were walking: the frantic waddle of a schoolchild told not to run in the halls. Nemesis must have been out for lunch or looking the other way, for Nina spotted a taxi stand. Incredibly, five taxis waited to take her wherever she wanted to go.

Somehow Nina managed a convincing impersonation of a woman who could step confidently up to the first taxi in line and open the door and slide in and name her destination. White bristles sat like a soft pelt on the cabdriver's layered chins. He peered at Nina in the mirror. She repeated the Hotel Danton's address.

It *must* have been a whorehouse. How else to explain the driver's searching gaze as he twisted around to face her?

Did he want to discuss this? Hey, Nina would discuss it! First they would establish that the Hotel Danton was indeed a house of prostitution. Then she would ask him what he thought of a man who flew his girlfriend to Paris to stay in a swell place like that.

But no such discussion seemed required. The cab pulled away from the curb and went less than a block before the driver hit his horn, then his brakes, and then they sat for ages amid a silky cloud of diesel exhaust and the hum of idling engines.

There was a lot of traffic, the cabdriver said, in French. Farmers from the provinces had dumped truckloads of oranges onto the roads, blocking the highways to the airport. You couldn't blame the farmers, they were just trying to live. But the traffic, my God. Taxi drivers had to live too, Madame. . . .

Oranges on the airport road? Had Nina heard him correctly? Her French left so much room for misunderstanding.

The driver made a series of sharp furious turns, and at last they took off. They seemed to be flying down the same streets Nina had walked along earlier, so that riding through them was like seeing a film played backward, fast. This couldn't be the most direct route. Was this thieving son of a bitch running up the meter? Taxi drivers had to live too, Madame. . . .

The cab made a smooth landing at the curb in front of the Hotel Danton. Coming in from the airport, Nina had been too numb and tired—and also smart enough—not to let herself notice how squalid the hotel was. She'd been wise to ignore it then, because by now she didn't care. The Hotel Danton was home to her now. She was overjoyed to see it.

She paid the driver and went inside. A new person was at the desk. A hatchet-nosed, haughty young man surrendered Nina's key despite his evident opinion that her asking for it was gauche. Where had Nina seen him before? At the desk in the Rodin Museum? Maybe not the same young man, but close enough for Nina. So this guy was the other half of what Paris was offering her this time: grieving heartbroken women and sleek disdainful young men.

Nina peered around the corner into the breakfast room. Madame Cordier wasn't there. What sane person would be? The room had stopped playacting with its coffee, butter, and jam and had revealed its true nature as a place where, at three A.M., any insomniac could stumble in, so desperate for a drink that he or she would be glad to unstick the furry bottles of cheap brandy and fruit liqueurs.

When the elevator door closed, Nina pressed her arms into her sides. This country would be hell on a claustrophobe; the whole continent would be. The truth was—and why not admit it now?—Leo was claustrophobic. He rode elevators to high floors, but if they were staying on the lower floor, he always took the stairs. He said he needed the exercise, but Nina had seen him in elevators, where she'd learned not to talk to him. He was much too tense to listen.

They could never mention this. Hush now, don't explain. She could understand his embarrassment. Men were supposed to face down wild animals, bandits, vicious bullies, and killers. They were not allowed to fall apart in small enclosed windowless spaces. But Nina's endlessly flexible love had more than enough tensile strength to effortlessly embrace the fact that Leo was claustrophobic. When you loved someone, you loved him at every age he ever was or would be, and the Leo who so feared elevators was Leo as a small boy. Who else could he find to love him so much— to love every weakness and failing?

Nina unlocked the door with difficulty that stopped this side of panic. She switched on the light and saw with dismay that someone had cleaned her room, dismay because of how the bed was made, the blankets tucked haphazardly under the lumpy pillows, the bedspread hanging down on one side and rucked up at the bottom, with none of the practiced rigor of a hotel chambermaid: the hasty way a bed might be made by a resentful family member.

The breakfast tray had been removed, but the half-empty water bottle remained to give Nina one last chance to drink the backwash some stranger had thoughtfully left her. No point even looking for a chocolate on the pillow. The shutters were still open, which made Nina suddenly anxious, as if someone might be spying on her through the dusty, thin white curtain. Someone would have to hover there—and what was there to spy on? A nervous American tourist pacing until she collapsed, fully dressed, on the bed and fell asleep watching TV.

She looked out the window and down at the deserted roof. The cats must have settled their disagreement over the plastic-wrap mouse.

Madame Cordier had said that a prostitute died, leaping from this window. But the roof wasn't very far down. She must have broken her neck. Had Madame said it was this room? Or had she just *not* said it wasn't? Had she told Nina that the girl was dead or just that she'd jumped out the window?

A gust of chill air blew in from outside, and suddenly Nina was sure: The girl was dead, and her ghost was faking the record-breaking orgasms. It wasn't healthy to think this way. It was time to be a real person. "Be a real person, Nina," Leo used to say. She was never certain what he thought a real person was, but she understood that he meant she was being paranoid and irrational.

Nina leaned out to tug at the shutters, which finally banged shut with the chilling finality of jail-cell doors in films about innocent men on death row. Suppose they never opened again? Fine. What did Nina care?

She decided to take a hot bath, a long blissful soak. Blissful? She must have been imagining a bath in some other bathroom, perhaps a tub in one of those heavens where she'd stayed with Leo—surely not this swampy noxious cave, stinking of mildew and piss. She found the stopper, rinsed it off with what passed for hot water, and wedged it in the drain.

The faucet choked and spat out several splats of brownish liquid that sank thin flakes of sediment to the bottom of the tub.

Nina ran the water until it was semiclear, then looked around for some soap. And now her mind *was* mercifully taking her back to another bathroom, another hotel, a hotel she'd stayed in with Leo. She recalled every shining detail of the shampoos and gels and lotions, each a different pastel color in a clear glass bottle. Everything—the conditioner, the soap dish, the cotton puffs, the snowy bathrobes—whispered of comfort and luxury and the promise of sex.

Not to be outdone, the Danton offered two identical thin rectangles of hard, tightly wrapped airplane soap. Every detail seemed designed to communicate cheapness, dirt, and deprivation.

How could this be a whorehouse? A whorehouse was supposed to have at least some theoretical relation to pleasure. Though Nina had seen photos of brothels in Bombay, the cramped cells, the filthy mattresses, the dangling lightbulbs that served as focal points for the prostitutes to stare at while they lay on their backs and worked. No wonder the poor woman who labored nights at the Danton felt she had to compensate for the hotel's flaws with her high volume, nonstop pornographic sound track.

Nina slipped off all her clothes at once, like a carapace, noting with interest the baggy pouches, the stains and streaks that had gravitated to her outfit. Anyone would think she'd been using her good black skirt for an ashtray.

She lowered her hips down into the tub and scooted under the water and watched her body flatten into a white blurry fish.

Leo had a strange habit. Often, when Nina took a long bath, he'd knock on the bathroom door and ask if she was all right.

He'd learned it from his mother, he said. When his mother was a girl, a neighbor's kid drowned in the tub. So his mother had called into him whenever he took a bath, which was extremely annoying, because he was usually masturbating. It had never occurred to him that he would grow up to be just as crazy. But he'd been programmed; he couldn't help it. He was afraid *not* to check periodically when someone he cared about was in the tub. Suppose someone he loved fell asleep and drowned and Leo let her die just because he was afraid of turning into his mother.

Someone might be irritated at being interrupted just as she slipped into the warm, enveloping fog one wanted from a bath. But if Nina minded, it was only for a second, a burr of irritation quickly washed away in the flood of erotic surrender and over-whelming awareness of her love for Leo, annoying tics and all. Leo cared about her! That was what Nina heard, even though—it occurred to her now—what Leo actually said was that his bathtub-drowning neurosis was about being Jewish; and Nina, not being Jewish, would never understand. He had never specifi-cally said that he was worried about *Nina* drowning. The fear was that "someone he cared about" might slide under the water. Only now did Nina allow herself the depressing thought of Leo inter-rupting a long succession of women, each at the point of losing herself in the pleasures of the tub.

She could stay in the bath forever now! She could fall over and drown and no one would bother her, knocking timidly at the door. But suddenly, bathing began to seem like a strange thing to do, soaking in your own dirt, as shower-takers said.

Nina got out and dried herself with a thin towel that reeked of candy-sweet disinfectant. She gathered her clothes and put them back on, which was not a good sign. At least she put on clean underwear except for the same black tights, whose baggy feet gave off puffs of grayish dust. Then she switched on the television and lay down on top of the bedspread, clutching the remote control.

The only interesting program was about Soviet breakaway republics, street fighting and guerilla warfare between two warring Asiatic nations whose names Nina couldn't catch. *This* was what Nina should be thinking about: genocide, savage local wars, world peace. That all she could think of was Leo further lowered her self-esteem. She told herself that her failure to focus on the important issues, to concentrate on the news was not a moral but a linguistic lapse; she was missing too much of the French. Her language skills must be degenerating, because she'd always found it easier to understand French on TV than in life. Even though they spoke quickly on television, you weren't expected to answer and could try to comprehend without the pressure to compose a grammatical reply.

Soldiers lay on their stomachs in bombed-out rooms, plugging away at mortars; the charred bare windows of government buildings emitted clouds of smoke. Stretchers raced by too quickly for Nina to see who was on them. Toothless grannies beat their chests and fell on the graves of husbands and sons.

The remote control worked if you shook it and kept hitting the plus button. Nina switched to a channel on which there was some sort of talk show. These people sat on high stools, as if at a kitchen counter, smiling dementedly and breaking off their rapid-fire chat to sing snatches of songs that inspired the audience to fits of raucous applause. Who were these people? What were they saying? Nina had been wrong to assume she understood their language at all.

So it didn't matter—in fact it was a relief—that the next show was in Italian. Strip *Jeopardy*, as it turned out. If the all-girl contestants missed a question, they had to remove an item of clothing.

A tall blond (on Nina's TV set, white-haired) woman lost everything but her underwear and was looking troubled until the kindly quiz-show host tossed her a thigh-length satin robe. She embraced the avuncular host and covered his face with kisses. He wore a slightly longer robe in a shiny dark silk.

Most of the pretty hotels in which the famous dead had slept provided robes for when the living emerged all wet and warm from the tub. During that last trip, it had often been hard to tell when Leo and Nina's lovemaking started or stopped, hard to remember specific events apart from a general feeling. But there was one evening Nina remembered, or a part of that evening: Nina had stepped out of the tub and thrown a robe over her steaming skin. Leo was lying on the bed and, as she crossed the room, he watched her very intently, then shut his eyes and tipped back his head, and she knelt and kissed his throat.

Nina must have fallen asleep. A trail of drool slicked her pillow. Had someone changed channels while she'd slept? Could she still be dreaming?

It seemed to her that on TV a pig was about to die.

As a child she'd had a recurring dream that began with her mother or father calling her name in their gentle familiar voices. When she heard that, she knew what was coming next: A ghostly figure, a translucent chalky silhouette would drift closer and closer to her bed, and just before it reached her, she would wake up, rigid with terror.

That's how it was about the pig. She knew what was going to happen although there was no pig around.

On television a peasant couple sat side by side at a picnic table in the courtyard of a palatial stone barn. A stooped man in a cardigan and beret, his wrinkled wife in an apron, they lived in the Auvergne, *la France profonde*, in a stone house in a magnificent valley.

The couple held hands as they told the interviewer how many generations of their families had farmed that fertile soil, *mon grand-père, ma mère*. Each time they mentioned a generation or referred to the land, the camera rose into the air and swooped over the lush fields and treetops to make sure the viewers saw what they were describing.

They loved each other, they loved their farm, and despite everything that was about to happen, they loved their pig. How did Nina know what was about to happen? There was still no pig to be seen, and just because of the other pigs, the ones in Provence and Alsace, that didn't mean that another poor pig was slated to be slaughtered.

But now, at long last, there was a pig. The camera had rooted it out, tracked it to its hiding place, a boggy spot near the barn door. The pig was half buried in the dirt, wallowing in mud, looking alternately like a hog or a miniature hippo.

Nina knew it was a pig. She knew what was going to happen. And so did the couple who loved their pig, and so did the camera crew, and so did everyone except for the pig, which slowly hauled itself from the mud and trotted over to the woman as she sweetly sang out its name.

"Mizu mizu mizu," she sang. The pig lowered its snout and nuzzled her hand. The camera zoomed in on the old woman's hand, cradling an apple. The pig lowered its head and bit the apple. The old woman stroked the pig's forehead and warbled into its ear. A look of sheer bliss came over its face. The woman seemed happy, too. Only now did the camera pull back to reveal the farmer holding a rifle. He hesitated a moment, then raised the gun to the pig's head and shot.

This pig had the best death, the most conscious, humane, and loving demise. Nina felt she was meant to admire this scene, the happy death of this barnyard creature, this couple who had lived in this place for so many generations and found through long trial and error the best way to slaughter a pig. An apple on its tongue, a hand on its chin, a bullet in its temple.

The audience was supposed to admire these peasants and their pig. But if so, why did the filmmakers indulge in ironic arty gestures, for example, playing Puccini's "Un bel dì" on the sound track as the animal died, grinning. They kept stopping the film and running it back and repeatedly showing the pig death footage. With each replay the death appeared less serene and idyllic, and by the third time looked more brutal than the violent mindless deaths of the Alsatian and Provençal pigs.

Someone knocked on Nina's door.

"Nina?" a man said. "Nina?"

"Excuse me?" she said. "Who is it?"

"Nina," a man said. "It's me."

Nina opened the door.

It was Leo.

Well, maybe it was Leo. That is, he looked exactly and nothing like the Leo she remembered, the Leo she had been thinking about every minute of every day while making such an effort not to think about Leo. She knew that it was Leo, but at the same time couldn't help feeling that this imitation Leo didn't resemble anyone she knew. At first she felt unnaturally calm and then so weak in the knees that when Leo opened his arms she slumped and fell into his chest.

Nina burrowed into his neck. She wasn't ready to look at him yet. First she had to touch his wide back and slightly rounded shoulders. Second, she had to smell him.

It was definitely Leo.

Only lovers had that pride in knowing each other's smell, which was so much more basic, more true, she and Leo agreed, than how most humans identified one another, with shallow questions about where they were from and what they did for a living. Lovers got past that, way past that, back to the essential, down to the primordial sniffing of cats and dogs in heat. That too was something you didn't share with every stranger you met.

"I missed you," Leo said huskily.

"I missed you, too," said Nina.

Leo knelt and picked up his valise and walked past Nina into the room. He put down his suitcase.

He said, "What is this place? A whorehouse?"

Laughter diffused the tension long enough for them to face each other. The strain and fatigue of travel enhanced Leo's haggard good looks. And as Leo studied Nina, he seemed to like whatever he saw and not to notice or care that she was wearing the same outfit she'd been sleeping in for days. Nina's clothing meant nothing to Leo, though he was vain about his own. Their romance still had nothing to do with clothes. Only at a later stage did lovers begin giving each other fashion advice, after the beloved's once attractive eccentricities began to seem like embarrassing reflections on one's self.

"This place is wild," said Leo.

"You noticed," Nina said.

"Adele Cordier's a real piece of work," Leo said. "She called and specifically promised that this place was charming—and remodeled top to bottom."

It lightened Nina's spirits that Leo talked about Madame
Cordier like any hotel owner, someone to do business with—
or not. But maybe it should have worried Nina to hear Leo
speak that way about a former lover. How would Leo talk about
Nina in their separate futures—futures that seemed less imminent and less separate now than they had just a few hours before?
Normally, Nina and Leo never mentioned past loves, except
for that poor woman having all-day sex with plants. Leo's passion for history did not extend to personal history. Once Leo
told Nina about a man he knew whose new wife asked him
to make a list of all his previous girlfriends; he said he'd go to
his office and do it—and he never came home again. The warning
in Leo's story was clear: He and Nina had no romantic pasts
before they'd met. He was right, it was wiser not to consider
the time they'd wasted, the years they could have spent together.
The only subject more taboo than the past was the subject of the
future. . . .

Leo said, "Adele's an old friend from when I lived here. She
buys and redecorates hotels now. I thought: Why not do her a
favor, check out her new hotel. We could go to Paris and write
the whole thing off."

We? When had Leo ever said *we?* Also, hadn't he said that a
friend in London has recommended this hotel? And what about
the other hotel Madame Cordier owned, the one in which Sarah
Bernhardt had stayed and, more recently, Leo and Nina? Did she
recommend that one, too?

Madame Cordier had insisted that she'd told Leo that the
Danton wasn't fixed up yet. One of them was lying or had a
twisted idea of the truth. But it was surprisingly easy to let one's
ideas get twisted. Yesterday, had anyone asked, Nina would

have insisted that Leo had told her that she was going to Paris without him.

"I met her. Madame Cordier," Nina blurted out.

"How predictable," said Leo. "All these hotel owners—these innkeepers—believe in the personal touch. Poor slobs. Their job depends on sending up fruit baskets and champagne, and conning writers into saying something complimentary, or at least listing the joint in *Allo!* Remember that guy who kept calling our room and we kept blowing him off and finally he came and knocked on the door when we were fooling around in the tub? Where was that? Was that Oscar Wilde's room? I only remember the tub."

Lucky Leo could still recall events like that without the searing pain that such memories had begun to cause Nina. But why should it be painful for him? He hadn't just lived through days—no, weeks—since they'd broken up. He hadn't known they'd broken up. He thought they'd been together all along.

"What are you doing here?" Nina said.

"What do you mean?" asked Leo.

"I thought you weren't coming to Paris."

"You did? Why? I can't believe it," said Leo. "I thought we agreed I couldn't leave New York until yesterday evening. But our frequent-flier miles expired the day you left, and if we didn't use them by then we'd have to pay for your ticket."

Frequent-flier miles? Separate flights? Surely Nina would have registered these fairly complex arrangements. But she didn't remember Leo mentioning frequent-flier miles. Often such questions did come up, requiring him to work out some thorny air-travel snag. So maybe he *had* explained all this, and it had scooted right past Nina.

If only she could reconstruct the details of that afternoon in his office, what he'd said and didn't say that made her think she was going alone. She started off assuming the opposite: that they were going together. Something must have made it plain enough for her to change her mind. She saw herself looking out his window, heard his "Nina, I'm over here." Could you feel so strongly and suffer so deeply because of a misunderstanding? What a ridiculous question! Wars broke out for less. . . .

Always, in the past, she and Leo had barely tipped the bellboy and locked the door before they were glued together, stumbling toward the bed. They joked about Leo's jet lag cure, which often began on the flight, under the airplane blankets, with quasi-accidental touches that escalated into furtive groping. If some prudish fellow passenger disapproved—well, so much the better! And so when they reached the hotel rooms already falling into each other, it wasn't the beginning but rather a stage in what had begun with a kiss before takeoff, clasped hands during landing, and evolved into long starved looks in the taxi from the airport.

But now they were starting off cold, so to speak. They had to find out where they were.

Leo kissed her, then kissed her again, seriously enough so that Nina toppled slightly and held up her hands, as if to regain her balance.

Leo sat down on the edge of the bed. Nina almost sat on his lap. But her guardian angel must have yanked her back seconds before Leo twisted around and reached for the remote.

Leo stared at the TV. Nina sat in a nearby chair.

No need to change the channel. The Auvergne pig was dying again. That was what got Leo's attention. The old woman was still singing its name. Mizu mizu mizu. Had they been repeating this scene, replaying it over and over during the time it had taken Nina and Leo to get from the doorway to the bed?

The end, hoped Nina. One final loop. The apple. The opera. Blam.

"Would you look at this?" said Leo. "Right-wing propaganda. *La France profonde.* Our peasant *grand-mère* and *grand-père.* Doing things the old way, the French way, not the Turkish or Senegalese or Algerian way. Voting the right-wing agenda is a vote for the peasants, for delicious French sausage made from French pigs hand-fed and hand-raised on French apples. Voting the straight right-wing ticket doesn't mean a vote, as one might ignorantly suppose, for deporting foreign workers, firebombing guest worker hostels, protectionism, high tariffs. Not at all! . . . It's a vote for sausage! You know what the pig's name should be?"

"Mizu?" said Nina.

"Dreyfus!" Leo laughed. "This lovely film about the lovely French farmers is all about the coming election. And that's why it took me two goddamn hours to get in from the airport. There was a demonstration on the Orly road, gangs of rednecks from the provinces dumping oranges on the highway. Crates of Moroccan oranges. How many oranges can *France* grow?

"But of course you can't blame them, the poor bastard farmers are broke, right along with the rest of the world, except for a few corporate slimeballs. The time is ripe for some fascist shithead to get the trains running on time and everyone eating pure French pork like our pure peasant grandparents. French sausage! You don't have to be Sigmund Freud—"

"I heard about that demonstration," Nina said. "The oranges on the road."

"Sure," said Leo. "Everyone heard about it. And I got to be the lucky guy sitting in traffic with the meter running."

"Was the flight all right?" said Nina.

"Hellish," Leo said. "The airline must have held a contest: free tickets for the most colicky infants and hyperactive toddlers. All the winners got to travel together on one flight to Paris—*my* flight, needless to say—with their passive parents, heavy into the drinks cart. The kids were all shrieking and punching each other and racing up and down the aisles. I insisted on being bumped up to business class. I flashed some back issues of *Allo!* until I found a steward who knew what *Allo!* was.

"There were some empty seats in business. They put me next to a teensy old lady. I figured she'd be no problem. She'd tell me about her grandchildren and then pass out over the pretakeoff champagne. It turned out she was a German who'd lived most of her life in Estonia. She'd done time in a Russian detention camp. Obviously a Nazi. What was she doing in business class? I knew I should have stayed in coach; at least the kids were harmless.

"One glass of champagne and she's telling me that every evil act the Russians committed was all because of a Jewish plot, and the Jews will never get enough of making Germany pay. I told her I was Jewish. She said she was sure I'd want to know the truth. This was before they'd even turned off the no-smoking sign."

"How terrible," said Nina. What a spooky coincidence! She too had come over on a plane of unrepentant Nazis. Was the international Jewish conspiracy the popular topic right now on transatlantic flights? Nina couldn't say this to Leo. He would be too quick to inform her that what had happened to her wasn't the same thing at all. Because Nina wasn't Jewish. Better not to mention her flight. Not for now, anyway.

"She drove me insane," said Leo. "I wound up getting crazy. As soon as we reached cruising altitude, I went into the toilet and wrote a line of numbers in blue ballpoint on my arm."

"Oh, dear," Nina said.

"Like a concentration camp tattoo."

"I realize, Leo," said Nina.

"And when I went back to my seat I casually pulled up my cuff and reached across her for a magazine. I made sure she saw."

"What did she do?" asked Nina.

"Nothing," Leo said. "If she was going to apologize, she would have done it when I announced I was Jewish. But at least we didn't have to talk for the rest of the flight."

"That was a blessing," said Nina.

"A lifesaver," Leo said. "Later I went and washed the numbers off, and I made sure she noticed that, too."

A jumble of images on the TV caught the edge of Nina's attention. The Auvergne pig had stopped dying, and the film had moved on to a group of farmers milling around with the transfixed stares of spectators at gambling casinos, though what they turned out to be watching was some sort of sausage-eating contest: French peasants at a table stuffing ground meat into their faces.

Leo said, "Ahem. Nina, are you with me?"

"What?" said Nina.

Leo said, "No doubt Adele Cordier told you all about our long tortured passionate love affair, and how I ditched her and ruined her life."

"Something like that," said Nina. "She said you kidnapped her from her husband in Tours and brought her back to Paris."

"I rest my case," said Leo. "The husband was my friend. I went down there for a political rally. We got arrested. The week I got back to Paris, she showed up at my door with a suitcase and a half-dozen kids. What was I supposed to do? I phoned the husband, my friend. I said, 'Come get your wife.' That clever son of a bitch, he said, 'You got her. You keep her. She's yours. The bitch is driving me nuts.' That was 1968. Things were still pretty retro. Two guys could still get together and decide some perfectly capable woman's fate."

"Didn't you live with her?" Nina asked.

Leo shrugged. "I let her stay. I probably slept with her once or twice. Soon she was driving *me* crazy. Was I going out? Where was I going? When was I coming back? Why had I said that? Done this? I was paralyzed with terror. You can imagine, Nina."

All too easily, Nina could. Soon after they'd become lovers, Nina made the mistake of asking Leo where he'd spent a weekend during which he hadn't called. He'd put a finger to her lips and said, "People say it's hard for passion to withstand the effects of time. But I don't think the problem is time, do you? I think it's . . . micromanagement." Was it micromanagement to want to know where the person you loved had spent the last forty-eight hours?

Leo said, "She was always bathing some naked child in my kitchen sink. They were pretty good kids, I guess. Not noisy or destructive."

"They were probably scared of you," Nina said.

"Of me?" said Leo. "Why? Hey, I caved in. Surrendered! I gave her the apartment and left. I went to Arles, I got a summer job breaking horses in the Camargue. I fell off twice, and after that I was a regular cowboy. By the time I got back from the South of France she'd found some new guy and was living with him. I think they even got married when her divorce from my friend came through."

Leo, a cowboy in the Camargue? Madame Cordier didn't mention that. Didn't she say he'd gone to the South to work on his novel?

"She told me you wrecked that happy home," said Nina. "She told me you showed up and swept her off to a hotel for one afternoon, and that was the end of that guy."

"She said *that*?" Leo bugged his eyes. "She said one afternoon with me was the end of some other guy? I'm flattered." He laughed. "Unfortunately, it's not true. Memory plays weird tricks. One consolation for aging is that you can rearrange the past and make it happen whatever way you wanted. Adele's a very smart woman, very shrewd, very creative. And every male can breathe a giant sigh of relief that she's put that energy into wheeling and dealing hotels."

Nina felt less like a woman talking to her lover than like a bewildered juror assigned to a case so contradictory that it bordered on the metaphysical. You couldn't tell who was on the same side, or which side was which. Maybe Nina and Leo were allied against the delusional Madame Cordier, or maybe Nina and Madame Cordier should unite against Leo and the tricks he'd been using to bend women's minds all these years. Probably Madame Cordier always exaggerated or lied. Probably Nina had misunderstood what Leo said that day in his office.

Leo said, "I can't believe we're talking about this, digging up shit from the past that's bound to make us both unhappy."

"Okay," Nina said. "Let's stop it."

A while later, Leo asked, "What else did she say about me?"

"That you played her the Billie Holiday," said Nina.

"Huh?" said Leo.

" 'Don't Explain,' " said Nina. "You played it for her."

"I don't think so," said Leo. "Maybe a different Billie Holiday song. Over the years, my favorites have changed. I could have played her 'I Cover the Waterfront.' Which I pretty much did in those days."

"Hilarious," said Nina.

"Not 'Don't Explain,'" said Leo. "Not that song. That one's way too tough, way too . . . close to the bone for me to have played for *her*. Did she say *that* song?"

"I don't know," said Nina.

"Christ, Nina, what is this? Be a real person, okay? Are you going to make me spend the rest of my life paying for the sins of the frequent-flier program?"

That wasn't what Nina was doing. This wasn't about separate flights. But what if it *was* all a big mistake? What a relief *that* would be! And Leo said 'the rest of my life.' Did he mean to spend it with Nina? Who else would make him keep paying . . . ?

Leo said, "Come here." He held out his arms.

Nina stood and crossed the room. Leo pulled up her skirt and rolled down her tights and set her, facing him, on his knees.

What was *that?*" said Leo, after their hearts had stopped hammering, and their breathing had slowed to normal.

Why was he asking Nina, just because she'd been there? She could summon up some pornographic snapshots that could make desire kick in again, but they were only details. A cyclone had picked them up—like that!—and set them down somewhere else. Nina was a different person from the weepy lovesick wimp, the pathetic alien spirit who, until a half hour ago, had been in possession of Nina's now relaxed and pleasurably tingling body.

All that was prehistory. Her time alone in Paris already seemed like a rough patch in someone else's life, some dippy fool who had squandered her grief on a silly misunderstanding. Anyway, that was over. Now they were communicating on such a deep cellular level that a mistake about travel plans hardly counted at all.

Leo gathered her to his chest. "One good thing happened when you were gone. *The Red Shoes* was on cable. I remembered your saying that it was your favorite film."

So Leo had remembered something Nina had said—remembered it for months! Did this mean that he had been thinking about her when she wasn't there? Once Nina had read that until babies reached a certain developmental stage, they assumed that when people left the room they disappeared forever. And it had struck her that most men lived and died without progressing beyond this plateau. Of all the inequities of gender, the one that seemed most unfair was that women could be obsessed with a man for months, years, a lifetime, while men busied themselves with useful activity and rarely wasted a precious hour of sustained attention on the women they claimed to love. Nina's pleasure in the possibility that Leo had thought about her, however briefly, delayed the startling realization—

"Leo!" she said. "The strangest thing! Yesterday some guy started talking to me in front of a store. And he was talking about *The Red Shoes*."

Leo said, "Great. Is this what you've been doing here, picking up French guys in front of shoe stores?"

She hadn't said it was a shoe store. Had she? How did Leo know? Was Leo staging brief scenarios in which he hired strangers to appear out of nowhere and chat about subjects that Leo would then bring up, as if by chance? Did anyone do that except in Hollywood thrillers about wicked gigolos who marry lonely rich women and drive them mad to collect their fortunes? Why would Nina let herself slip back into that stew of paranoia she'd been soaking in before Leo knocked on her hotel room door? Another possibility was that this coincidence proved that she and Leo had never been out of touch, even with an ocean between them.

"It wasn't like that, Leo. Don't you think it's weird? I was in Paris talking about a film you were watching in New York."

"Yes and no," said Leo. "I'm sure there's some incredibly obvious boring explanation. The guy saw the film on TV in New York. Or it went up on a satellite and showed in both countries at once."

It was troubling to imagine Vickie, the tormented ballerina, dancing *The Red Shoes* for all eternity in stratospheric orbit. But now, in Leo's reassuring presence, Nina could once again see the film as art, as compelling drama and not just a depressing tale about a woman so torn between two men—*and* their ideas of what she should be—that the harsh whistle of an oncoming train sounded like a Siren's song, an invitation she couldn't refuse. Leo was right, there was probably some simple explanation. Nina's mention of *The Red Shoes* had made Leo think: shoe store.

Leo switched on the night-light, then rolled on his side and looked at Nina and turned off the light again. They made love and fell asleep and awoke at the same moment.

This time, when Leo turned on the light, they finally saw the room. And now at last they could afford to apprehend its full unexpurgated horror, a vision too grisly to have faced alone, though together they could risk it. A room from a Weegee photograph or from a horrific nightmare. A room where a murder had taken place or was just about to happen.

"It's the ugliest room I've ever seen," Leo said. "Do you think it's really a whorehouse?"

"That's what I thought," said Nina. "And your old friend,

Madame, said it used to be one. She said that a prostitute killed herself jumping out of that window."

"I doubt it," Leo said. "Probably it's some sales thing, like those hotels capitalizing on the famous dead who slept there. Soon all the new hotels in Paris will be claiming to be recycled whore-houses, and the most expensive hotels will be the tackiest former. . . . But this place is impossible. I can't believe you slept here. Poor Nina, my poor little baby. Reach me the phone book, will you? Let's blow this dump right now."

Nina rolled over, groped under her night table, and touched something sticky. Gum!

"Oh, disgusting!" she said.

"What is it?" asked Leo.

"Gum on my hand."

"Get the phone directory, Nina. Then worry about the gum."

She would have done anything he asked in any order he sug-gested. She was so thankful that he'd taken over and called her his poor little baby. What if Leo hadn't come? Nina might have stayed here forever, checked in and not checked out. But that seemed unlikely, and not only because she couldn't keep running up the bill. She'd had a plane ticket back to New York, a life and a job—at *Allo!*

"It's in four volumes," Nina said. "Do you need them all?"

"I don't care," said Leo. "Hand me any two." His attention had drifted back to the silent TV. Was this the same or a different film about war in Soviet breakaway republics? Were these different grannies wailing over different loved ones in different coffins, different men on their stomachs, shooting different mortars and guns?

"Who's next, I wonder?" said Leo. "It could happen anywhere.

We want to think that these people aren't like us. But vicious ethnic warfare could begin tomorrow in the streets of Crown Heights. We could teach the Balkans a thing or two about . . . ugh. I don't want to imagine. It starts to seem like a matter of time. So I, for one, am determined to seize every moment of pleasure I can before the shit hits the fan."

Leo took the phone book and dialed. He was patient with the receptionists and found an acceptable room on the second try.

"Bingo," said Leo. "Let's pack."

"Shouldn't we shower?" said Nina.

"Not in this shithole," said Leo. "Besides I want to think of us walking around smelling like sex, like we do now."

There was nothing to pack. Leo hadn't touched his suitcase, and Nina had only to get her toothbrush from the bathroom.

"I was sleeping in my clothes," she said. "The whole time before you got here."

"Jet lag," Leo said. "You were in critical condition without Doctor Leo's jet lag cure."

They got dressed. Neither wasted a motion. They were ready to leave in no time.

As they left, Leo grabbed Nina's wrist.

"This is hotel hell," he said. "Whatever you do, don't turn around or look back as we walk down the hall."

Were they playing Lot and his wife, or Orpheus and Eurydice? Both of them practically tiptoed along the long dim corridor.

At the elevator, Leo said, "I'll walk down."

Nina heard his receding footsteps. How desperately she had missed him. How amazing—how fortunate—that he would be waiting for her downstairs. That is, she *hoped* he'd be waiting.

She'd misunderstood once before. Suppose she rode the elevator down and Leo was nowhere in sight?

The elevator took forever. Nina should have walked with Leo. She clung to her suitcase, which seemed to have gotten heavier since she'd checked in, as if the Danton's resident demons had packed it full of stones. The elevator hit the ground floor and bounced. The doors balked, then slowly opened.

Leo was talking to Madame Cordier, who was standing behind the desk. Leo leaned toward her. His elbows dug into the counter. Madame's eyes looked red-rimmed and raw. Leo was flushed and winded. They seemed to be breathing in staggered rhythms, as if there wasn't enough oxygen for them both.

Leo stalked out the front door. Nina still had the room key. Also she felt obliged to thank Madame Cordier, or at least say a few words. She walked across the lobby.

"L'addition?" she said meekly.

"Monsieur has paid your bill," said Madame Cordier. "But he has refused to pay for tonight and tomorrow, even though it was made very clear that we have a cancellation policy. . . ."

Was that why they had been arguing? Nina was relieved. Their conversation had seemed more passionate and freighted with history than a quarrel about money and checking out two days early. But how much else could have happened in the few minutes it took Nina to follow Leo down in the elevator? Nina smiled placatingly at Madame Cordier as she handed her the key.

"Merci," said Madame Cordier. "I wish you good luck."

"Thank you," Nina said. "I'm sorry."

"It is nothing," said Madame. "But really, what can one expect? Léo, il est juif."

"Jesus Christ," said Nina. She threw down the key hard enough so it bounced and fell off the desk. Madame knelt and was groping for it as Nina rushed for the door. She was still shaking and out of breath when she found Leo waiting outside.

"What's the matter?" said Leo.

"What a bitch!" said Nina.

Leo raised one hand and hailed a cab.

"We're history," he said.

As the taxi sped them toward the sixth arrondissement, Nina felt as if she were only now arriving in Paris, and that her time here without Leo had been a grotesque hallucination. Leo and the driver switched between French and English as they discussed the truckloads of oranges dumped on the road to the airport. The driver didn't think anything should be dumped on the road. People had to go places, Monsieur, especially to the airport. It only made things more confusing for those who agreed with the poor farmers unable to sell their produce because of cheap, low-quality fruit from Morocco, Tunisia, Israel, Spain, Brazil. . . . The driver listed every country with a warmer climate and darker-skinned population than France's. In the back of the taxi, Leo took Nina's hand and suggestively stroked her thumb.

When a red light delayed them in front of a movie theater, the driver said, "All American films."

"Bad ones," Leo said.

"People pay," the driver said, rubbing his fingers together.

"It's all about money," said Leo, and the driver beeped his horn in agreement. Nina was proud of Leo for having charmed this grumpy Parisian, who began driving more recklessly as he told Leo this story: Early one morning, recently, he'd arrived at the taxi garage to find that some Turkish drivers had slaughtered a lamb for a holiday and were divvying up the bloody meat.

Was this like the pigs dying on TV? Nina knew what the driver would say. The Turkish lamb killed on the sooty floor of a smelly Paris garage was the polar opposite of the pig who had generously given up its idyllic life somewhere in rural France. A foreign lamb, a shifty conniving lamb, a lamb that would sell itself cheap and make everything harder for the noble, pure, patriotic French pig.

From the outside, the Hotel Monastère gave off gleaming seductive hints of more brightness and comfort within: its name engraved on a polished brass plaque, a newly sandblasted granite facade, a foyer like a Japanese painting, with a vase like a swollen seed pod, sprouting a tall spray of pink gladiolus and lilies, their beauty heightened by the promise that they would be dead by tomorrow morning.

Leo and Nina squeezed into the same wedge of revolving door and wound their arms around each other as they crossed the lobby. This was lost on the desk clerk, who could have been the first cousin of the disdainful young men at the Rodin Museum and the Hotel Danton. But now this species had lost its power to scare and intimidate Nina.

This young man was also sorry, in this case to inform them that their room was not yet ready. Surely Monsieur would understand. Monsieur had only just telephoned, after all.

Leo and Nina exchanged quick looks. Their rooms were *always* ready. Leo called ahead and told the hotels when they would arrive. Leo liked things arranged in advance. One challenge of travel, he said, was making many random events fall more or less into place.

But now they both seemed faintly relieved that their room wasn't ready, perhaps because it liberated them from the question of whether or not this trip would be like the last one: a dreamlike crawl from hotel to hotel and directly from bed to bed.

"Fine," said Leo. "Can we leave our things?"

"Let's get something to eat," said Nina.

They exploded from the hotel like children let out early from school. Nina hung on to Leo's arm as he steered them through the streets. No more hesitation, no more getting lost and then found, now that Nina *had* been found, at least for now, by Leo.

"I thought I handled that pretty well," Leo said. "I mean, not blowing a fuse because our room wasn't ready. I know I'm not the most spontaneous guy in the world."

"You were fine," said Nina, squeezing his arm. How dearly she cherished and loved him!

"Let's find the closest place that looks good," Leo said. "Something right nearby."

"Great," said Nina. She would let him choose and thus avoid either credit or, more likely, blame.

But soon they'd passed the closest place and the closest after that, as Leo guided Nina through a maze of progressively narrower streets.

At last, he said, "How about here?"

"It looks terrific," lied Nina. In fact its windowless faux-brick facade looked notably less terrific than fifty places they'd just passed.

Inside, scores of radiant people chatted and laughed and chewed under heavy aphrodisiac clouds of cigarette smoke, wine, and garlic. Everyone seemed to love it here. How delighted they were with their food!

"This is fine!" said Nina.

Would there be an empty table? Nina braced for trouble. Encouragingly, the stout owner wiped her hands on her apron and showed them to the table for two near the back of the room.

Nina and Leo settled into their seats. Nina glanced around. On every side were couples, tempestuously in love, staring into each others' eyes, letting go of each other's hands only long enough to tuck into plates of chicken in glossy brown sauce and creamy mashed potatoes. Imagine if Nina had come here alone! Everything that so cheered her now would have driven her mad with self-pity!

This place had been created for them: a full-sized mechanical bistro, paused in suspended animation, waiting for Leo and Nina to walk in and switch it on. And they had just wandered in—on instinct, on bistro sixth sense. Such were the joys of discovery, of striking out for new terrain. This magical place existed in the lives and dinner plans of these lovers, but not in any tourist guide: terra incognita. But Nina couldn't say that lest Leo think she was criticizing him for so rarely allowing chance to influence their choices. Besides, Nina should really stop playing the airy free spirit, the spontaneous brave explorer. She hadn't been so adventurous before, all alone without Leo.

"This place is from central casting," Leo said.

"Abracadabra," Nina said. "Nineteen-fifties Paris."

"That's what the city does for us," said Leo. "Remember our last time here?"

"Yes, I do," said Nina, forgetting to breathe for a moment.

Leo's presence was putting the city in a state of mild arousal, and as attraction sometimes—rarely—does, bringing out its best behavior. Leo was forcing it back to being the Paris of pretty hotels and hearty bistros, not the city of Camille Claudel, the city of broken dreams, of brothels and anti-Semitic madames watching pigs get whacked on TV.

"Nina!" said Leo. "What's the matter? You look terrible!"

"Oh, do I?" Nina said. "Sorry."

This was not the time to tell Leo about Madame Cordier's parting words. Their mood seemed volatile enough, though Nina couldn't say why. A certain stale tension lingered between them. No doubt it was Nina's fault. Perhaps she couldn't shake the many negative unhelpful emotions left over from when she'd believed that Leo had ditched her. Wouldn't it be ironic if they broke up now because she had misunderstood Leo and thought they already had?

The *patronne* brought their wine and a gravy-stained menu. It would be torture, they agreed, to pick only one dish for each course. The candlelight flattered Leo. Nina was ravenously hungry. He had restored her appetite. The patient was recovering.

The menus kept them occupied the whole time the *patronne* was gone. Nina ran through a series of possibilities and decided just as the owner appeared. She ordered the grilled sweetbread and mesclun salad, the duck confit, Leo the terrine of skate and andouille sausage and fried potatoes. Then they sat back and drank their wine and basked in the promise of wonderful food.

"I have a confession," said Leo.

Nina felt her chest tighten.

"I'd heard about this place," said Leo. "Our coming here wasn't entirely an accident."

That was Leo's confession? Nina's midsection unclenched.

"Who cares?" she said. "I love this place. Who told you about it?"

"Adele Cordier," said Leo. "Back at the hotel. First I asked her if she knew a great bistro—and then I informed her that we were checking out two nights before we were scheduled to go. Surprise! She said she felt especially ripped off that I did those two things in that order. Like asking a girlfriend to lend you money and then telling her you're breaking up. But I wasn't ending a love affair, I was checking out of a hotel. She was extremely unprofessional, and besides, I couldn't see what difference it made, asking for restaurant advice and then telling her we were leaving."

"No wonder she was pissed," Nina said uncertainly. What about Leo's refusal to pay the full bill? And hadn't Madame Cordier spotted his valise when he'd first come downstairs? Right away, that should have suggested that Leo and Nina might be departing. Perhaps she hadn't wanted to see the suitcase. Nina knew how such things could happen.

Nina was almost grateful that at the very last moment Madame Cordier had revealed herself as a foul anti-Semite. It was easier to discredit the rest, everything that had fueled Nina's old doubts—or started new ones—about Leo.

"She's been pissed off for twenty-five years," Leo said. "She was probably born that way. Anyhow, she should be ashamed.

Imagine, expecting civilized humans to stay in that dump of a whorehouse. What else did she say about me, Nina?"

Nina swallowed. Miraculously, the *patronne* brought their first courses. Leo couldn't expect Nina to answer a tricky question like that with her mouth full of sweetbreads and feathery pale greens.

Leo admired his striped terrine. "It looks like a Rothko. Better than a Rothko. Tastes better. Try some."

Nina leaned forward obediently, permitting Leo to feed her. He gave her time to savor the terrine's barrage of sequential flavors. Then he said:

"What else did she say about me? I know you know something, Nina. I can see it in your face."

Only Leo knew her face well enough to read such detailed messages there. This proved that they were still in love. Nina took a deep breath.

"She said you were writing a novel."

"Excuse me?" Leo said.

"She said when you lived in Paris you were writing a novel."

"God. You know, I think she's right. How embarrassing. I'd forgotten."

"It's not embarrassing," Nina said, though she'd certainly thought so when she was looking for reasons to despise and patronize Leo. But now it didn't seem corny at all. Young Leo in Paris writing his novel seemed very touching and sweet.

"Did she mention what my novel was about?"

"She didn't know," lied Nina. "I mean she didn't say."

"She did," said Leo. "You're protecting me. Go on, spit it out, Nina."

"She said that all the American guys had come to Paris to write novels about American guys who'd come to Paris to write novels."

"Bitch," said Leo. "Absolutely untrue. It's all coming back to me now. It was science fiction. *Brave New World. 1984.* I remember, it was about mind control and a race of aliens that take over the television networks and tell everybody what to think. They convince the world about what reality is. They send everyone on the planet nightly subliminal signals with racist and nationalist subtexts—and pretty soon a million small local wars break out, and aliens conquer the planet. I wrote this in the sixties. Everyone was paranoid then. Once again, I was way ahead of my time. Thirty years in advance of the landing."

A perfect subject for Leo. Leo, the mind control expert. Telling *Allo!* readers what to think, trying to do the same to Nina, informing her that she would adore a cheap whorehouse of a hotel, trying to convince her—*convincing* her—that he'd said he was coming to Paris with her.

That ex-girlfriend of Leo's who was having perpetual sex with the plants and rocks and trees recently sent him a letter about how, after a lifelong struggle, she was no longer susceptible to certain kinds of mental oppression. She had finally come to realize that she had power over her own brain. Shouldn't it worry Nina that Leo's former girlfriend was talking about getting out from under a lifetime of mental bondage? The old girlfriend always turned out to be the one you should have listened to. In which case, what about Madame Cordier . . . ?

"It's happening now," said Nina. "The worldwide mind control, I mean. Not the part about the space aliens, of course. But the right-wing nationalist propaganda. All those dead pigs on TV."

"All those dead pigs? All *what* dead pigs? Earth to Nina. Hello-o."

"Remember?" said Nina. "The documentary? The peasant couple killing the pig? You said the pig's name was Dreyfus."

"Ah, poor Dreyfus," Leo said. "Was there more than one pig?"

"Before you got here," said Nina. "There was one dead pig a night." But already, those nights and those pigs had receded so far into the past that Nina half-wondered if she'd imagined the nightly pig executions.

"How can you know *what* to think?" Nina said. "Everything you think is real could be flipped around by one essential fact you learn only later on. It could all turn out to be totally different from whatever you'd thought."

"Meaning what?" Leo said. "I'm not sure I see where all of this is going. Meaning that reality is subjective? Did you just discover this, Nina? Congratulations!"

"Meaning that before you got here," said Nina, "I thought you weren't coming to Paris, and everything looked hopeless. Miserable. Gloomy. Tragic. Everywhere I looked, I saw women with broken hearts smashing their sculpture, women videotaping hateful guys and getting bit on the face by parrots."

Nina stopped, out of breath. This was the closest she had ever come to a declaration of how much she needed Leo—or at least how much she mourned for him when he wasn't around.

"Bit by parrots?" said Leo.

"In a pet shop," said Nina. "But now the whole city seems fine again. Everyone is happy and in love and eating wonderful sweet-breads and skate. I guess you could say I was having a world-class epistemological crisis. First I thought one set of things was real, and then I found out it was something else. . . ."

"An ontological crisis, no? Reality's the issue here. Not episte-mology—how we know what we know. I adore you, Nina. But if that's the problem, then really, you must still be having your crisis. We *all* are. Constantly. Daily. Can you say for sure what's real right now? What's real is that none of us can hope to be certain about anything for longer than half a minute. Obviously, I'm delighted that I could so thoroughly brighten your day. But are we still on the tiresome subject of your thinking I wouldn't join you, that I was shipping you off to Paris to make you languish here without me?"

That was exactly what Nina thought, though she hadn't said so, exactly.

"And whose face got bitten by parrots? Nina, why are you being so—"

The owner took their empty plates with a gesture that promised that their main courses were only a heartbeat away.

Oh, why had Nina ordered duck? It required so much chewing and concentration when she needed her wits about her just to figure out what Leo was saying.

"What beautiful potatoes," Leo said.

He was right. The potatoes were ravishing: small wedges fried golden brown and flecked with fragrant mites of parsley, pepper, caramelized onion, and garlic. Leo forked up two chunks and put them in his mouth, chewed. . . .

Tears began streaming down Leo's face.

"Leo, what is it?" cried Nina. She had never seen Leo cry. Upsetting visions danced before her, fiendish recipes from hell involving handfuls of cayenne pepper or a splash of carbolic acid instead of the balsamic. But Leo didn't seem to be in pain—just terribly unhappy. Nina thought that if she stared at Leo and didn't let her attention waver, her focus might somehow generate a protective bubble around them and spare Leo the added pain of strangers watching him weep.

But finally Nina couldn't help herself and surreptitiously checked around. Two booths over, a handsome woman wearing a black-and-white checked turban, and with spaces between her front teeth that made her mouth look checked as well, sat across from a small wrinkled dog, curled up in its chair. The woman's lips were moving. Was she talking to the dog? With a shiver of panic, Nina realized that the world around her had ducked back behind the fright mask it had worn before Leo got here. So Leo was right once again: Her crisis was ongoing.

By now Leo had calmed down enough to speak. It seemed that in Nina's absence he'd seen a television program in which a noted forensic pathologist discussed his most famous cases. Many of these involved the last meals found in victims' stomachs. Of all foods, said the medical examiner, potatoes took longest to digest. Now Leo was eating potatoes, the apotheosis of delectable fried potatoes, and all that he could think about was the doctor saying how long potatoes lasted in the stomachs of the dead.

Leo said, "Everything's like that now. Why not just admit it? Everywhere I look, I see nothing but mortality and death. It doesn't matter if I'm with you, Nina. In Paris or New York. The old Estonian lady on the flight, she was going to die, and the children on the plane, they were dying, we're dying. I'm dying, minute by minute. . . . It's not exactly news, I know. But sometimes it just kicks in."

"Sex and death," Nina chirped with artificial brightness meant to hide the fact that she was reeling from the shock of hearing Leo say it didn't matter if he was with her or not. Relax. All he'd said was that Nina's presence didn't diminish his awareness that someday he had to die. Well, all right. Nina could live with that.

"What else is there besides sex and death, Leo?" she said.

"Death and no sex." Leo sighed. "Death's been on my mind, is all. Before I was even conscious of it. Why else would I have gotten the idea of staying in famous dead people's hotel rooms? And poor Nina can't even take a bath without my thinking she's drowned. It's because I'm Jewish. I envy you, Nina. I do."

"Envy me what?" said Nina.

"Not being Jewish," said Leo.

Was Leo saying that Protestants didn't fear death? They'd brought skulls and hell to New England before the Jews even got there. But maybe Leo was right—at least about Nina. Lately, she rarely thought of death. She'd known her plane wasn't going to crash without the Hasidim's prayers. Death wouldn't waste its grim surprise on her when she was already so wretched. And how could she possibly find the time to worry about her mortality when she needed every waking minute to wonder if Leo loved her?

"Get this," Leo said. "One of the hyperactive kids on the plane was eating a candy bar, a chocolate-covered mummy with red button candy eyes. And you know what the brand name of the candy was? Give up? Ready? 'To Die For.'"

"To Die For?" Nina repeated.

"A chocolate mummy," said Leo.

"You must be kidding," Nina said. But she knew what it was like when you were thinking of something and the world conspired to inundate you with examples of what was already on your mind. Hadn't Nina spent days grieving over Leo in a city populated solely by lovesick abandoned women?

Scrubbing the last gravy streaks off his plate with a thick chunk of crusty baguette, Leo seemed mostly recovered from his grief over the potatoes. He said:

"So I thought: Why not take it all the way? Why not do a piece for *Allo!* and call it 'Paris Death Trip.' We'll go to the Catacombs. The cemeteries. Père Lachaise. Maybe buzz through the Cluny and look for some great medieval woodcut of Death in his hooded cloak mowing down the population with his giant scythe. I thought of someplace else. Just a minute. Right. We'll check out the Conciergerie, the prison where Marie Antoinette spent her last night. There's an established tradition of morbid cemetery tourism. Isn't there a Mark Twain book where they go to Europe and after a while you realize: All they're seeing is graveyards?"

A few tears still glistened in Leo's brown eyes. Nina stared at him adoringly. "Paris Death Trip" was a great idea, exciting, a little subversive. Go to the Catacombs, skip the Louvre, head straight for the boneyards and the prison. . . .

But was Leo serious about writing this for *Allo!*? Surely he must know that his loyal subscribers—retired schoolteachers and former middle managers from the New Jersey suburbs—had no desire to spend their precious time in Paris inspecting stacks of femurs, guillotine blades, graves, and crumbling headstones. Sooner or later, Leo would come to his senses and realize that "Paris Death Trip" was not for *Allo!* but was something he had to work out for himself, his own personal pilgrimage.

But for now, what did that matter? Nina was happy to tag along. To go anywhere, with Leo.

They would start tomorrow morning. They had work to do. Right now they were free to have dessert and coffee and pay the check and get their coats and walk to their hotel.

Their room was ready. They were directed across a courtyard and up two flights of narrow stairs to a door that admitted them into a courtesan's bedroom from the 1920s or '30s, everything painted or upholstered in silk of the palest robin's-egg blue.

"This hotel used to be a monastery," said Leo. "Until the Revolution. Then they made it into a bordello. A high-priced historic whorehouse. And now, inevitably, a hotel . . ."

On the wall above the bed was a reproduction of an Ingres, a woman with a gray satin dress slipping off her plump shoulders clear down to the hollow at the base of her spine. Nina scooted across the bed to get a closer look. She thought of the Rodin Museum, the statue of the bending woman, the smooth marble back she'd run her hand over when Madame Martin wasn't looking.

"Something happened," Nina said. "I went to the Rodin Museum." She caught herself, too late. She hadn't meant to tell him yet. Leo could get competitive if he thought you'd done something more interesting than he had: another wise reason for making sure to do everything with Leo.

"Excellent," said Leo. "Maybe we'll go this time."

"They mistook me for someone else," Nina said. "This old woman thought I was some . . . writer she was expecting. And she took me—she took whomever she thought I was—to a storage room and showed me their collection of Rodin's erotic drawings."

Leo said, "Are you telling me that some batty Frenchwoman thought you were someone else and took you on a free guided tour of Rodin's erotic drawings?"

"That's what happened," Nina said.

"You lucky stiff," said Leo. "Were they beautiful?"

"Really beautiful," Nina said.

Leo was silent for a long time. Then he said, "Do you think your little old lady ever goes back there and jerks off?"

"Leo," said Nina. "I don't want to think about that."

"Wouldn't you, if you worked there? I know I certainly would."

"I guess so," Nina conceded. "I don't know. I don't want to know. Anyway, listen, Leo. Another thing the old woman told me. When Rodin was fucking his models in his studio, he used to put a sign on his door that said: Absent. Visiting Cathedrals."

"Excellent," said Leo. "Absent. Visiting Cathedrals. I love it." And then, after a moment, "What were the drawings of?"

"Oh, you know," Nina said. "You've seen them in books."

"I know. I've seen them," said Leo. "But I want you to tell me."

Nina said, "There was one. A woman—"

"Wait," said Leo. "Show me."

A woman's scream awoke them. They sat up, clutching each other, until they were awake enough to distinguish ecstasy from terror.

"Not again," said Leo. "Wouldn't you think that this exceeds the statistical probability? Every time we come to Paris we get to hear some lucky couple fucking each other's brains out."

Especially if you counted Nina's neighbor at the Hotel Danton. Nina had almost forgotten that woman, who hadn't made a peep after Leo arrived. Maybe it was the dead prostitute's ghost, exorcised by Leo's presence.

Tonight their next-door neighbor was very much alive and well. Their courtesan's bedroom had a mirror on the wall across from the bed, and the woman's cries—and the man's low groans—seemed to seep through the mirror. Without Leo, the noises of sex had annoyed and depressed Nina, but with Leo she found them comforting, then amusing, then erotic.

Leo said, "I love this."

The woman next door began to laugh.

"Someone's having fun," said Leo. "What do you think he's doing to her?"

"What do *you* think?" said Nina.

Leo reached for her in the dark.

These Catacombs are babies compared with the ones in Rome. These date from the eighteenth century when the cemeteries got so crowded that the stench . . . Well, there was public pressure to dig up the dead and start over. Some genius remembered these quarries that were mostly mined out. They dug up the bones and dumped them here. And when the Revolution got going, you can bet they were glad for the space. Come on. I think it's this way."

Self-assured and chatty, Leo grabbed Nina's hand and waded into the traffic. He was unrecognizable as the wreck who'd wept into his fried potatoes. Well, who wouldn't feel better after a whole night of making love, then breakfast (good coffee, fresh orange juice) in the pleasant hotel bar with its damask chairs and clear Plexiglas floor over an ancient stone foundation?

But now the entrance to the Catacombs was hiding from Nina and Leo, impishly shredding their patience until they were both nearly frantic. In their search, they made several scary runs across the traffic circle.

Finally Nina saw a long line of people waiting on the street.

"Could that be it?"

"I doubt it," Leo said. "All those people lined up to see the Catacombs in November?"

But the map said the Catacombs were here. There was nothing else nearby that these tourists could have come to see. Sheepishly, Nina and Leo took their place at the end of the line. Nina felt a bit deflated because her happiness that morning was partly about going somewhere that only Leo would think of going.

At least the tourists weren't all American. Most were German families with infants and school-age children.

"Am I hallucinating?" said Leo. "Or are these the kids from my flight? I don't know if I'd take my kids here. With everything there is to see in Paris, I don't think I'd take them to see a heap of rotting bones."

"I wouldn't either," Nina said. "Though kids would probably love it."

Closeness percolated up out of their shared conviction that children should be protected from this, even if they might enjoy it. It was as if they'd made a parental decision about their own children, though they'd never once mentioned the possibility of having children. This too was part of the etiquette. How could they talk about having a family if they weren't allowed to admit that it mattered whether they traveled together or alone? Did Nina want to have children with Leo? She'd started taking birth control pills again, which must mean: not yet. She certainly couldn't decide something like that standing on the sidewalk in line to get into the Catacombs. Though maybe this was the perfect place to make that sort of decision.

The elderly German couple in front of them wore matching safari suits. They opened their umbrellas, though it was only misty, not raining.

Leo said, "These Germans must think this is the French equivalent of Teutonic ancestor worship. The bones of the glorious warriors who died for the Fatherland. And the irony is, they're right, though some of these bones died fighting the Gestapo. Do you think they have any idea that the Catacombs were the French Resistance headquarters during the Occupation?"

In Leo's secret dream of himself he was a French Resistance hero, running urgent dispatches through the Catacombs and sewers, wearing his good leather jacket. It was a sweet dream for Leo to have, heroic and romantic.

Leo said, "Look, Nina. Everybody's got flashlights."

"They do?" Nina said quietly. "Aren't the Catacombs lit?"

"I'm sure they are," said Leo. "I'm sure if we needed flashlights I would have read about it somewhere."

Two American tourists joined the line behind them, a matched pair of muscle-bound blond guys in baseball caps and hooded Syracuse University sweatshirts. They also carried flashlights.

"Hi there," Nina said.

"Yo," said the boys.

"What's with the flashlights?" said Leo.

"It's supposed to be pitch-dark down there," said one.

"Creepy," said the other.

"Way creepy," agreed the first. "They say it really sucks if you're the least bit claustrophobic."

"Leo, we can come back here later!" Nina said. "Some other time! When we have flashlights!"

"Don't be silly," Leo said. "Don't be ridiculous, Nina! Even the stingy French government will have sprung for lighting down there. This country has lawyers, like everywhere else. Nobody's looking for litigation."

Leo resumed his mini-disquisition on the history of the Catacombs that he'd started as they'd crossed and recrossed the place Denfert-Rochereau. But now his raspy monologue had a pizzicato rhythm as it looped around to include the subject of death and burial customs in general.

"Our culture is the most squeamish," he said. "Tombstone toppling may be big at home, but grave robbing never caught on. Everywhere else, the graveyard is like a mall. The dead are underground commodities. Money in the bank. Though it takes a pretty smart cookie to successfully market the dead. Eva Perón did some heavy postmortem traveling. For centuries every monastery that needed quick cashola would dig up the local saint and sell off prime chunks of bone. In Greece they exhume their loved ones after ten years and bury them somewhere else. Apparently that's getting harder, stickier, so to speak, because chemical food preservatives also keep bodies from rotting, and the relatives are finding some nasty new surprises."

So Leo hadn't recovered. He was still overwrought. And he and Nina were about to descend into claustrophobe hell.

The line moved very slowly.

Nina said, "How come they're letting in only a few people at a time?"

"We're better off not knowing," said Leo.

"Spooky, dude," said one of the Syracuse guys.

"Nasty," said his friend.

Then suddenly everyone craned for a look at the woman at the ticket window, who was shouting at the younger woman collecting tickets at the turnstile. The younger woman yelled back, even louder. Stalled at the entrance, a tourist family looked on with rigid horrified grins.

"What's the problem?" Nina said.

"I can't hear," said Leo. "Something about a lunch break. The idea is to make us even more impatient to get away from all this screeching and to be down below with the nice quiet dead."

Nina stood on her toes to kiss Leo's cheek. His face was damp and salty.

"Are you sure you want to do this?" Nina said.

"What's wrong with you?" asked Leo.

Finally the young woman waved Nina and Leo through the gate. Nina's smile was meant to convey that she had sided with *her*, no matter what. The ticket taker tossed her head so that the beads woven into her dozens of tiny braids clacked like a beaded curtain lightly disturbed by the breeze.

Leo marched in front of Nina with the headlong determination with which yesterday's pedestrians had plowed through the rain. He made a quick turn and stopped short.

Nina came up beside him at the top of a staircase. They might have been standing on the edge of a cliff, that's how steeply the stairs corkscrewed down the hollow, chilly stone stairwell. Nina could see down the steps for a couple of turns but no farther, so there was no way of telling how far down it went, though a blast of loamy air rushing up suggested it might be some distance.

Leo took a deep breath and plunged ahead. Nina followed him down. The stone steps were very narrow and steep, the spiral extremely tight, so in addition to climbing straight down they were turning in small circles.

Leo said, "I feel like Alice falling down the rabbit hole."

"It's like a mailing tube with steps," Nina said. "Or an ancient parking garage."

"It *is* an ancient parking garage." Leo voice rose up.

"Leo, wait for me," bleated Nina.

As they descended, the spiral seemed to constrict until they were spinning more rapidly, round and round. Nina was conscious of having to resist the magnetic pull that dares you to leap off bridges and out of skyscraper windows.

"I feel a little weird," said Nina.

"How long does this go on, Nina?" Leo's disembodied voice floated up the stairwell.

Why was Leo asking Nina? He was the one with the answers. Leo's question—and his tremulous tone—heightened her dizzy unease.

"Forever and ever and ever," Nina said.

"Jesus Christ," said Leo. "Is that your idea of a joke?"

"Sort of," murmured Nina, but Leo didn't hear. Just ahead, he stumbled and held on to the wall. He paused a moment, then straightened and, with a rattling sigh, went on.

"You wouldn't want to fall down this!" Nina forced herself to sound cheery. "Though you probably couldn't find a more convenient and considerate place to break your neck. They wouldn't even have to move you, just roll you onto the last pile of bones. Leo? Leo, are you okay?"

"I'm fine, goddamn it," said Leo.

Was Leo having a claustrophobic attack? Nina couldn't ask him, so she couldn't determine how serious it was, or if there were any way she could help. Oh, theirs had to be the absolute worst, the most deficient romance in the world! Everyone knew that communication was essential—basic! But Leo and Nina couldn't talk about the largest or least little things.

How many times had the stairs twisted down? Forty? Fifty? Sixty?

"Are you finding it hard to breathe?" Nina said. "I mean, I can hardly get any air."

Leo didn't reply.

"Leo?" said Nina. "Are you all right? Do you want to go back?"

"We can't," Leo said through clenched teeth. "People are coming down."

"I don't hear anyone," said Nina.

"Shut up and listen," said Leo.

Nina was becoming caught up in the rhythm of spiraling down, almost as if she'd surrendered to the centripetal force that spun the possessed at voodoo rites in diminishing circles until they dropped, twitching, to the ground, foamed at the mouth, and passed out. Would she and Leo have the strength to stop turning if they ever reached bottom? This was terrible! Terrible! To think that they'd paid money to let themselves be punished this way!

Leo was panting raggedly. Nina's legs felt wooden—it was partly exertion, she knew, but also tension, vertigo, the fear that it would never end. She could ward off panic if she could just keep from thinking that later they would have to climb this far to return to street level. Oh, let there be an elevator! Please, just let there be that! Nina's heartfelt prayer concluded with a promise that she would become a better person and never again have a doubting or suspicious thought about Leo.

"You know what I've been thinking about?" Nina's voice

emerged in high pinched bursts between spasms of shallow breathing. "Orpheus and Eurydice. Ever since we left that room at the Hotel Danton and you told me not to look back. I've been thinking about Orpheus. You want to know what, exactly?"

Leo didn't answer. He kept on going downstairs. There was a funny pitch in his walk. What if he froze and couldn't move? Then they would sit down and wait calmly on the stairs, perhaps till the Syracuse students came and bailed them out. Leo must not be made to feel like an aging neurotic, dependent on the dumb healthy strength of two blond meathead Vikings!

Nina said, "Everyone assumes that the Orpheus myth is about how the power of art and music and love and sex is stronger than the power of death. But obviously, death is stronger than all the rest put together. I mean, death is making the rules, love can only bend them. Or maybe it's a warning about love, not to let it get out of hand and obliterate everything else. No matter how clearly Orpheus is warned not to look back until they're out of Hades, nothing's real for him but Eurydice, and he turns around and loses her. . . ."

It was becoming harder to talk, but Nina couldn't stop babbling any more than she could have quit corkscrewing down those endless stairs. Why had they done this to themselves? In the name of what? Curiosity? Pleasure? Why would a chronic claustrophobe with a serious death fixation decide that he had to come here— here, of all places in Paris?

Nina sensed that Leo was listening and wouldn't interrupt. Fine! Just let him keep breathing and not stop dead or fall down. Maybe it wasn't true that she'd been thinking about Orpheus and Eurydice ever since Leo warned her not to look back at the Hotel

Danton. All right. She was thinking about them now, and she wanted to tell Leo.

"The other thing, Leo, and excuse me for saying this, is that maybe it's not about love but about men. Maybe Eurydice was just an excuse for Orpheus to take on Death, to pit his music or poetry against Pluto or whatever. Because the point at which he looks back is when they're almost out of hell, and he wants to make sure that Eurydice knows what he's done, accomplished, achieved for her—the whole bright living world! So maybe it's a warning about that tendency some men have, wanting to show women the world, to tell them what's real and what's not.

"I said *some* men, Leo. Or maybe it's a story about women, too. Aren't there versions where Eurydice wonders why he won't look at her? Doesn't he love her anymore? Of course there's a reason, but all she can think about is love love love love love, and so she keeps calling and calling him until he turns around and looks and she loses him, loses everything . . . so maybe it's also a warning to women."

By now Nina's breathlessness came as much from excitement as from oxygen deprivation. She felt she understood something; she'd arrived at a realization. So what if she'd made it up on the spot to prevent Leo from flipping out and to quiet her own anxieties? Sometimes extreme situations inspired revelations. The yogis who lay on burning coals might want to experiment with a brisk little trot down these stairs.

And now Nina recalled another version of the story, the most common, the most human: Orpheus begins to worry that Eurydice might no longer be behind him, and he turns instinctively, helplessly. . . . Poor Eurydice! Imagine how she must have felt, condemned to eternity in hell because the guy got nervous. This was the version that Nina couldn't mention to Leo, lest he imagine she was commenting on their present situation.

"Leo, what do you think?" Nina said.

"I think we're saved," said Leo.

They had reached the bottom of the stairs. They stood in a dimly lit passage, no less narrow and close than the stairwell, but at least horizontal.

Leo bent over and clutched his knees, taking deep hungry breaths, then straightened his back and shook his head and held out his arms to Nina.

"What do I think?" he said. "I think you're an angel. I was having a pretty tough time on those steps. I don't know . . . Dizzy, oxygen deprived, I guess. And it was such a help for me to hear you burbling on about . . . what was it, Nina? Orpheus and Eurydice?"

"Yeah," said Nina.

Leo kissed her on the mouth, and they embraced right there in the middle of the corridor leading to the Catacombs. So then, it was settled: Sex was stronger than death.

"What's the matter?" Nina said.

Leo said, "Something dripped on my head."

"Ugh. Let's keep walking," said Nina.

They set off through the gloomy tunnel lit by dangling bulbs that, separated by long intervals, cast down small tarnished coins of light. As the passageway curved, Nina and Leo groped through the blackness until they rounded a corner and reached the next pale circle.

"We should have brought a goddamn flashlight," said Leo.

"This isn't so bad," Nina said.

"Oh, isn't it?" said Leo.

Under their feet, wet gravel crunched with a sound like rattling bones.

"I stepped in a puddle," Leo said. "Jesus, this *is* hellish."

Nina's eyes had given up trying to distinguish darkness from near darkness and had begun to suggest an array of alarming alternatives: shadowy afterimages and flashes of phosphorescence.

"Leo," she called. "Where are you?"

O Lord, she prayed, don't let it be true that Leo was insane and that this whole trip was a plot he'd hatched that day in his office, a scheme to drive her crazy, to make her think they'd broken up and then find her and fuck her and ditch her in the Catacombs under Paris. That did seem highly unlikely. What would the purpose be? Only Nina would dream up a paranoid melodrama like that. She was the insane one. And what if Leo did run off and leave her down here now? She would go the end of the tunnel and get a cab and somehow find her way back to the hotel.

Why was she still thinking like this? She'd thought she'd successfully navigated those treacherous straits of doubt in which every word of Leo's cried out for close interpretation. The visible universe no longer had to be dissected into its component parts in order for Nina to distinguish what was real from what was Leo. Now that they were together, their reality was the same. Or was it?

"Where do you *think* I am, Nina?" Hearing Leo's voice, Nina felt something like the relief she'd seen on the faces of mothers reunited with toddlers who'd wandered off in the supermarket. "We're practically falling all over each other. What is wrong with you, Nina? You sound completely hysterical."

At least Leo was no longer panicking, as he'd been on the stairs, but only cranky and skittish in a way that required Nina's unceasing vigilance.

Had they walked a half mile? A mile? It seemed considerably longer, perhaps because of how their spirits sank every time they left a ring of light and headed into the darkness and into the silence broken only by the osteoid crunch underfoot. They should have learned their lesson from the stairs: Everything has an end. But the fact that they'd stopped descending didn't prove that they would ever stop going forward. There had to be a finite depth to which you could bore down into the earth. But how could one know that this tunnel wouldn't continue forever?

Finally they reached an archway. Over the door a sign said: STOP! YOU ARE ABOUT TO ENTER THE EMPIRE OF THE DEAD!

"Well," said Leo. "I'd say their empire extends all the way back to the top of those fucking stairs."

They'd been traveling for ages—and they'd only reached the border of the empire. They passed a few historical exhibits, a tiny city carved from stone.

"It's so beautiful and weird. Like a dollhouse," said Nina. "Who built it?"

"Some quarry worker," Leo said. "Then the poor guy got the bright idea of building steps so that people could come down here and pay a few centimes to see his little project. And guess what? He got flattened by a cave-in. Shouldn't that have sent a message? Well, I guess it did—that there was money to be made. What was one more dead body? They dug the guy out and promptly raised the price of admission."

Now the walls on both sides were interrupted by niches, each containing thousands of bones, neatly stacked or arranged in decorative bands of thick femurs and delicate tibias. There were crosses made of skulls and columns of skulls winged with curving ribs against a playfully rococo background of pelvic arches. There were street signs on the wall: QUARTIER DES INNOCENTS, RUE DE MONTROUGE. Leo told Nina that they referred to the original graveyards from which the masses of dead had come.

"No Jewish bones here," said Leo. "You can bet on that."

The bones encouraged Leo. They provided company of a sort, and suggested that he and Nina might be making progress. And wasn't there something that Nina should be learning from these bones, perhaps some Buddhist precept about how our individual lives finally amount to no more than an anthill of calcium dust? The sheer numbers of skeletons should free her from the prison of self. But she had already escaped that prison. Her new jailer was Leo, and she kissed the hand that had locked her up and thrown away the key.

As they passed between the walls of bones, the corridor took a series of turns that let them glimpse other sightseers, several bends farther on: the first indication since they'd started that they weren't entirely alone. How happy Leo and Nina were now to see the very same tourists they'd scorned in the world of the living— and to hear them having such a rollicking good time. The crow-like caws of children echoed through the tunnel. Where had these people come from? Nina turned and saw the two Syracuse students rapidly gaining on them. She and Leo squeezed to one side to let the boys pass by.

"This is sick," said one of them.

"My buddy here wants out," said the other.

Now they were on the rue Danton.

"Danton again?" said Leo. "That fanatical fucker is following us this whole trip. These must be the dead from the Revolution. Do you think the dead aristocrats are stacked up with the dead workers and the dead middle class? I'd say not. If I know the French, they've got it all neatly divided."

"Look! That corridor's blocked off," Nina said. "I wonder what's down there."

"Hiding places," said Leo. "How about it, Nina? We could find our little niche and never go back to New York. Imagine fucking in the Catacombs! Talk about sex and death!"

The acoustics gave Leo's voice a ringing metallic overtone. "Sometimes when Resistance people got fingered by the Gestapo and couldn't get out of Paris, the Maquis would stash them down here, often for months at a time. I read a memoir by a guy who hid out in a passageway surrounded by mounds of skulls. He wrote that at first the skulls were just skulls, but soon they developed personalities. Some were hard to get to know. Some were friendly, some weren't. And when his Resistance girlfriend came to sleep with him on his cot, some of the skulls would get jealous and throw themselves off the walls."

They were standing too far from a lightbulb for Nina to see Leo's face, but she could tell from his dreamy tone that he was putting himself in the scene. He was the anti-Nazi hero whose only hope of survival required a solitary indefinite stay in the empire of death. In Leo's fantasy, he was Yves Montand making love to Simone Signoret surrounded by the suicidal crashing of jealous brittle skulls. Who was the woman Leo imagined braving Nazis and tunnels for him? And who was the Leo he pictured down here, the unclaustrophobic courageous Leo, living in a cul-de-sac, making friends with skulls? Certainly not the Leo who

THREE PIGS IN FIVE DAYS   *183*

barely made it down the stairs and still seemed very unsteady as
they made their way through the tunnel.

The gap between Leo's fantasies and the actual Leo moved
Nina so powerfully that she knew she would do anything—anything at all—to protect him, to keep him from having to face the
abyss between his lofty ideal of himself and the Leo she knew and
loved. She would go the ends of the earth for this man, risk her
life to be with him, just like the Resistance heroine, weak and thin
from wartime shortages, threading her way through this ghoulish
maze to spend one night with her lover. And in fact she quite
liked the idea of never returning home and having Leo for all
eternity in their underground love nest.

They would never mention Leo's episode on the stairs. Hush
now, don't explain. It was better that way. The incident would be
forgotten, Leo's dignity left intact. Maybe noncommunication
was a synonym for good manners. Maybe Leo was right.
Analysis—in fact, any mention of what transpired between
them—was not merely the death of passion but a shameful waste
of time. Instead of investigating the causes and symptoms of Leo's
claustrophobia, instead of going on about whether Leo had meant
to ditch her in Paris, she'd had a series of revelations about
Orpheus and Eurydice, though already she could hardly recall
what had seemed so revelatory. A fat drop of cold liquid hit
her forehead. Tears of insult sprang to her eyes.

"What's this shit dripping down on us?" she said.

"Don't ask," Leo warned her.

Leo stopped in front of one of the wall plaques that appeared at
intervals, brass squares engraved with quotations on the subject of
death. Unnecessarily, Leo translated the French for Nina,

" 'Remember every morning that you may be dead by evening. Remember every evening that you may be dead by morning.'

"Terrific," said Leo. "Just what I needed to hear." He gripped Nina's upper arm.

"I'm getting through this," Leo said. "But I'm not enjoying it, Nina."

The stairs that restored them to the living (not that the living paid them any more notice than the dead) were also long and steep but, despite what Nina anticipated, less arduous and exhausting. Perhaps the promise of daylight made the climb seem easier, combined with the added assurance that this nightmare would soon end. On the way up, they paused prudently to rest and catch their breath. And in a short time, they popped out onto the noisy street and were blithely dodging the taxis that screeched and careened around the circle.

Had Leo and Nina been changed by their underground ordeal? Certainly the world had. How fragrant the smell of diesel seemed now, how lively and skilled the drivers, how graceful the veiled Muslim girls who brushed past them, shouting and giggling. This time, Orpheus had succeeded and left the underworld so far behind that he and Eurydice could already laugh at their recent perils.

Apparently, Nina and Leo had had a *great* time down in the Catacombs!

"Pretty amazing," said Leo.

"Amazing," Nina agreed. How instantly the thrill of escape transforms the memory of imprisonment.

Leo said, "Wait till I encourage droves of *Allo!* readers to have massive coronaries humping up and down those stairs. Of course, I'll say it's only for travelers in tip-top physical shape. But show me one flabby American who doesn't think he's in tip-top condition."

Often, when Leo wrote for *Allo!*, he amused himself with a private game: At least once per article, he'd recommend some crummy dive or smoke-clogged brasserie, some roach-infested truck stop with abysmal food, some seedy Montmartre strip joint, places *Allo!* readers would automatically hate unless they chose to imagine they were slumming, seeing the insider's Paris. Maybe no one actually followed Leo's and Nina's tips; surprisingly, no one ever wrote to complain or cancel a subscription. Demographic studies showed that the typical *Allo!* subscriber was married and retired with a median pension income of seventy thousand a year.

Nina said, "Are you sure you want to do that? What if someone died—and sued you? Us."

Leo let that *us* go by. "I'll find out the exact number of steps," he said. "And put that in the article. That way, I will have covered my ass. They can't say they weren't warned."

Leo often claimed that he was doing his readers a favor by

keeping them on their toes, sending them to some bistro where penniless students ate wedges of packaged cheese and sandy salads with charred croutons and chunks of cold salt pork. He was doing his public a service by making them decide, at least once per trip, what they really liked or hated. Had he been doing Nina a similar favor by making her think she was traveling alone and staying in a lovely *hôtel de charme?* Was it kindness or cruelty? Love made it so hard to tell. Had it all been a test, and had Nina passed or failed? What was in it for Leo? Another successful experiment in female-mind control?

They were passing through the neighborhood not far from the Hotel Danton. Perhaps that was why Nina found herself stuck in this grating repetitive groove; perhaps these minor chords of paranoia and self-pity still lingered in the air.

"Where to?" Nina piped up.

"Père Lachaise," said Leo. "Let's walk awhile, have an early lunch and go the rest of the way by metro. Maybe stop at the Cluny to try and find some especially gorgeous and grisly depiction of the Grim Reaper, hard at work in the fields."

Nina was silent a moment, then said, "Leo, where is Simone de Beauvoir buried?"

"Oh, isn't that wild?" said Leo. "We talked about that, didn't we? Nutty women from all over the planet leaving flowers and letters on her grave, those poor crazy girls deceiving themselves with that mother-of-us-all bullshit. None of them seem to have heard what everyone's known for years: All the time de Beauvoir was writing about how women should call the shots, she was being Sartre's handmaid and pimp, editing his manuscripts, sending him her cutest girl students—not even getting laid! To say nothing of the charge that de Beauvoir collaborated during the Occupation. I'm pretty sure she and Sartre are buried in Montparnasse. Which we're actually passing near. But we'd better not stop. How many graveyards can I put in this piece? I'd hate to be late for lunch."

"Can't we go there?" Nina asked. "As long as it's on the way? I've been thinking about de Beauvoir's grave. Ever since you told me, Leo. Before you got here, I was thinking about it, Leo. I'd really like to see it, Leo. It would only take a minute, and then we could be on our way." Saying Leo's name so much had not been a good idea. It had made Nina seem like an imploring whiny child. In response, Leo sounded like a tolerant parent at the limits of his patience.

"Don't tell me," said Leo. "You want to leave a note on the grave. 'Please Simone, don't let Leo notice that my historic hotels article for *Allo!* is already two weeks late.' "

"The piece is in!" cried Nina, wounded. Didn't he know? Actually, Leo never said if he liked her writing or not, but he printed it unedited, so she'd always assumed. . . ."I handed it in the week before I left."

The way Leo changed the subject was truly sleight of hand. You could easily miss the moment at which the conversation veered past you, and it took great stamina to try and change it back.

"Who else is buried in Montparnasse?" persisted Nina.

Leo said, "I don't get it, Nina. Since when are you such a de Beauvoir fan? I thought you were a sensible person."

"I'm not," she said. "I mean I am." Years ago she'd read *The Second Sex* and found it passionate but boring. She knew the less attractive facts of de Beauvoir's life but was still moved by the idea of her—a serious intellectual who wrote books *and* had love affairs with writers, a woman who made mistakes and cheated and was cheated on, but still kept loving, kept working, kept going. . . . Yesterday she'd felt guilty for reducing this brilliant writer to yet another bleeding female heart. But yesterday she'd had the chance to visit her grave—and it had simply slipped her mind. So why was Nina digging in her heels and insisting on doing what hadn't seemed urgent enough to do on her own?

Maybe the reason she wanted to go was that she *had* thought of it yesterday. The impulse was like a sudden desire to revisit a childhood home, to forge or discover a link between the present and the long-lost self, or in any case her recently discarded pre-Leo-in-Paris self. But what did she want from that paralyzed drip, unable to get out of bed, seeing Paris and Rodin's sculpture as a clutch of demeaning private communiqués about her failed romance with Leo?

Perhaps what Nina wanted from that earlier self was its two-week head start, getting over Leo. But why was Nina still thinking like a woman whose boyfriend had left her or was about to leave her when new evidence suggested that Leo wasn't planning to leave her—at least not in the near future.

"Maybe we could go to Montparnasse and skip Père Lachaise," Nina said. "How many graveyards *do* you need to put in 'Paris Death Trip'?"

Surely, Leo must have realized by now that this article would never be written unless he had some subconscious desire to permanently alienate his faithful *Allo!* readers. To kiss *Allo!* good-bye, so to speak.

"What's so funny?" said Leo. "What are you smiling at, Nina?"

"Nothing," Nina said.

Leo would never agree to this seemingly minor, spontaneous change of plans and actual major disruption in his whole way of being. Nina caught up with him and grabbed his arm with such force that they teetered and clumsily rocked to a stop.

"Whoa," said Leo. "Easy, big fella."

"It's important to me," she said. "I want to. I mean it, Leo. I've been thinking about it for a while. We can just run in and check it out. It would be unfair to me not to. I never ask for anything. And this is nothing. You know that." Nina was as shocked as Leo by the intensity in her voice.

"Fine," said Leo. "Fine. Okay. You win. We'll go to the Montparnasse Cemetery. It's going to throw the whole day off, but fine, if it makes you happy."

"It's not about happiness," said Nina. "It's about obligation." What was Nina saying? Obligation to what? What did she care about Simone de Beauvoir's grave? Nothing, less than nothing! This was some superstitious tic, some fear that she would be consumed with regret if she passed so near and didn't go see the grave.

Nina said, "Leo, you of all people hate to know you've been near something great and not stopped to see it. This would be like going to Chartres and not looking at the cathedral, like visiting Agra and skipping the Taj Mahal. . . . Well, okay. Not exactly like that."

"Okay." Leo sighed. "This makes no sense at all. But fine. I already said you win. All right? Satisfied? Let's cross here."

He yanked her hand and she followed, stepping off the traffic island and into the empty street just as the light turned green and the taxi drivers hit the gas and headed straight for them, forcing them to hurry, then run, as they threaded through traffic, like pinballs slamming through a maze of harsh bells and flashing lights.

The dead were polite in Montparnasse, not only silent but considerate, lying modestly under their neutral-colored stones, shrinking back from the pavement, from the tidy edges of the narrow paths and the broad tree-lined alleys so that you didn't have to step over them or even think about them as you passed right by their dwellings. You could pretend that the place was something else, some other sort of city, with neighborhoods and families, grandparents, bachelors, children, pets, all making room, getting along, overcrowded but civic-minded, law-abiding and peaceful.

Nothing and no one would bother you here, not even the cats that sat on the tombs and watched without seeming to see you, then snarled and took off running when you made the slightest move. Every motion was a blur across the edge of your peripheral vision. Was that a feral cat or the beating wings of a stone angel or a puttering three-wheeled truck bristling with brooms and rakes? No one would harm you, nor would anyone help—if, for example, you'd got here and realized that you had no idea where, in this city of graves, Simone de Beauvoir was buried.

People sat on benches along the wide cobbled avenues: a dessicated old lady in a black coat and lavender gloves, two middle-aged sisters with matching small dogs. Clasped together, a pair of young lovers in blue jeans and sweaters flung themselves across their bench, their limbs at the floppy angles of the dead or gravely wounded. Everyone seemed insubstantial, flat, like pencil drawings or ghosts, and gave no sign of noticing Leo and Nina. Especially not the young couple, whom Nina and Leo hurried past with an uneasy and, it seemed to Nina, jealous haste. Why should they be jealous? They'd made love almost all last night.

On another bench a natty old gentleman in a dark tweed jacket rotated his head and shoulders in small obliging increments so a photographer could shoot his distinguished face from every flattering angle.

"Who is he?" asked Nina. "Do you recognize him?"

"I don't know," said Leo. "A poet, maybe. He looks like Buster Keaton."

He looked to Nina like someone they could ask for directions. What would it cost Leo to ask? He needn't mention Simone de Beauvoir. He could say that they were looking for Sartre. This old man would know and gladly explain where to find Sartre's grave. But it wasn't in Leo's nature to ask, certainly not in this case. And since his French was so much better than hers, Nina couldn't ask, and was reduced to glaring at Leo as they passed the old man and walked on.

"Where is the goddamn grave?" Leo said. "If you know it's in this cemetery, why don't you know where it is?"

But it was Leo who had said that de Beauvoir's grave was here. Leo was never wrong about such things. It was Nina who made mistakes.

"Let's forget it," Nina said. "If it's too hard . . . maybe it's not here . . . this is taking too much time."

"We're here," said Leo. "Let's find the goddamn grave if it's so goddamn important. It's not like I haven't told you the truth about de Beauvoir, just like I have to tell you every goddamn—"

"Tell me *what*, Leo?" said Nina.

"Nothing," said Leo. "Sorry. Let's keep on looking for the grave. We've wasted the goddamn time already."

Oh, this was awful! Awful! They were practically never like this, like a married couple with decades of practice in detesting and boring each other! The reflexive squabbles of intimacy were what they most wanted to avoid.

Nina scanned the names on the tombs. Who would have thought that Death had undone so many? It was like trying to find an old friend whose address you had misplaced by checking the names on every door in a large foreign city. In a regular city, a living city, Leo's directional sense was useful. But it wasn't working in the dead's hometown, and Leo wasn't pleased.

"This is just like yesterday," Nina said. "I kept getting lost. And then I'd surface on some boulevard and I'd know where I was, more or less."

Leo didn't answer. Nina observed—did Leo?—that they seemed to be walking past the same graves they'd just passed. Oh, they should have skipped this and gone to Père Lachaise, where Leo would have known where to find every grave worth finding.

"Look!" Nina said. "Who's buried there? Look, Leo! It's Baudelaire."

Even in the graveyard the famous dead retained some cachet. From far away you could sense that a particular grave was special and gave off a sort of aura, like celebrities at parties. Did the dead still have personalities? Certainly Baudelaire did, as did Maupassant; both their graves were surrounded by force fields, palpable from a distance. Wouldn't *Allo!* readers like knowing where to pay their respects to great French writers, and maybe snap their loved one's photo beside the tomb of—

"Let's bag it, Nina," Leo said. "Sartre and the girlfriend must be somewhere else."·

But they were here. They had to be, or Leo wouldn't have said so, twice. So what? It wasn't worth it. Coming here was a giant mistake, and now it was time to correct it.

They needed lunch. Then on to the Cluny and Père Lachaise. She and Leo would forget this, just as they had already forgotten their miserable trek through the Catacombs. Though of course they hadn't forgotten and were only pretending, which only made their misery and frustration seem cumulative and more depressing.

They were heading toward the gate when Nina looked down a wide path and saw a grave that looked from a distance like a homemade shrine, decked with flowers and bright objects. This grave gave off, with unmistakable force, that indefinable aura that preserved the dead's reputations even here in the graveyard.

"I think I see it," Nina said. "Over there! Leo, look!"

Leo turned. "You may be right," he said dully.

They approached the graves cautiously as if they *were* at a party and were inching toward a group of guests surrounding de Beauvoir and Sartre.

Two simple plaques lay side by side. Sartre's grave was bare.

De Beauvoir's was covered with flowers, votive candles, marble
eggs, handwritten notes pinned down by rocks, and a confetti-
like sprinkle of punched metro tickets, faded and bloated by sun
and rain. These were tokens pilgrims left as proof they'd completed their mission. Nina had no metro stubs. She and Leo had
walked here. Should she leave their punched Catacombs tickets?
Leo probably had them, but Nina couldn't make herself ask.

"Like the grave of a fucking voodoo queen," Leo said. "These
French feminists are just like their grandmothers, lighting candles
to the saints. They should sell actual relics. I'll bet there'd be a
market for the finger bone of Saint Simone."

Most of the notes were illegible, puckered by yesterday's rain.
But two handwritten letters, both on fresh notebook paper, must
have been left here this morning. One was in Cyrillic. Nina hesitated briefly, then knelt so she could read the other, which turned
out to be in English. The top corner was folded down, hiding
parts of the text. It seemed wrong to touch it. Nina read what she
could.

"Blank blank Pakistani student," Nina read. "Thank you, dear
Simone. Thank blur, big blank. Thank you for being the first."

The first what? The first woman to write her own books *and*
edit her lover's manuscripts, schedule his romances and intercede
with girls he'd tired of but couldn't bring himself to reject,
including several he'd agreed to marry only because they'd pro-
posed. . . . That couldn't be what the Pakistani woman meant. But
why was Nina dwelling on that? De Beauvoir had managed to
write her books, and now her lover lay beside her, and hers—not
his—was the grave heaped with presents, metro tickets, and
flowers.

Someone had left a book on the grave, a paperback sealed in a clear plastic bag.

L'Amour fou. Roman.

"Perfect," Leo said. "A big literary best-seller by some sex-crazed woman novelist about her brief obsessive love affair with a married Russian double agent. *All I did was wait for his phone call. And then he went back to his wife.* That sort of hooey. Bad Jean Rhys. Bad Edna O'Brien. Boring. Jesus, who cares?"

Worn out from the effort of deciphering Leo's utterances and decoding his shifting moods, Nina had grown so inattentive to her own responses that it took her a while to understand why her spirits had just plummeted.

All I did was wait for his call—wasn't that the story of Nina's stay in Paris before Leo arrived? Leo was right, it was tedious. Who wanted to hear about women strung out over guys? Men thought it neurotic and trivial; worse, it made them feel guilty. And women considered it bad luck to even mention that there *were* still women like that. Women whose hearts could be shattered by men were an embarrassment to their sex. It was bad for the image of Liberated Womanhood to admit that such women existed!

Leo must have said something. He waited for Nina's reply.

"Excuse me?" Nina said.

Leo didn't answer. He and Nina stood in silence, looking from Sartre's grave to de Beauvoir's and back.

"His name is on top," Leo said.

"I saw that." Nina liked it that Leo noticed, too. But what did that signify, really? His paying—and calling—attention to this gender inequity beyond death might just be another trick, a technique that worked on women, like playing Billie Holiday songs and peering into their passionate souls. If that fooled women, anything would! Women were so pathetic. Poor Simone de Beauvoir with her hopeless love, her galley proofs and girl students!

By now the silence had lasted too long to be comfortable even for lovers, if that's what they were. Nina felt compelled to speak, although she had nothing to say.

"Sex and death," she said. Her faux-casual wave took in the two graves.

Leo said gloomily, "Death without sex turns out to be the actual story."

Why couldn't Leo stop it? For now, for a day or two at least, they could have sex without death, if Leo would just quit ruining everything by being so gloomy and morbid.

"You know what these two lovebirds did in the war?" Leo said. "Sartre decided to start the Resistance. Like it was his idea. It never occurred to him that anyone would think of it without him. So he formed his own cell to discuss Resistance theory and tried to recruit other members—guys who were already *in* the Resistance, but who wouldn't tell Sartre because they thought he was just some fruitcake who liked to sit in cafés and run his mouth. . . . When de Beauvoir lost her teaching job for corrupting the morals of female students, she got hired to write for the collaborationist radio station."

"I know that, Leo," Nina said quietly.

But Leo went on, "De Beauvoir always swore she wasn't anti-Semitic. I mean, she had affairs with Jewish guys. As if that proved anything at all!"

Nina flinched, though she knew this wasn't meant personally. At least she hoped it wasn't. Once, as if it were an abstract matter of mild interest to them both, Leo had mused aloud that he didn't much like the way Nina pronounced the word *Jewish*. He claimed that she pursed her lips as if she were sucking a lemon. After that, she tried not to say the word at all.

Leo was hardly ever like this! He put his energies into good living, sex, food, and travel, not into harboring venomous hatreds against dead existentialists. Like poor Camille Claudel, silenced by death and helpless to defend herself against Madame Martin, Sartre and de Beauvoir had to lie there while Leo stood directly over them and told the worst stories he knew. And it wasn't their fault; he wasn't mad at Sartre and de Beauvoir—he was angry at Nina for dragging him here and making him change his plans.

Leo said, "You want to know the truth? The truth is, I'm jealous. I'm jealous that they're immortal, that the faithful are still making pilgrimages to their graves. Who the hell's going to visit the grave of a guy who wasted his life editing newsletters for hypochondriacs and cheap greedy retiree tourists from Connecticut and the Jersey suburbs?"

I will, thought Nina. I will, Leo. But it wouldn't have helped to say so.

"They're not immortal, Leo," she said. "As a matter of fact, they're dead. And it doesn't make them any *happier* that people are coming to see them. They don't know about it, Leo. You know as well as I do. The point is to be happy when you're alive. . . ."

Nina's voice trailed off, and she looked searchingly at Leo. Was this too much passion for him? Surely, their ban on expressed emotion didn't include helping Leo deal with his fear of death.

After a silence Leo said, "Gather ye rosebuds? Is that your point, Nina? The grave is a fine and private place, but none, I think, do there embrace. All right. Brilliant. Can we go now?"

"Sure," said Nina, blinking back tears. Before Leo joined her in Paris, she'd prayed to have him here with her. And for what? To have this dreary argument over Simone de Beauvoir's grave, to have Leo act like she was a fool for trying to make him feel better?

"Let's beat it." Leo sounded cheered by the prospect of leaving.

One good thing about Leo was that he didn't hold grudges and had a mercifully short memory for quarrels and moments of strain. As soon as they left the Catacombs, they'd acted as if it had been fun, and now that they were escaping Montparnasse Cemetery they could forget this sniping over the graves, those fits of temper and annoyance when they'd thought they were lost.

Retracing their steps, they took the broad empty avenue bordered with benches, trees, and graves. They walked so quickly that the headstones they passed seemed to flip over like rows of collapsing dominoes. The squat trees were bare, with skinny fingerlike branches vertically clawing the air. Giant gnarled cankers grew riotously over their trunks. Their bark had a metallic sheen, gold and silver, peeling like the wallpaper at the Hotel Danton. A few papery leaves clattered along the cobblestones.

Someone turned a corner and came toward them.

A young man. Then another.

Another.

Another.

All skinheads.

That Nina could read them so quickly was part of the effect: the stubbly hair, the leather jackets, the jeans, the peaked caps and black Doc Martens. The skinheads spotted Nina and Leo, and began walking toward them.

"Jesus Christ," said Nina.

"What's the matter?" said Leo.

"Here comes trouble," said Nina.

"Don't be paranoid," Leo said. "Just keep walking. Nothing will happen. It's not like we're . . . Moroccans."

Two tall lumpy guys with faces the color and texture of cooked cauliflower walked on either end. The other two, in the middle, were slighter and more tense.

"Couples, do you think?" Leo whispered. Why was he so relaxed? Leo, who always insisted he wouldn't be surprised by a flat-out Nazi resurgence within the next five years. Why couldn't Leo see what was obvious to Nina, that these boys intended to rape her and make Leo watch, and afterwards kill Leo and make Nina watch that. Or else they would rape and torture Leo and then get around to Nina.

But maybe nothing would happen. Maybe it *was* paranoia. Nina put her hand on her chest to quiet the buttery thump of her heart. How could Leo accuse her of feeling safe because she wasn't Jewish? If fear, as Leo claimed, was a Jewish emotion, then Nina was the Jew this time. How could Leo have been scared in the Catacombs when they weren't in danger and so stupidly serene now when they were about to be sodomized and killed? Who said Leo was the sensible one? The one who knew what was real?

How did Leo and Nina look to these guys? She rarely thought of herself from the outside. It was hard enough being inside herself, and trying to see inside Leo. The only time she was conscious of their appearance was when she and Leo flirted in public, and that was not an aspect of themselves that they wanted to show a gang of neo-Nazis.

Nina was blond. Okay, Aryan. That's how Leo described her. And Leo? Not American. French? French gangster? Jewish? It was possible, though not certain, that the skinheads registered that. Or maybe that didn't matter. Maybe this wasn't about religion or race but about social class. Maybe the skinheads wouldn't have cared if Leo and Nina were Africans or Arabs but simply wanted to kick the shit out of anyone with a good wristwatch. Nina would be useless in a fight. Leo was strong, compact enough. But this was four against one.

No one said a word. Then suddenly, as if on command, the four guys walking toward them fanned out and blocked the road so that Nina and Leo would have to pass between them.

It was almost comic, like a scene from *West Side Story*, as if they'd learned gang behavior from watching Hollywood films.

"Relax, goddamn it," Leo said. "I can hear you breathe from here."

"I'm nervous," said Nina.

"Don't be," said Leo. "It doesn't help. They can smell it, like dogs."

So Leo knew there was trouble. It was not just her paranoia. For a second Nina felt better, confirmed—and then instantly worse.

She looked around. There was no one near. Should she look for somewhere to run?

Two of the boys could catch her while the others grabbed Leo. Could that happen here without anyone seeing? This was not the wilderness, but a cemetery in central Paris, where people came to eat lunch, to make out, or to visit the dead. A three-wheeler filled with garden tools might trawl past at any minute.

Jolts of panic alternated with the hope, no doubt false, that everything would be fine. They wouldn't get beaten or raped or killed. No one would touch them. Maybe these boys were just strutting, muscling pedestrians out of their path. What a lucky surprise that would be: much too lucky to hope for.

It was all Nina's fault. For once she'd made a decision, insisted on something *she* wanted. They wouldn't be here if not for her. But how could she have avoided this, how could she have fore-seen it? And couldn't Leo have caused it with his obsessive belief that he would be facing the Nazi hordes at some time in the near future? It was so mean of her to suspect, even for a moment, that Leo was enjoying this because it was proving him right. For Nina to even imagine this was paranoid magical thinking. Four guys rounded a corner, that was how it began: nothing mystical or mysterious—nothing more complex that that.

The tallest thug let a few inaudible words slide from the corner of his mouth. His upper lip rippled meanly, creasing his fat bristly chin.

"What was *that* about?" said Nina.

Uh-oh. She shouldn't have spoken.

All four heads had turned toward them with a choreographic snap. Once more Nina thought of gangs in '50s and '60s movies.

Nina and Leo kept walking. The boys sauntered menacingly toward them, slowly converging on Leo.

Nina heard herself moan softly.

"Shut up," Leo said. "Just shut up."

"You shut up," Nina said.

"Bonjour," Nina said to the boys.

They glared at her. One laughed harshly. Then they returned to the business at hand, which was staring down Leo. Small shiny badges—swastikas!—glinted on their leather jackets.

With narrowed eyes, Leo stared into the middle distance. He

too looked like an actor, Gary Cooper or Clint Eastwood. Leo and these guys were playing out their separate movies, while a real person could get hurt or killed, and that person could be Nina.

The young man who stepped forward was Leo's height and size, one of the hopped-up, whippetlike ones. His head had a pleasing bullet shape under its fuzz of dark hair. Was Nina shallow? Sex-mad? How could it even cross her mind that this vicious punk was handsome?

He walked up to Leo and stopped a few feet short of nose to nose. It still wasn't entirely clear that anything would happen. Leo and the kid faced each other. His friends gathered around, at a distance. No one paid attention to Nina, a spectator like themselves.

Something happened too quickly for Nina to catch. Were words or a glance exchanged? Leo turned away from the guy, as if he were going to sneeze. He brushed past him so close that their arms touched. The young man laughed, shrugged at his friends— and let Leo pass.

One by one they roused themselves and ambled off much more slowly than Leo and Nina walked away from them.

"What's the rush?" said Leo.

"That was terrifying." Nina took Leo's hand.

"I knew nothing was going to happen," he said. "Those fucking sons of bitches. Nazi dogshit."

Nina flung herself on Leo. Nothing did happen! she wanted to cry. No one was hurt or disgraced. Leo had handled himself so well, his palms weren't even wet. What could have been a bloody mess had turned out to be nothing. She stared at Leo's familiar beautiful face. How well she knew that mouth, those eyes, in what ranges of lights she'd seen them: interested, worried, impatient, blurred and slack with passion. How deeply Nina loved him! She was stunned, as she often was, by the force of her feelings for Leo.

Leo said, "All they wanted was the fear. The fear was what they were after. As soon as they got that, they could go away—"

"But you didn't seem scared," Nina said.

"You did," Leo told her. "You knew I couldn't protect you. And that was good enough for them."

She knew he couldn't protect her! What was Leo saying? Was he accusing Nina of doubting him? Of having been disloyal? And he was right! The truth was: Not for one moment had Nina pictured Leo, like some kung fu superhero, fending off a whole gang.

Nina couldn't speak. She pressed herself into Leo, who hugged her, with less fervor. Almost at once he pushed her away. She could tell he'd seen someone behind her. Dear God, had the skinheads returned?

"Pardon?" a man said softly.

She pulled her face out of Leo's neck. The voice turned out to belong to the elegant old man they'd seen getting his picture taken. His Buster Keaton eyes conveyed the regrettable fact that he'd witnessed their encounter with the thugs.

"Je suis désolé." He regarded them closely. "You speak French? Both of you?"

"Oui," said Leo.

"We're American," said Nina.

"In English, then," said the old man. "These boys did not live through the War. It is a national shame. Especially it is a problem here at the Montparnasse Cemetery. They come to visit the grave of Pierre Laval—the prime minister of the collaboration government during the Occupation."

"Laval," said Leo. "He's buried here? My God!"

"Over there," the man gestured. "Lousy filthy bastard. He was worse than Pétain. He was the one who masterminded the roundup of the Jews and hunted down the Resistance with a special . . ." The old man licked his lips in a way that suggested a taste for blood.

Leo's gaze was steady, worshipful. Had this man been in the Resistance? Nina knew that Leo wondered but couldn't think how to ask. Gosh, were you in the Maquis?

Leo said, "Laval got what he deserved. Wasn't he sentenced to death, and took poison, and they pumped his stomach and shot him right in the middle of his suicide attempt?"

"Yes, well," the old man said. "After the war we didn't want him here. But people think it looks bad, staying angry at the dead. Maybe there was also some feeling that the fellow had suffered enough, dying that terrible death; they had to prop him against the wall for the firing squad. Myself, I don't think he suffered enough. We were right not to want him buried here. His grave has become a pilgrimage spot for these neo-Nazi bastards."

Leo stared at the old man. He was seeing himself as he would have been had he lived the life he wanted to live and fought with the Resistance. The old man was sent to rescue them. He'd taken an unpleasant incident—a humiliating encounter—and given it a wider political context. Their run-in with the skinheads was larger than Nina and Leo, far more serious than whether Nina had thought that Leo could protect her. It was about the future, the past—the history of Europe!

"You have been to visit Sartre's grave?" the old man said. He'd seen them there, too, Nina realized.

Leo didn't answer. Nina knew what he was thinking. Suppose this elderly Gallic hero lectured these silly Americans on what a fake Sartre was. As if Leo didn't know! As if he hadn't told Nina!

The old man looked at Nina.

"Yes, we have," Nina admitted.

"And Simone de Beauvoir's grave?" he asked Nina.

"Yes, I guess so." She guessed so? Nina smiled. The old man didn't smile back.

Now he regarded Leo with new compassion: sympathy for this poor American whose girlfriend was another deluded devotee of a sour man-hating lesbian. His mobile face expressed all this; nothing had to be said. The old man shrugged, Leo shrugged. For an instant they reminded Nina of the cardplayers on the plane, with their very clear ideas about who was part of their group, and who wasn't. It was terribly unfair, this sudden surge of fellow-feeling about the trouble Simone de Beauvoir had made for the innocent male population. Why wasn't Leo protecting her *now?* In fact he was betraying her. He'd gone over to the other side.

Nina and Leo and the old man had fallen from innocent grace and no longer felt warmed by the pure light of angelic rescue. Leo avoided the old man's eyes, nor could he look at Nina.

"I am sorry," said the old man. "What just happened with you and those boys is happening all over Europe. It is extremely unfortunate. Enjoy your stay in Paris. I am sure you will. And now I must leave. *Au revoir, Monsieur. Madame.*"

"*Au revoir, Monsieur. Merci,*" Leo said.

"*Au revoir,*" said Nina.

They watched the old man grow smaller. The skinheads were

nowhere around. A three-wheeled truck drove by, its sputtering engine announcing that real time had resumed.

"It was my fault," Nina said. "It would never have happened if I hadn't made us come here. And for what? I'm sorry, Leo."

"Why should you be sorry?" Leo said. But his voice wasn't forgiving. It was syrupy and ironic. *Nina, I'm over here.*

Leo walked on. Nina rushed to keep up. Dizzying stutters of dark and light blinked from the alleys of trees.

Walking ahead, Leo called back, "Why should you apologize? Fascism wasn't your idea. It's hardly your invention, Nina."

They left the cemetery for a busy street of empty market stalls littered with rotten salad, swatches of newsprint and orange peel, reassuring proof that the living were still buying vegetables, at least as of this morning.

Leo put his arm around Nina. He said. "So far this hasn't exactly been our most romantic trip to Paris."

Nina wished he hadn't said that. So many things *were* better left unmentioned. But Leo had simply stated a fact. This trip wasn't their most romantic . . . that is, if one defined romantic in the most narrow way. A panic attack in the Catacombs, a squabble over Sartre's grave—if that wasn't romantic, Nina would like to know what was. Why did things keep going wrong? Leo would be sorry he joined her in Paris. Perhaps he would really leave Nina now after that practice trial run, which must have shown him just how simple the real letting-go could be.

Nina slipped her arm around Leo's waist—insinuatingly, she hoped.

"Parts of it were nice," she said. "It could still turn out okay."

"Sure it could, Nina," Leo said. "And pigs could sprout wings and fly. I wish this market were happening. I'd love to put that in my article: Where to buy provisions for an intimate picnic in a cemetery and neo-Nazi pilgrimage spot."

Just beyond the market was a picturesque street of bakeries and groceries, windows stacked with pyramids of blue-veined cheeses stabbed with price tags written in spidery French numerals. Another window held Parma hams, air-dried beef, quail and guinea hens plucked clean around the middle but retaining their feathered heads and wings, red beaks, and yellow feet.

Bread, cheese, ham, cheap good red wine. Nina could drink a whole bottle! She looked up at the buildings around her, searching for an apartment for her and Leo to rent. They could shop for food every morning in this charming street!

"Let's buy stuff for sandwiches," said Nina. "And take it back to the hotel." Hadn't she learned her lesson about suggesting they change plans?

"Definitely." Leo pulled Nina close. "I could use a nap."

They leaned together as they walked, then drifted to a stop. Leo took Nina's shoulders and turned her around and kissed the nape of her neck. She arched her back against him, right there in the street.

This heat followed them, like a draft of warm air, into the butcher's and baker's. Selecting and purchasing meat, cheese, wine, bottled water, lacy cookies, gleaming orange clementines, they agreed at once on everything, and all it of seemed delicious. Obviously, they were lovers on a brief furlough from bed and not office colleagues dispatched to buy provisions for their coworkers' lunch. The erotic sparks they struck showered on the crusty baguettes, the neat packets of translucent ham, the satiny wedges of Brie.

As soon as they got back to the hotel, they unwrapped the

shiny white packages and were not only astonished by how much they'd purchased but by several tasty surprises neither could remember buying: hard sweet pears, boar salami, a tiny volcano of goat cheese coated with the ash of a recent eruption.

Leo had a pocketknife. He sat at the delicate table in the pale blue bedroom and carved hunks of bread into sandwiches and handed Nina hers. With its winning mixture of taking charge and taking care, Leo's sandwich-making filled Nina with a languor that made her stretch like a cat in the sun of intimacy and surrender.

They ate. They finished lunch. They talked. The liquid undertow of talk drew them steadily nearer, then lifted them up and out of their chairs and into each other's arms.

They made love and stopped and started again, long after they thought they couldn't. At one point Nina noticed they'd moved from the bed to the chair. They lost all track of time. They slept and woke and slept. . . .

Nina opened her eyes. The clock said three. Had they slept for an hour or thirteen? The only thing she knew was that making love with Leo was more important, more serious and far more real than all the mental calisthenics and contortions she put herself through during the hours she squandered not making love with Leo.

Leo groaned and jumped out of bed.

"Come on," he said. "We've just got enough time to make it to the prison."

"Prison?" said Nina. "Jesus, Leo."

"The Conciergerie," said Leo. "Get with the program, Nina."

It took her a while to remember: Marie Antoinette's last night.

The Conciergerie, the Revolutionary Prison—the final phase of Paris Death Trip.

"We can take a cab," Leo said. "The prison must stay open till six."

"Can't it wait till tomorrow?" Nina said.

"Why should we? We're here. We're awake."

Nina was only half awake.

Leo turned on the TV.

"Look at this," he said, as he buttoned his shirt. "A *boudin noir* festival."

At a table, farmers were eating blood sausage; dark sticky crumbs of breading stuck to their mouths and chins. No need to watch a pig get killed. These pigs were dead. Long dead. A herd, a small private army of pigs must have given their blood for this.

Hiding her face in the pillow, Nina thought about fairy tales in which a hero imagines he's completed his Herculean tasks and can finally wed the princess, only to learn that the hardest task of all still remains, saved for last. Since this afternoon in bed, she'd thought that they were home free—and now they were remanding themselves to the Revolutionary Prison and more of the hostile gloom and doom of Leo's Paris Death Trip. How cold and depressing the jail would be, how massive, damp and chilly, what unpleasant walks they would have to take through its seeping caverns and halls.

Only a hopeless lunatic would leave this warm soft bed and go there.

"I'll get a taxi," said Leo. "I'll meet you outside in two minutes."

Nina imagined Marie Antoinette rolling toward these iron gates, sitting backward in a cart, a creaking wooden tumbrel, eliciting the naked curiosity with which people stare at horse trailers barreling down the highway. Nina imagined the wobbly cart bouncing over the cobblestones, approaching the massive prison with its cylindrical turrets and conical witch's hats. She knew that her imaginative leap was all melodrama, play-acting, as she suspected it must have been for Marie Antoinette and the thousands who knew they were going to die here but couldn't truly believe that these massive stones would really grind them up and never spit them out.

Leo steered Nina through a courtyard and into a vaulted granite hall. He went to buy tickets while Nina leafed through a cheap glossy photo book of Paris tourist spots under a postcard-blue heaven. Already she felt like a prisoner staring at pictures of sky, only dimly believing that blue sky still existed.

THREE PIGS IN FIVE DAYS   *225*

She studied a poster advertising a ticket book with coupons for admission to more monuments and museums than anyone could want to see. Why couldn't Leo do *that* for *Allo!*? Buy a coupon book and dutifully go every place that it let you visit. Why couldn't he write something educational, helpful, and pragmatic, untouched by personal terror of extinction and death?

Leo appeared to be arguing with the woman at the booth. Their voices echoed through the antechamber as they politely took turns exploding in bursts of furious French. Nina went to investigate, but Leo had already given up, paid, grabbed the tickets, and intercepted her halfway.

"Fascist bitch," said Leo.

"What's the problem?" Nina asked.

"We have to take a guided tour. We can't go around on our own."

"Why?" said Nina. "I hate guided tours."

"Bomb threats," Leo said. "They can't have all those sleazy Arab terrorists wandering wherever they please, stashing little packets of Semtex in French national historical monuments."

They passed through a narrow opening in a barrier of metal grillwork crowned with spikes. First Leo and then Nina tripped down the invisible step that led into a gigantic room surrounded by dripping stone walls the color of auto exhaust. The emptiness and vastness of the underground cavern made Nina feel like a nervous spelunker, or like an astronaut cut loose by mistake and floating weightless in outer space.

The room was too dark to see very far. And why would anyone want to? Hundreds of briefcases tied with rope could be ticking away in the shadows.

"The Hall of the Men-at-Arms," said Leo. "This is where they kept the prisoners during the Terror when they overflowed every abbey and holding pen and subhuman jail in Paris. That bitch at the ticket booth claimed this place is always being targeted by terrorists, but I'll bet it's a lie so they can herd us like sheep and save a couple of sous."

But how could it save money to pay someone to take them around? Nina threaded her arm through Leo's. How dark and glacial it was!

Near the gate, facing each other, were two backless wooden pews so punitive and unyielding they might have been the originals on which prisoners awaited their rides to the guillotine. A woman and a girl of about ten sat on one of the benches. Nina and Leo nodded at them and walked on without stopping.

They drifted around the huge hall. Each thick stone arch, each stone pillar was exactly like the others. There was no reason to be anywhere instead of anywhere else. There was nothing to say, and besides, it would have felt strained and artificial to stand in the midst of that echoing void and fake a conversation. They circled around and sat down on the bench across from the woman and the girl.

Under a wide mane of tight dark curls, the woman's handsome features asserted themselves despite a patina of makeup that took on a slightly orange cast in the dim available light. With her olive skin and glossy black hair, the girl was obviously her daughter, and at the same time looked slightly Eurasian. Their very different sorts of beauty transmitted a sexy message: The woman hadn't just cloned herself but had slept with a man to conceive the child.

"How much time do we have to wait?" Nina said.

"Twenty minutes," Leo answered.

Leo stared at the woman and the girl. Nina had nothing against the child, but wished the woman would have the grace to disappear or die. This was what it meant to be with a man, with any man, with Leo: to see this otherwise winsome picture vandalized by jealousy and envy, turned into a personal reproach on the themes of fertility and beauty. Nina wasn't as pretty, she had no daughter, Leo would register that. Poor Leo, who hardly did anything to make Nina jealous! Leo didn't use other women to control her and make her suffer—at least he hadn't yet. And Nina might have envied the woman even if Leo weren't with her.

Suddenly Nina experienced an unsettling premonition: If she valued her present life, she should just grab Leo and run. She felt quite certain that this woman disguised as an innocent tourist would eventually reveal herself as a screeching Fury who would swoop down, clawing at Nina's poor heart, fouling it with birdshit, enfolding Leo in her wings, like the hag in the Camille Claudel sculpture.

"The prisoner," said the mother.

"*La prisonnière,*" said the girl.

"*Bon,*" said the mother. "The guillotine."

A merry grin illuminated the girl's face as she chopped her upturned palm with the blade of her other hand.

"Great," whispered Leo. "The Addams family."

Nina laughed, a bit hysterically.

Ostensibly to Nina but slightly louder than necessary, Leo said, "Marie Antoinette was brought here after her failed escape. The royal family disguised themselves and took a carriage to the Austrian border. But they were so stupid, they couldn't travel except in the style to which they were accustomed, with a giant entourage, a whole court, coaches, and horses. Of course, everyone who was supposed to help them screwed up—royally, so to speak. Her hairdresser—that's right, her hairdresser!—sent the loyal soldiers away. They were stopped and recognized before they could cross the border. The driver of the coach was Marie Antoinette's lover, which made things even more complicated—"

The woman placed a restraining hand on her daughter's forearm and flashed Leo and Nina a broad smile that created an opening wide enough for her to say, "Well, maybe. And maybe not."

"Excuse me?" Leo said.

"Count Axel Fersen." The woman leaned forward. "Maybe he and the Queen were lovers. More than likely they weren't. Probably the story was part of a whisper campaign about Marie Antoinette's sexuality. The rumors of adultery, lesbianism, promiscuity, nymphomania. The usual sexual rap sheet hung on powerful women. Nymphomania! What a concept! She and her sister-in-law were accused of teaching the Crown Prince to masturbate! It was said to be a plot to drive the Prince insane and ruin his health forever."

Hold on! Where was this woman *from*? Nina's first guess was that she was an academic. A marginally with-it, American feminist French historian. But what kind of feminist was she, playing so obviously to Leo with the casual mention of masturbation and that derisive superior sneer at the whole concept of nymphomania? There was nothing she couldn't talk about freely and probably nothing she wouldn't do. Nina knew she was being unfair—the woman wasn't playing to Leo. She was addressing them both, carefully rotating her head and fixing her animated dark eyes on one and then the other. It wasn't her fault that Leo suddenly sat up very straight.

"You seem to know a lot about it," he said, and for a moment

Nina hoped futilely that he was being sarcastic instead of admiring. Were he and this woman bonding over Marie Antoinette trivia?

"I'm a director," the woman said. "A theater director. We're doing *Danton's Death* this spring. I'm using that as an excuse for Isadora and myself to do some research in Paris."

Her tone communicated self-assurance and career success. It was Leo and Nina's social duty to ask what theater she worked with, what plays she'd brought to the stage. Nina wasn't going to ask, though out of solidarity she should have. Men—even Leo—so rarely inquired about a woman's work. The woman gave them time to do so, then sighed and went on. "For months I've been doing nothing but reading about the French Revolution."

Nina said, "What a coincidence! I mean, isn't it strange? I stayed at the Hotel Danton my first few nights in Paris."

"Well, I'm sure there must be quite a few of them," said the woman, trying kindly—if a bit patronizingly—to make Nina's non sequitur sound marginally less brainless. "Though possibly, there aren't. One can't help noticing how little in this country is named after Robespierre and poor Charlotte Corday."

"*Danton's Death*," murmured Leo. "What a brilliant play!"

"A work of genius," said the woman. "I'm surprised you know it. Are you by any chance in the theater?"

"I'm a travel writer," said Leo.

"I'm Nina," Nina said.

At first Leo seemed unsure about this, but after a moment confirmed it. "This is Nina. She writes also. We work together on a little private-subscription newsletter called *Allo!*"

Work together! thought Nina. Was that all they were? Coworkers?

"How American we are," the woman said. "Telling each other what we do for a living. By the way, I'm Susanna Rose."

"Oh! I'm Leo! Sorry!"

"Where are you from?" said Susanna Rose.

Leo said, "New York. And you?"

Susanna Rose said, "Manhattan. Where else?"

Leo and Susanna Rose exchanged knowing smiles. Nina gave a chuckle, louder than she'd intended.

"What's masturbation?" said the little girl, Isadora.

A seismic ripple disturbed Susanna Rose's dark curls as she shook her head and laughed, not *at* her daughter, but as if she and the child were old friends sharing a favorite joke. "Sweetie, you already know the answer to that. You just want me to say it in front of these new people."

Found out, the child gave the same fresh smile she'd given the word *guillotine*, the smile of the tolerant mini-adult amused by her silly child self. Did all little girls have this knack of flipping from child to grown-up? And did every mother have as much skill and precision at making them do it?

"Bad spin doctors," said Leo. "Bad image. That was Marie Antoinette's problem."

"There were many problems," Susanna Rose conceded. "But that was one of them, yes."

"Nowadays, she could hire someone to watch the polls and give her fashion advice and take care of damage control after she said to let them eat cake," Leo told his new friend.

Hello there! What about Nina? She longed to make some possessive gesture, like putting her arm around Leo or, if this turned out to be full-scale war, resting a hand on his thigh. (Though that was also risky—Leo could shrug it off.) As a compromise, she reached for Leo's hand. Leo moved it away.

What a monster jealousy was! In the taxi Nina had liked it when Leo charmed the driver. But now it drove her wild to see him trying to win this woman over. If he had a portable CD player, he'd be playing Billie Holiday. But why was Nina thinking of Leo in this suspicious, ungenerous way? Why? Because he was flirting with this . . . stranger, not caring that Nina was right there!

"The French press is a bit more complicated," Susanna Rose said. "It's just as corrupt as our media but more sophisticated, less simpleminded."

"Like the French in general," said Leo. "And also more full of itself—"

"Ask me some more French," Isadora said.

"*Le lit,*" said her mother.

"The bed," said the girl.

"*Magnifique!*" said Leo.

The child regarded him without interest.

"Another word," demanded Isadora.

"*Le cauchemar,*" said Susanna Rose.

"That's a hard one," said the girl. "Not fair."

"Think about it," said her mother. Then, turning back to Leo, "These latest French elections are scary."

"Again it's public relations," said Leo. "Popular perception. The right wing whipping up those poor dumb bastards into dumping all those oranges on the airport road."

"Like with the pigs on TV," said Nina.

Leo and Susanna Rose turned to stare at her.

"I'm missing some connection here," Susanna Rose said. "Enlighten me. Tina, is it?"

"Nina," Leo corrected her gently, before Nina could, less gently.

Nina said, "My first few nights in Paris, every time I turned on the TV, I saw a documentary about peasants killing pigs. Leo explained about the elections, about the TV networks showing the peasants and their pigs as a way of drumming up sentiment for pure, old-fashioned peasant French ways—" She stopped. Why was she telling Susanna Rose how brilliant Leo was? There was another song Leo played, a blues song. *Women be wise, keep your mouth shut, don't advertise your man.* Leo had a whole repertoire of songs about women not talking!

But Nina should have taken the song's advice—don't advertise your man. Because now she had only herself to blame as Susanna Rose fixed Leo with a dewy gaze and said, "Of course, you were right. Don't you just adore it? How fabulous these people are. Deconstructing pigs on French TV. Right-wing semiotics."

Why was Susanna Rose so admiring? What did she want from Leo? Nina watched a smoggy haze of attraction rise and hover between them, gleaming with tiny particulate flakes of curiosity and desire.

"Nazi pig propaganda," Susanna Rose said.

"I'm afraid so," agreed Leo.

"Pigs," mused Susanna Rose. "Danton was trampled by a herd of pigs. Also gored twice by bulls. His face was a mass of scar tissue. Women loved him despite it. So I'm being a tyrant about not prettying up our Danton. And we're having a hell of a time finding an actor who'll play him. Actors are such peacocks. . . ."

Other sightseers were assembling now, waiting to take the tour. Two American tourist couples tried, as Leo and Nina had, to find some reason to stroll around the vast depressing hall. Soon they gave up and gravitated toward Leo and Nina, close enough for Nina to overhear one man tell another, "Before this vacation, I didn't know nothing about France. Except French fries. French toast . . . French kissing."

"He don't know nothing about French kissing," said the man's wife. "I can tell you that."

Leo smiled at Susanna Rose. *He* knew about French kissing. And Nina already knew he knew. No point smiling at *her*.

A group of American college students drifted in and immediately felt compelled to try out the acoustics by hooting like owls; they lapsed into stunned silence when the stone walls hooted back. Soon afterwards, a slight, round-shouldered woman materialized from the shadows wearing a belted tan raincoat, a flowered kerchief tied in little points under her chin, and shoes that managed to be both geriatrically sturdy and perilously high-heeled. Calling out, *"Mesdames et Messieurs?"* without the least hope that anyone would reply, she raised one hand and shook it as if something were stuck to her fingers.

Eye contact wasn't part of her job. She addressed the air in a voice just loud enough to collect the English-speaking tour.

"Welcome to the Conciergerie," she said. "The infamous Revolutionary Prison. Right now we are standing in the Hall of the Men-at-Arms. Built in the thirteenth century, it was—"

The group assembled in front of her. Isadora was the first to rise from the bench, then Nina, then Susanna Rose and finally Leo. The little girl ran over and weaseled her way to the front. Several students patted her head as she wriggled past.

Nina, Leo, and Susanna Rose stood off to one side, and as far back as they could.

Leo said, "I'm waiting for this babe to tell me something I don't know."

"I despise tours," said Susanna Rose.

"Me, too," Nina said.

A common rebellious spirit united the three of them. They might not be permitted to go through the prison unescorted but they didn't have to cooperate with this fascist guided tour.

"Many famous people," said the guide, "passed through the gates of this prison. Marie Antoinette. Charlotte Corday. Danton. Robespierre. If you turn around, you will see the grill to which Madame du Barry clung when they carried her in."

Everyone turned except Nina, Leo, and Susanna Rose—they weren't about to roll over and do what they were told—so that the rest of the tour wound up staring at *them*. All except the college kids, who weren't even pretending to listen. A British boy pinched his sister, which started a punching match that engulfed their parents in a firestorm of furious whispers.

"It's all Nazi totalitarian shit," Leo told Susanna Rose. "You know what happened to us this morning?"

"How would I?" asked Susanna Rose.

"Tell her, Nina," said Leo.

"No, go ahead," said Nina, dully.

"We were in the Montparnasse Cemetery," Leo said.

"I love it there," said Susanna Rose. "So restful."

"To see Simone de Beauvoir's grave," Leo said.

"Wasn't it inspiring?" Susanna Rose said. "She may have been full of baloney, but she really galvanized millions of women—"

"I know." Leo interrupted her. "I agree. I'm sure you've seen the touching notes that women leave on her grave. It's really quite extraordinary. She's become a sort of patron saint."

Edging closer to Leo, Susanna Rose nodded as if he were a slow, sweet-natured child she was trying to encourage. What was Leo saying? This was worse that outright lying! Didn't it bother him to imply he'd *wanted* to visit de Beauvoir's grave, to pretend in the presence of someone—Nina!—who knew he'd been dragged there kicking and screaming?

Their guide said, "During the Terror, thousands of prisoners were brought through this hall every day."

Peering into the darkness, Nina listened for some residual echo of the victims' groans and sobbing. In the face of that, it was senseless to get so bent out of shape because her boyfriend was misrepresenting himself to impress another woman.

"We ran into a gang of skinheads," Leo said. "At the cemetery. Apparently they've turned the grave of Pierre Laval into some sort of neo-Fascist shrine."

"Oh, God in heaven." Was Susanna Rose pretending to know who Pierre Laval was? Was that something every . . . theater director . . . knew as a matter of course? Nina had never heard of him until today in the graveyard.

"God in heaven indeed," said Leo. "It was very unpleasant. Luckily, they knew not to fuck with me. But it could easily have gotten ugly."

"Well, I suppose it's just a matter of time before every local minority gets picked off and slaughtered." The dolorous resignation with which Susanna Rose accepted the brutality of her fellow man was leavened by a shiver of anticipatory excitement. "It's just a fact that the peasantry—French, German, Polish, whatever—never had a problem rounding up and turning in Jews."

Certainly there must have been *some* peasant who'd had a problem killing Jews. Leo and Susanna Rose knew it, too, but that wasn't their point. And Nina couldn't say so. They might think she was anti-Semitic.

They. It struck her with the force of a slap that Leo and Susanna Rose were Jewish—and were using that fact to exclude her. But what about Leo and Nina, excluding the rest of the world on the immensely sensible, rational basis of sexual attraction? What about Leo and the old man in the graveyard, shutting out Simone de Beauvoir and an entire gender of hysterical, nagging females? And the cabdrivers, each xenophobic in his own way, and Madame Cordier and Nina, joined together in an aggrieved, exclusive sisterhood: Leo's current and former lovers.

Everywhere on the planet, people were agglomerating in gummy alliances based on sex or nationality, ethnic origin, history, or religion, some of it more or less violent and all about us versus them. It was naive to imagine a world without combination and exclusion occurring constantly, unstoppably, on the lowest biological level, a world of humans running about, pretending to be complex organisms but really no more than gametes swimming toward fertilization, toward that moment, that shattering pop between the sperm and the egg that signals all the others to just keep on swimming by. . . .

I'm losing my mind, thought Nina.

The guide was reeling off numbers: thousands, hundreds of thousands of men and women arrested, imprisoned, tortured, numbers of prisoners guillotined per hour, per day, per week. The college kids were with her now. They could relate to this.

Leo told Susanna Rose, "I'm trying to get back here later this year. They're celebrating the fiftieth anniversary of the liberation of Paris. And I can't help wondering if there's going to be a fuss about the French not exactly . . . hesitating to help deport the Jews."

What trip to Paris later this year? Was Leo coming back with Nina?

"What's the name of that town?" said Susanna Rose. "Help me. My memory's going. Somewhere near Lyons? It was the staging place for the deportation of all those children. And the commemorative plaque doesn't even mention the fact that the kids were Jewish."

"Izieu," said Leo.

"That's right," said Susanna Rose. "That's right. Izieu."

This was vile. Vile! Nina couldn't believe it! Using the deportation of the French Jews as a sexual come-on!

Yet everything they were saying was true. And was it any more outrageous than Nina standing in this vast hall from which so many thousands of wretched innocents were dispatched to their deaths and having a jealous fit because her boyfriend was flirting? No wonder every new day presented a new ontological challenge as you kept trying to see the world as it really was, while the world's face kept changing, and sex kept you from seeing at all, kept your eyes from focusing unless you had the beloved beside you, covering you with kisses and signs of physical devotion.

What did Nina expect to happen now? Did she for one moment imagine that Leo would leave her for Susanna Rose, exchange her right here in the prison like a worn-out pair of sneakers? I think I'll wear the new ones, you can wrap up the old ones, or better yet, if you wouldn't mind, just toss them in the trash. Anyone but the deeply disturbed would predict that they would have their little conversation, take their little guided tour, and return to their separate lives: Susanna Rose to her daughter and her play, Leo to his magazines and Nina.

Leo and Nina would never mention this. And when he wrote about the Conciergerie for *Allo!* it would not be as the place where he'd flirted shamelessly with a fellow tourist, but as the historic landmark in which Marie Antoinette spent her historic last night on earth.

"*Allons*," said the tour guide, and everyone nervously regrouped as she shepherded them from the huge reception-detention hall into a corridor that was slightly less dark but exceedingly narrow. Not so narrow, Nina hoped, that Leo would get claustrophobic, though she assumed he'd keep it together around Susanna Rose and the others.

The passage was only wide enough for two. Suppose Leo and Susanna Rose paired off and left Nina to tag behind, like their duenna, their chaperone, like Eurydice again, this time with Orpheus walking ahead to chat up another woman.

Susanna Rose left off her desultory conversation with Leo and peered anxiously over the heads of the crowd. As if summoned, her daughter sidled up and burrowed under her arm.

"On the third of Thermidor," said the guide, "one hundred and thirty-eight prisoners . . ."

"Did you hear what the guide said before?" Isadora asked.

"What, dear?" said Susanna Ross.

"They guillotined this woman? And after they cut off her head, they picked it out of the basket and one of the jailers smacked her face? Slap slap." The little girl backhanded the air.

"Please, dear," said Susanna Rose. She and the child skipped off, arm in arm, down the hall.

"Wait!" Leo called after them, and they paused for him to catch up. "Remember Orpheus! The one rule is: Don't look back." Leo's voice was low and confiding, but even so, Nina heard.

They had made it through the corridor and were walking along a portico and had just picked up speed when the guide stopped short and once more raised her hand.

"The so-called rue de Paris. Four hundred and fifty meters long, it was for many prisoners the last march to the guillotine. During the worst of the Terror, the condemned were obliged to walk past as many as five hundred prisoners sleeping on the rue de Paris, as well as a miniature city of errand boys, barbers, cooks, vendors, nurses, and lawyers who lived off the prisoners housed here. At one point there were two hundred and sixty lawyers for half that many prisoners."

The tourists laughed harshly, placatingly, but the numbers were not to be stopped. Numbers were their guide's true subject, the statistics of the dead. Meticulous records had been kept, all very proper and bureaucratic.

They passed a guillotine blade no bigger than a meat cleaver. Were human heads smaller then? The rusty iron inspired the guide to a new barrage of numerals, the precise dimensions and weight of the axe, the bills for daily corpse removal, carting, and disposal.

It was perfect for "Paris Death Trip." But Leo seemed to have forgotten the article he was researching. At that moment, he wasn't brooding on death. Which was a blessing . . . or was it? Which was preferable, sex or death, if the sex was with someone else, if he wanted Susanna Rose. . . ?

"Through that door," said the guide, "was the prison kitchen. The wealthiest prisoners brought their own cooks, but in some cases that was denied. For example, in the case of Danton, the great orator and cruel revolutionary leader who sent so many innocents to the guillotine . . ."

"Bullshit," Susanna Rose said, just loud enough for Leo and Nina—but not the guide—to hear.

"Hardly bullshit," Leo said. "The guy was heavy-duty."

"With Marie Antoinette," the guide continued, "known during her imprisonment here as the Widow Capet, there were very rigid controls on what the prisoner could eat. A servant girl tried to make the Queen some unsalted chicken broth. But that was not permitted."

The college students shook their heads. Now they saw how bad this was. No Big Macs, no French fries, no Mom's chicken soup . . .

"Animals," said the man who didn't know about French kissing.

"Relax, hon," said his wife.

At last they reached a bottleneck, a tunnel-like cul-de-sac they had to venture in and out of to see Marie Antoinette's cell. Moving in an orderly line, they approached the opening where they waited for the others to inspect the Queen's last room and to come back through the corridor and pop out like champagne corks. Couldn't the Revolution have foreseen this eventuality and housed the Widow Capet in a cell with a separate entrance and exit so that a line of tourists could have filed past in one direction?

Once more, Leo and Nina separated from the group. Susanna Rose and Isadora also stopped, a short distance ahead.

"When they took the Queen's son away," Susanna Rose told Isadora, "when they came for the little Dauphin, Marie Antoinette kissed him and told him to be very brave. And then she let him go. But when they tried to take her daughter, the beautiful little Princess, the Queen grabbed her and wouldn't give her up and offered to die for her child."

"What happened then?" breathed Isadora.

"They took the Princess anyway."

"And after that?"

"Well, er, the mommy died, and the little girl lived."

Though Susanna Rose directed this intensely at Isadora, there was an aspect of theater about it, an address to a larger crowd as she labored to entrance her daughter and Leo, both at once. Nina recalled how, when they'd sat on the bench and Leo described the royal family's failed escape attempt, his voice had risen to involve Susanna Rose and her daughter.

A group of college kids emerged from the corridor, looking chastened and perturbed, blinking until their bland faces set like individual puddings. Leo held Nina back and let Susanna Rose and Isadora precede them to see the Queen's cell.

In their absence, Leo and Nina could hardly look at each other. It was as if the two of them were rejected spouses whose more attractive partners had just run off together.

Finally Leo said, "Did you hear that crap? That was pure feminist bullshit! I'll bet that's not what happened. No one in those times gave a flying fuck about little princesses, Marie Antoinette included. It was the Prince—the royal heir—she tried to save, the Prince she offered to trade her life for. What's her name, Susanna Rose, was just jacking that kid around, inventing some elaborate psychodrama so that poor girl would believe that *her* mother would gladly die for her, too."

Leo's handsome jaw clenched. Why was he so enraged? Was

he jealous of Isadora? Otherwise, what did he care if a woman told a harmless lie about a long-dead mother and daughter?

And what did Leo imagine that everyone was doing: he and Nina, Susanna Rose, her daughter, the tour guide, and her group? Drifting like a pack of zombies around this monstrous prison, madly pushing each other's buttons, trying to distort or manipulate their listeners' sense of the world with appalling statistics and selected snippets of information? And how was that different from people everywhere since the beginning of time, from the revolutionaries who'd spread lying gossip about Marie Antoinette, from the TV stations showing documentaries intended to persuade you that peasant couples killing their pigs and making their blood sausage would lose their whole way of life if France allowed foreign workers and oranges from Morocco?

And what about Leo, the mind-control king! What had he thought *he* was doing, preparing Nina to adore the disgusting Hotel Danton? Where had he gotten *his* information? From that bigoted slut, Madame Cordier? Who in turn had wanted Nina to know some important facts about Leo.

And now Susanna Rose and Isadora reappeared with staring eyes and nearly identical looks of exaltation and distress. Both seemed on the verge of tears, and when Leo said, "How was it?" Susanna Rose held up one hand and steered her daughter past them.

At last it was Leo and Nina's turn to peek in at Marie Antoinette's cell. Two mannequins shared the cramped room with a cot, a table, a washbasin, a pen, an inkwell, and paper. In a black dress and bonnet, the Queen sat in a woven rush chair with an ebony rosary pinched between her hinged fingers. Diagonally across, a statue in a military jacket and breeches stared absently through the glass, standing guard over empty space.

Marie Antoinette was meant to look either composed or dejected, Nina couldn't tell which. It wasn't a lifelike dummy. There was no illusion of suspended motion, no waxy skin seeming to breathe. Just two grimy mannequins behind a dusty window.

The Marie Antoinette dummy was wearing plum-colored suede shoes. Somehow Nina knew that these same shoes had belonged to the Queen. This was the only touching detail: the idea that she had kept those shoes until the end, an extreme example of women's faith in the magic of shoes to change their luck and save them.

What had so transformed the college students that they'd come out blinking like possums? What on earth could have moved Susanna Rose and Isadora too profoundly to speak? For Nina, seeing the tableau had reduced the tragedy of Marie Antoinette's final days to moth-eaten taxidermy.

Nina and Leo trudged out of the corridor to find that they were alone; their so-called guide and her ragtag band had wandered ahead and left them. For a couple that hadn't wanted to take the tour, they were unreasonably disturbed by the prospect of being left behind. Hurrying, they caught up with the group in a pebbled courtyard landscaped with a few patches of dead grass and a scrawny tree beside a dry fountain and a stone trough.

"*La cour des femmes*. The courtyard of the women," said the guide. "Here the female prisoners came to wash their linens and groom themselves in whatever pitiful fashion they could manage. Sometimes two hundred women were packed into this yard. And there, behind that iron grill, the male prisoners gathered to watch. Even at the hour of their death, they took time for harmless flirtation."

Well, speaking of flirtation, here was Susanna Rose again, dragging Isadora behind her as she zoomed over to Leo.

"Did you see it?" Susanna Rose asked breathlessly.

"See what?" Leo asked.

"Danton's cell," she said.

"Marie Antoinette's," corrected Leo.

"No, no," said Susanna Rose. "Not that. Not those stupid dummies. You were meant to keep going past the Marie Antoinette room and on to Danton's cell. It was unbelievably powerful. Really incredibly moving."

"We must have missed it," Nina said glumly. "We didn't know there was anything beyond—"

Leo wheeled on her in silent fury. Missing something by accident was Leo's personal hell, worse than capricious changes of plans, worse than someone else having an experience he envied.

The guide's voice dropped and faltered as she reeled off one last list of statistics: deaths from starvation, malnutrition, disease, from torture and execution. Probably her job required that she offer the facts of French history without praise or blame, free from partisan sympathies for Jacobins or Girondins, above pity for the victims or censure for their killers. But that could hardly be possible after spending day after day in this prison, serving out a sentence not unlike that of the Revolution's casualties, though with the hope of parole every evening, Sundays, and national holidays. The staggering numbers were her way of giving her story emotional content, of adding moral judgment to a presentation that was meant to be factual, unimpassioned, and historically objective.

They left the courtyard for another large stone hall, a shade less dark than the others. The show was over. The house lights had come up. The guide stood near the far door, expressionless and glazed over. She wasn't even going to tell them what this room was for.

Before she'd finished thanking them for their time and attention, the college students were tripping over each other in their rush to escape. The other tourists trudged past, mumbling *"merci merci,"* without looking at the guide, their faces frozen in the abashed social smiles exchanged by flight attendants and passengers filing gratefully from an airplane.

Leo and Nina, Susanna Rose and Isadora paused to thank the guide. Had they become a group of four? Oh, please, God, no, prayed Nina. Don't let anyone suggest that Nina and Leo and their new best friends go out for a drink or a meal.

"Plus ça change," said Leo.

"Pardon?" The guide's moist eyes found Leo.

"There are always massacres," Leo said. "What happened here was simply standard operating procedure. Actually quite neat and orderly compared with what was going on in the rest of Paris. Isn't it true, Madame, that no one knows how many people were hacked to death in the streets?"

The guide knew Leo was talking to her. She wanted to be polite but couldn't control her yearning gaze after the departing tourists.

Leo went on. "The mobs were grabbing everyone in nice clothes or a fancy hat, bludgeoning and dismembering them, cutting out their hearts and stuffing their testicles in their mouths, while people danced on the corpses, up to their ankles in blood, and for months the whole city reeked of rotting flesh. That was only two hundred years ago. Hardly prehistory, right? But now everyone acts so shocked when it happens in Europe, Bosnia, Russia. And by the form it takes in *our* country: some nut goes into a fast food joint and blows away fifty kids . . ."

Nina, Susanna Rose, Isadora, the guide—one by one they forgot themselves and let their jaws go slack as Leo raved on. Finally, he ran out of steam. No one said a word. A low thrumming could be heard from the depths of the prison, like the sound of the ocean trapped inside a shell.

A long time passed. Then Susanna Rose said, "God, you're right. I couldn't agree with you more."

What was the little girl making of all this? And the guide? Was she marveling that this addled American was comparing the glorious Revolution to a shoot-out in a McDonald's? None of them could have known what Nina was thinking about: Leo's earlier speech that day on the subject of bloody mass murder.

That afternoon, at the hotel, they'd just finished their sandwiches and were satisfied and sleepy from lunch and the bottle of good wine. Leo started talking about the fact that their hotel had once been a famous abbey. Not just a famous abbey, but the site of a famous slaughter, the massacre of more than fifty priests during the Revolution. A mob had dragged them from their cells and herded them into the courtyard—the same garden where now, in the warmer months, guests enjoyed their coffee, croissants, and jam. Several monks tried to hide in the cellar. But the killers dragged them out and hacked them into chunks. The courtyard was littered with body parts, the paving stones slick with blood.

Somehow this story had segued into Leo and Nina having sex.

Not in some obvious corny way: the violence turning them on. It was all more accidental, less linear, less clear. Leo had fallen silent a moment, and something in their glance just *caught*, the way a sleeve or a lock of hair can snag on a button or coat hook.

Leo had reached out and taken Nina's legs and lifted them onto his lap. It was exciting in itself that he could do that if he wanted, the intimate hint of possession implicit in his freedom to move her around.

At some point (they were kissing) Nina thought about the abbey, and it did make Leo's kisses seem more caustic and sweet. It intensified her desire to have so much pleasure in a place that had seen so much pain. Sex obliterated all that, along with everything else: the history of the hotel, Nina and Leo's past, the room, the pillows, the cool crisp sheets, time, everything but their bodies. All five senses were distilled into one molten drop of sensation. Then Nina was outside herself. Absent. Visiting Cathedrals.

You had to trust someone to let yourself get to that place where you were so wide open, so dangerously unprotected that anyone could sneak up on you and bop you over the head with a mallet. You could wind up like the French pigs, let's say the Auvergne pig, lumbering over for apples and love and taking a bullet instead. The farmer's wife's voice had been so musical as she sang out her darling pig's name. "Mizu mizu mizu," she had called. Nina could hear it still.

And what if no one killed the pig but just tortured it awhile, alternately stroking and cuffing it, making it behave one way, then changing the rules completely. The poor pig would go mad, like Camille Claudel, better off in the nuthouse, or like

Nina, who chose to think of herself as a sensible person even as she drifted through an unreliable world that might transform its whole appearance at any given moment, depending on what Leo said, and if she thought he loved her.

A rubbery snap of awareness recalled Nina to herself. How amazing that she was here—not in their room, in bed with Leo, but in the vast dark chilly hall of the Revolutionary Prison.

In the time that Nina had taken for a quick mental jog back to their hotel room, Leo had fallen silent. And now it was, apparently, Susanna Rose's turn. Maybe she hadn't liked Leo's impassioned operatic aria about wholesale slaughter, after all. Because now, unaccountably, she seemed to be showing off for the tour guide, as if the guide were their teacher and she was set on being the smartest kid in the class. A better student than Leo, better than her own daughter, better than Nina, who didn't count and was at any rate out of the running, having been spaced out entirely in some sexual other dimension. Or maybe Susanna Rose's attraction to Leo was entering some new phase that looked, to the casual observer, like cutthroat competition.

"The Revolution was all about sex," Susanna Rose was saying. And though this was a reprise of a topic that, even in their brief acquaintance, Nina had already heard Susanna Rose address, she felt responsible, as if, with those radar signals that thoughts of sex emitted, her meditation about Leo had somehow made Susanna Rose say this:

"The Revolution was entirely about the rumors people spread concerning Marie Antoinette and her so-called lovers and her incest with her son. It was all about Danton adoring sex and Robespierre and Marat hating everything to do with the body.

Once Danton and Robespierre had a fight about the meaning of virtue, and Danton said that virtue was what he did in bed with his wife. Finally Danton quit going to the long boring political meetings and just stayed home and made love to his wife all day. Naturally, that was the end of him." Susanna Rose tipped back her head and slashed a finger across her lovely throat.

"Bravo!" Leo said.

Leo might have been one of the mannequins in Marie Antoinette's cell, that's how startled Susanna Rose was when he opened his mouth and spoke. She had a watery unfocused look. She'd almost forgotten their existence. In theory she was speaking to them, but in fact she'd been talking to herself.

But what was she trying to tell herself? What did Danton mean to her? And how could Nina hope to know what Susanna Rose was thinking? How would she cross that unbridgeable distance between one life and another, a chasm that deepened with every second, with every tiny exchange, with every quick impression that divided us one from another and made up the separate hours and minutes of our separate lives? How she could assume anything about this stranger when—after all this brooding obsession, all this pain, all this wasted time—she knew so little, almost nothing, about the man she loved!

Susanna Rose's voice grew soft and thick. Nina felt herself tense. Was this woman about to make some grandiose sexual claims on Danton's behalf? Susanna Rose took a deep breath. She could say anything, Nina feared.

"Danton's wife died suddenly while he was away," Susanna Rose began. "It took six days for him to get home. And when he got back to their village, he paid for her corpse to be dug up. It was no big deal in those days. In fact it was often a good idea, since a certain percentage of the population got buried alive by mistake.

"Danton's wife was dead, all right. Still, he held her in his arms. One of the gravediggers wrote about how that giant ox, Danton, lifted his wife and shut his eyes and softly kissed her forehead. The gravedigger wrote that Danton forgot that they were there, and he howled. The men were too scared to breathe or move or do anything to disturb him."

Susanna Rose slipped deeper into abstraction and gazed down at the gritty stone floor. Nina heard the sound of water, dripping somewhere in the prison. One by one, the adults glanced over at Isadora to check out her response, as if depending on the child to react to this for them.

After a considered pause, the little girl said, "Gross."

The tour guide seemed appalled by the whole performance. It was harder to read Leo. Perhaps he was less affected by the story than by annoyance at Susanna Rose for having upstaged him. Whatever fragile thread of attraction was being spun between her and Leo was snipped by their competition over who could get more exercised about the French Revolution. Nina knew better than to compete with him. He was so easily wounded. If Susanna Rose had meant to impress him, what a miscalculation!

It was Nina—and Nina alone—who was thrilled by Susanna Rose's story. The story of Danton and his wife had worked like a magic key, rolling back the stone prison roof like the top of a sardine can. Light had come streaming in along with this ghastly anecdote about an historic disinterment. About Orpheus and Eurydice, translated from Greek myth into modern history, from Hades to a country graveyard during the Revolution.

"*Merci, Madame,*" said Susanna Rose.

"*De rien, au revoir,*" trilled the guide.

"*Au revoir,*" Susanna Rose told Leo and Nina, and then she and her daughter were gone.

So Nina's premonition had been all wrong. She had mistaken Susanna Rose for a demon instead of a guardian angel. She had thought Susanna Rose would sow discord and erotic unrest when in fact she was offering help in the form of a grisly story that Nina hoped she could keep in mind after she and Leo left the prison and returned to their regular lives.

Nina felt like an explorer in one of those misty historical paintings of white men in armor or buckskins on the edge of a cliff from which some misguided native scout points out the promised land. Though what Nina saw before her was hardly a heaven on earth, but rather a desolate wilderness she would have to cross and would cross, out of faith in what waited (well, what *might* wait or what might not be there at all, who could possibly say?) on the other side. How she longed to bridge that chasm and find someone to trust, to know as well as she knew herself. And they *wouldn't* have to discuss their love, this time because what existed between them would be as tangible, as real, as simple and mysterious as a loaf of bread. She would—that is, she *hoped* she would—feel that way about someone. But it seemed unlikely that this someone would be Leo. . . .

Her desire for Leo would intensify, growing more obsessive and tragic the nearer it got to ending, to changing from a constant presence into a constant—and present—absence. Their passion would die, finished off by deepening misunderstanding, by their inability to exchange one unambiguous word, to break their sacred taboo against admitting the other mattered. Nina tried to tell herself: No. They would love each other forever. The love they'd made, the love they'd shared was a fact of nature, an entity that existed and had its own survival instinct. But Nina didn't believe that. She and Leo would edge apart. Leo wouldn't dig up her grave or come down to hell to save her.

Meanwhile it would help to think of Danton lifting his wife from her coffin. It would inspire Nina to keep her sights fixed past Leo. Danton's story was a light to steer toward without knowing where she was going, the light of a love that couldn't be argued with, nor told it couldn't succeed: Don't bother. Leave that dead woman alone. Stay out of hell with that lyre.

Nina imagined Danton hunkered down, his wide strong back muscled like a Rodin bronze. And her hands flew to her ears as if he really were howling—

Someone touched her, covered her hands with his own. Nina shuddered. It was Leo. She knew it was Leo. But her heart refused to quit hammering as he tenderly peeled back her fingers, starting with her thumbs. He leaned close and began to whisper, his warm breath on her temple. The guide was still there, though she'd moved farther on toward the exit, as if to urge them forward. Really, they should be leaving and let her get on her way.

Leo's chest brushed Nina's shoulder as he whispered in her ear. She longed to arch her back and rub up against him—that is, till she understood what he was saying.

He said, "The best part, the really terrific detail that what's-her-name, Susanna, left out was that Danton remarried within a year. *Within one year* of digging up his wife and howling over her grave. The second time, he married a girl of sixteen. Some nubile sixteen-year-old cutie . . ."

Nina took a few steps away and again covered her ears. Once again she shut her eyes, and once more she saw Danton.

She stood where the gravediggers must have stood and watched Danton, crouched and howling. She felt what the gravediggers must have felt. She tried not to breathe. She was determined not to move, not to disturb or stop Danton, not for fear of him but from respect for what he was doing, for the ambition, the foolishness of his doomed impossible hope, disinterring his wife from the grave, that grand ridiculous gesture that proved, despite what Leo said and despite any whisper of doubt, the existence of love beyond reason, beyond the reach of time's sharp blade: the love that—miraculously, narrowly—evades the arc of the scythe as Death stalks past in his hooded cape, mowing his way through the world.

THE LIVES OF THE MUSES
Nine Women & the Artists They Inspired
ISBN 978-0-06-055525-2 (paperback)

A brilliant, wry, and deliberately provocative examination of the complex relationship between the artist and his muse.

WOMEN AND CHILDREN FIRST
Stories
ISBN 978-0-06-050728-2 (paperback)

"A meticulously observed collection . . . Stories that glow with a burnished wisdom." —*New York Times*

HOUSEHOLD SAINTS
A Novel
ISBN 978-0-06-050727-5 (paperback)

"Prose brings off a minor miracle of her own in the rare sympathy and detachment with which she gives life to this poignant story. " —Jean Strouse, *Newsweek*

GUIDED TOURS OF HELL
Novellas
ISBN 978-0-06-008085-3 (paperback)

"Wit, knowingness, and an intimate familiarity with guilt and anxiety—Francine Prose has these qualities in abundance." —David Lodge, *New York Times Book Review*

PRIMITIVE PEOPLE
A Novel
ISBN 978-0-06-093469-9 (paperback)

"Francine Prose has a wickedly sharp ear for pretentious American idiom, and no telling detail escapes her observation." —*New York Times Book Review*

ALSO AVAILABLE BY
FRANCINE PROSE

THE GLORIOUS ONES
A Novel
ISBN 978-0-06-149384-3 (paperback)

The Glorious Ones travel the length and breadth of seventeenth-century Italy, playing commedia dell'arte in the streets and palaces with equal vigor. Founded by the ingenious madman Flamino Scala, the players endure kidnappings and passionate affairs, cabals, riots, and disgrace.

READING LIKE A WRITER
A Guide for People Who Love Books and for Those Who Want to Write Them
ISBN 978-0-06-077705-0 (paperback)

"A love letter about the pleasures of reading and how much writers can learn from the careful reading of great writers as diverse as Virginia Woolf and Flannery O'Connor." —*USA Today*

New York Times Bestseller

A CHANGED MAN
A Novel
ISBN 978-0-06-056003-4 (paperback)

"Riotously funny . . . Prose uses humor to light up key social issues, to skewer smugness, and to create characters whose flaws only add to their depth and richness." —*Booklist* (starred review)

Winner of the Dayton Literary Peace Prize

BLUE ANGEL
A Novel
ISBN 978-0-06-088203-7 (paperback)

Deliciously risqué, *Blue Angel* is a withering take on modern academic mores.

National Book Award Finalist in Fiction

THE PEACEABLE KINGDOM
Stories
ISBN 978-0-06-075404-4 (paperback)

"Smartly observed and deftly written, these eleven stories present the weird jungle of modern life through the eyes of a wry and mordant writer." —*New York Times Book Review*